DARKEST ROSE

THE INEVITABLE WAR

VERA MORGANA

To my lovely sister Uthara, who not only supported my writing more than anyone else, but became an inspiration in creating the character of Elizabeth. Without her, I would not have had the courage to pick up the pen in the first place.

PROLOGUE

She could feel the tendons in her legs tearing; gradually, she reduced her pace. They must have managed to catch up. She wasn't sure.

Bloodshot eyes, glares from hungry wolves, preying to pounce on her ... bright colours like mirrors of the moonlight with faces of murderers. For an instant, she yearned for help from humans. Her distinct camouflage betrayed her. They were going to wolf her down their throats.

The tree behind was the only alternative, but the branches pressed her downwards, bending and breaking from her weight. The rustle of the leaves as she fell to the ground drained all the energy she had left. Hiding was the only logical option, but those noisy leaves were giving it all away. Her thoughts of him overrode the idea of her freedom. Her death held no importance.

She had become prey for being different – those words reverberated through her. The only vivid image she could recall without any stress was when his voice echoed her name. Not her name. It was *the girl with the red hair* or *the cherry servant*.

At least someone saw her as human.

As the voice grew closer, she realized that even though faith was adrift, she held on to hope. Although it was too late to live, she could always find comfort in him – her love. She let every part of him explore her dying mind.

When he wrapped his arms around her for the first time, their giant secret hideout tree, slowly she drifted into darkness. As her eyes were closing, she felt an open locket fall off her chest.

Someone picked it up and closed it.

Her knight in shining armor. He was human, and she knew that for sure. He watched her as the fangs of his hungry pack sank into her skin. This was it. She wasn't going to fight anymore. Just as she gave in to the last gasp of death, she heard her name … not *the girl with the red hair* or *cherry servant* …

'Virgo …!!!'

CHAPTER 1

'Why aren't you dressed?' Lady Desouza asked.

It was a regular morning in the Desouza mansion. The budding sun kissed the edges of the clouds. Rays of warm, soft light peeped through the window. It was a morning with a bit of a difference. A girl of her age should have jiggled for joy, since it was her birthday. Still, no iota of fun or excitement crawled into her wandering mind, only memories of sitting in the rose pavilion and listening to musical sounds from afar.

A few feet down, it was all hustle and bustle, like the town market. Except that these weren't traders, only brightly dressed ladies who were craving the nod, smile, or glimpse of some handsome earl.

'I will ready her soon enough,' Nurse Marcie said.

The girl was fumbling with the pearl of her necklace. Calm as the still sea, her tepid self remained.

Marcie was handling both troubles, hers and that of

the celebrator. 'My lady. Your elegance is wasted here; feed it to the starving guests.'

'You sure know how to flatter ...'

A knock.

'Let yourself in,' the lady commanded.

'My lady, my lord requests your presence. As it isn't right to keep the Duke of Kroukhesta waiting.'

'The Duke? Why is that infuriating fellow here?' the little girl voiced out her first concern.

'To mark your coming of age.'

'You sure have a way of daubing my emotions with misery.'

'Hush, Ella. You shouldn't say that,' Marcie cautioned.

'You will perform your duties to our family's name. Nobles of your age are with their husbands.'

Ella picked up a matching pair of earrings. 'I would cheerfully trade this nobility for freedom.'

Lady Desouza let out a peal of wry laughter. 'Everyone awaits your presence. Don't delay,' she said as she walked out of the room.

She caters for every other person except me, Ella thought.

Edmund Gilmore finally got a moment alone from the blare and clatter of his kin. They were at home for his birthday. The feasting table had always been a stand for political standings and debates. The constant chatter between his father and uncles would sometimes get out of control. Edmund's mother was still quick to quench the inferno with a passionflower tea.

Lady Gilmore took longer than ever to serve the tranquillizing tea today. Unlike other days, she wanted to air her opinions concerning the strident discourse. The Gilmores shared similar detest for the Desouzas and for the mere reason that the Desouzas' only daughter, who was ripe for marriage, wasn't getting any advances.

Edmund sneaked into his room to embrace the comfort of his bed. The thought of his parents deciding his future due to some old rivalry he never understood made his head thump. It wasn't the first time they'd tried to outdo the Desouzas, but it was becoming infuriating now more than ever. Out of a thousand rivalry situations, one would sometimes become wild. So wild and riotous that the prince had to intervene.

Just as he tried to wrap his head around all of that, he heard a knock on the door.

So much for a peaceful day.

Ruffle-haired and desperately needing alone time, he made his way to the door. 'Just a minute, Father.'

Walking briskly to the door, he wondered why his dad had come knocking.

Maybe he perceived my absence.

He pulled it open, but no one was there except the empty door frame. 'Reveal yourself.'

The young lad didn't get any reply. He lazed back to his bed and once again, he heard a knock. 'One more time, and you'll see red,' he warned.

'Open the window, you flapdoodle! How much longer do you require me to hang on the tree?'

Edmund turned to see the mischievous figure through the window. He was hanging on the tree outside. 'Leofrick! From the look of it, you must have been here a long while,' he said.

While he opened the window to let him in, Leo was stuck on one of the branches, but he made it to the room with Edmund's help. 'Only burglars use windows.'

'And only a deafened one wouldn't observe me out the window.'

'I express my regrets for that.'

Leo's eyes and face were similar to that of the vermilion flycatcher's – a bird draped in human red fluid cloaked in black. 'You know, friend, I could be anywhere else but here, clinging on trees like that one.'

A mischievous smile plastered across Edmund's face. 'What other evil have you been preparing?'

'A whole heap, I have lost track,' Leofrick answered with a rogue snigger. 'Like I could get away with Hermes' slippers. Travelling to and fro in the blink of an eye. I would laugh at the horse's stride. Wouldn't that be a spectacle?'

Edmund raised a brooding eyebrow. 'I know you are as tough as an old boot, but you'll outdo yourself.'

'Well, I did climb a tree like a young lad toda—'

'What object is that?' Edmund gestured towards the locket hanging on his belt.

'Label me ancient, but this grey-haired could only think of this as a present for your natal day.' Leofrick handed him the locket.

Edmund held it high against the noon light. 'Thank you. What bothers me now is how ancient it is.'

'Three decades old.'

'How can you tell?'

'Whoever sold it said so.'

'And you swallowed it all.' Edmund began fastening his boots. 'Can we Hermes' sandals off now?'

Leofrick smiled. 'That depends on what is next.'

'I couldn't care less about what is next, and I just want to leave.'

'Wouldn't they observe your absence?'

'Yes, and I couldn't care less. How do we leave?' Ed asked.

'The same route I came in, but not all which comes up easily goes down the same.'

'Your horse?'

'Ready for your use, my lord,' Leo jeered unsuccessfully.

'We would be visiting one place we are never wanted.'

'The palace?'

Leo and Ed had their mischievous days. They once stole the king's ornamental armor just to cause a ruckus in the palace. The king had prohibited them from stepping into the castle ever since.

'No, the Desouzas.'

'Are you pie-eyed?' Leofrick asked, completely startled.

'My heart beckons to Sophie, and I need to see her. You know me well; nothing stops me.'

~

Nurse Marcie signalled to the lord of the house.

It was time, and Sir Desouza enjoyed showcasing his jewel to the world. He cleared his throat like he was about to make a toast. Instead, he channeled the attention to his daughter, who was walking loftily down the stairs. The chill golden handrails sent a spasm of nervousness down to her feet. Unknown eyes with hidden intentions trailed her every step. Her eyes were trying to avoid the gossip whispers.

Wilkin walked up to her, his sly smile irritating her. She held out her hands. 'You are striking, my lady. Like the sun's radiance piercing through the clouds, your beauty pierces my heart,' he said.

Ella faked a smile. She needed to flow with the tide. 'Thank you,' she whispered. 'I need not your support to take a stride,' she added.

Wilkin pulled in his hand like a leper. 'I hope to win your heart, my lady.'

'It can never …'

'Beautiful, isn't she?' Lady Desouza cut in.

'Yes, my lady,' Wilkin answered. 'My lady.' Wilkin gave Lady Desouza a hand-kiss. 'Excuse me.'

'I hope I didn't interrupt anything.'

'Not at all, Mother, he was just leaving.'

Lady Desouza led Ella to one of her guests; Baroness Sulley. A lanky loathsome widow married to the vile act of wrecking those she viewed as a threat to her troubled life. On the other hand, she was never to be ignored when social events like this were involved.

Baroness Sulley's sister, Swetiue, was the reeve of the district. She was a close friend to Lady Desouza and mother to Sophie. Ella and Sophie had been mischievous little imps since childhood, though they were more responsible now they were grown up. In a way, the only good thing about the party for Ella was meeting Sophie.

Lady Desouza and Baroness Sulley kicked it off with conversations about King Gilbert Atalon II, the reigning monarch of their Kingdom, Yovaria. It was high time she escaped this female political twaddle.

She took a step back, hoping that the heels of her shoes wouldn't give her away. Then another, till she disappeared from the presence of those two. She managed to hide in the crowd and found her way to her exclusive hiding place, the rose pavilion. She spread the grapevines at the entrance of the canopy so that no one would be able to find her, and sat on the bench. She loosened the corset around her waist, listened to the music, and slowly swung herself to the melody. She was finally alone.

Edmund was looking for a way to get into Desouza's mansion. The process was a bore for Leofrick. Nothing was stopping him from seeing Sophie except the guards. He had seen her once, her golden spun hair gleaming beneath the noon sun … bright grey eyes like the mirror of the moon in the sea. Memories of the beautiful Sophie wouldn't leave him.

After circling the mansion for the fifth time, he

found an opening – the most dangerous route climbing the creepers near the garden wall. The son of the head and future heir of the Gilmore House couldn't possibly waltz into the Desouzas' party. Both families were sworn enemies. As far back as when the foundations of the Kingdom existed. There was no way he was getting a formal invitation to this party. Not even if he begged for it.

Edmund was about to start climbing when Leofrick walked up to him. 'You've fallen so deep in the Abyss for this young lady. So much that you are willing to climb over walls into Desouza's hell?'

'I didn't fall for her.'

'No, you didn't. You plunged into Sophia.'

Edmund shrugged off Leo's sarcastic remark. 'I am just here to confirm my feelings.'

'Look at yourself. You are climbing a wall draped with treacherous grapevines. What other confirmation do you need?'

Ed smirked. 'Your days at the Faded Tavern are finally paying off. It is too early to be dead drunk.'

'I haven't had any wine. If word of this reaches your father, you'll—'

'It won't. Except if you plan on stabbing me in the back.'

Leo smiled. 'We have been a mischievous duo for a very long while. I would never soil that.'

'See you at Canary Lane,' Edmund called. He was half-way up already.

'See you, and try not to get caught,' Leo called out from below.

CHAPTER 2

Lord Desouza sighed, already tired of all the conversations he had been engaged in with the numerous guests in attendance at his daughter's party. Politics held little interest to him when all he could think about was the importance of Ella's first dance and how smoothly he intended it to go.

Where was this woman when he needed her? He wondered at his wife's disappearance. His eyes scanned through the crowd meticulously, and he finally caught sight of her doing what she knew how to do best with the Baroness of Hillsville.

He shook his head. Nothing in the world could break women and gossip apart. That he had learned quite early on. He walked up to her, interrupted them politely to ask for Ella's whereabouts and waited patiently as Lady Desouza called for Nurse Marcie. It was time for Ella's first dance.

When he was sure Ella would be summoned, he turned to leave only to come face to face with Sir

Wilkin, who handed him a glass filled with wine, quite similar to the one he held in his hand.

'It seems to me that you are losing your charm as a man if you ever had any,' Lord Desouza said to him.

Wilkin faked a smile. 'She has stopped avoiding me like the plague nowadays. I need more time.'

'Good. Take as long as you need, but time isn't what you have. You know her beautiful and noble self receives proposals from suitors every week. An ignoble nobody could sway her with words.'

'Never would that happen. This beauty I shall take as my wife. I have your blessing, and that is what matters,' Wilkin said in a measured tone.

'Her first dance will commence soon. This is your chance to increase her interest in you. You know what to do, right?'

'Of course, siyer, it will be a flawless spectacle with me in the picture.' Wilkin bowed slightly before leaving.

It was the third song the orchestra had played that evening, and Ella was sure people would begin to notice her absence soon enough. However, she was only ever able to control the growth of the roses better when she was alone.

When she was eight, the Emperor who ruled the entirety of their Kingdom had sent Duke Anselmus to all the noble houses to celebrate the birth of his second son, Prince Kai Sutcliffe. It was custom for the people of Yovaria to present a fully bloomed yellow rose to the royals when there was a new birth. Ella's mother had gathered a bouquet of yellow roses yet to bloom. She had left them on the table unsupervised and asked a maid to buy ones that had bloomed from the market. Out of curiosity, Ella had touched the gentle roses by the stalk. It was the first time Ella realized the power she had. She knew then that her touch had a spark of life in it. Lady Desouza had returned, assuming that the blooming flowers were that which the maid bought. She presented them for the celebration of the prince's birth without much thought.

It wasn't long afterwards that Ella noticed her *touch of life* – the name she had given her strange ability – hadn't just been a one-time thing. Petals of flowers responded to her call, and they grew and blossomed as long as she focused her energy on them. She had tried several times to show her friend Sophie but she never could get the right time to do so. She soon realized that it would only work if she was alone, but it felt different today. She was alone in the garden that had become her secret haven over the years, but the flowers refused to play around her.

No one else noticed them, but they had been filling the room with gracious tunes, housing them in perfumed harmony. She could hear them playing the third sonata in the great hall now. Unlike the orchestra, whose duty it was to create vibrant music, the guests would notice her absence soon enough. Ella had been experimenting with the *touch of life* since the occurrence on the day the second Prince, Kai Sutcliffe, was born. At first, she had thought it was the gardener playing tricks on her, or something else was causing the flowers to blossom, but it was tough to hide from one's self, so she accepted her plight.

She savoured each note of the sonata. Just like the host of the highest heavens, they filled the mansion with bliss. The garden sanctuary had a way of influencing her emotions. Still, she could feel no connection today; only the music coming from the castle had an effect on her emotions. Maybe she needed more time, something she couldn't possibly get. Not at this moment when she was expected to be on the dance floor or pretending to enjoy conversations with royalties and prominent figures of the Kingdom.

Her wandering mind was becoming hollow. Her thoughts numb, excitement flat. Each day had its ambience; some days she would soar through the skies of happiness on the wings of nature and other days she would delve deep into the crypt of dolefulness.

The grapevines were moving …

I am not the one doing this, she thought. Even if she was, the roses were stagnant. Roses would respond to the slightest energy of the *touch of life*, but not grapevines.

It didn't stop … it began shuddering violently. One of the vines tickled her neck, and she jumped off the bench. She looked up at the wall and saw what was responsible for the tremor.

Someone was climbing the wall.

Edmund used his last spurt of energy to place his leg over the wall just as he used his arms to pull his other leg over. Exhausted, he sat on the wall, closed his eyes and faced upwards, taking in the serenity of the wind gently blowing against his face. After what seemed like a whole minute, he opened his eyes and was quick to jump down when he noticed that a girl was looking right at him through bright hazel eyes.

'I … sorry to frighten y-you, miss,' he stuttered.

Ella exhaled, closing and opening her eyes as if to wake herself from a dream. Perhaps she had fallen asleep on the wooden bench and was now seeing things. She pinched herself. *Is this real?* She noticed his copper-red hair.

A Gilmore? They were well known for their red hair after all.

She shook her head so much at the impossibility that her sore neck threatened to fall off. Her hair and head got stuck between the vines.

Nurse Marcie shouldn't have picked this ribbon.

Edmund jumped down and landed close to her. 'Are you okay, miss?' He was going to free her from the baleful vine restraint. The texture of her blonde hair startled him. 'You have very smooth hair. I will untangle it in no time.'

Compliments from a Gilmore could never hit the right spot. After some of her hair got untangled, she was able to lift her head to see his face. It was apparent that he was more preoccupied with removing the thorns than noticing her.

'There. Done,' Edmund said as he stared into her

captivating bright eyes. 'My name is Edmund. Sorry about that.' It would be stupid of him to tell a Desouza his full name. He took a step back and bowed, which compelled a slight curtsy from Ella.

'I am Ella. Ella De—' She stopped, thinking it would be stupid of her to reveal to him that she was a Desouza when their families were sworn enemies.

The familiar sound of the baroque being played in the banquet hall forced her to come into reality. It was time for her first dance. 'I am sorry, I have to go,' she clumsily said, and began to run towards the mansion, her gown deftly held up by her dainty hands.

'Wait! Where are you going?'

She wanted to tell him that it was her first dance and her birthday. For some reason, she wanted to tell him everything; how she could control the growth of roses, how she didn't like Wilkin, but she pushed past her irrationality of confiding in a stranger and kept walking without sparing a glance back.

Edmund followed behind. He wasn't going to miss her, but when they got to the hall, she vanished into the crowd. Several couples had taken their places on the dance floor, then their attention was drawn to the middle. Sir Desouza stood at the top of the stairs, looking very much like a king ready to address his subordinates.

Edmund spotted the girl. He began making his way towards her.

'You cannot cut across the main event, young man. Wait till the dance is over.' Nurse Marcie held him firmly by the collar of his coat.

'I just want to know who she is,' Edmund replied, his gaze still fixed on the girl.

'And who might that be?'

He gestured towards Ella. 'The young lady over there. If I fail to know her, I may as well be a fusty goose.'

Who is this reckless lad? Marcie thought. 'That is Elizabeth Desouza, the only child of this very household. The daughter of the Emperor's eastern royal guard, Lord Derrick Desouza.'

At that very moment, Sir Desouza announced Ella's entrance. Edmund didn't hear a word, or maybe he did. The graceful train of appealing ladies in flawless yellow gowns was enthralling. Like an array of blooming daffodils, the slender ladies brightened the room. With elegant, meticulous steps, they travelled down the stairs. When reaching the last level, they spread out like a deck of cards. A dozen youthful menfolk met them with arms stretched, ready to lead them to the dance floor, except for Ella, and everyone knew why. She was the centre of attraction, and her eyes were expecting more than the regular chivalry others displayed.

Sir Desouza was boiling with fury, and Wilkin was nowhere in sight. Other girls had their partners, but Ella was dancing on her own. She wasn't worried, because her father was doing all the worrying for them both. The thought of the Gilmore boy filled her mind. She was looking around intently, hoping to catch a glimpse of the Gilmore intruder. A minute later, she felt someone hold her from behind.

'You better drop the courtly act before …' It was the Gilmore intruder, not Sir Bodolf. 'Oh, I am sorry.' Ella was quick to cover her seemingly aggressive trail of words. 'Why are you still here?' she asked, hoping he wouldn't comment about what just happened.

'It is a party, right?' Edmund asked rhetorically. 'Anyone can have fun, you know.'

'Everyone except you, obviously.'

'Why?' Edmund asked. He knew the reason, he just wanted to hear her say it.

'You know you can't be here an—'

'So you know who I am, yet you won't tell your father,' Edmund cut in.

'No, I don't want to.'

'It is fine then. Besides, I guess the real reason may be lying somewhere in your head.'

For some reason, the pink blush that had made its appearance on her pale cheeks bounced off and made its way to other parts of her visible skin. He was right. Edmund had been holding her hand and her waist for a while now. She didn't fight it. It felt cosy, like she had met him before now.

'Let's get out of here.' She pulled him away from the crowd. They made their way out of the dance floor towards the rose pavilion where they had met earlier. Heading towards her secret door, Ella waved her hand and the rose bush parted, revealing a wooden frame wrecked of age. Edmund stood still. 'Get in now!' she bellowed.

He walked in. 'You have magick?'

'They try to hide it, as apparently what I got was not meant to happen.' She waved her hand back, and the door vanished entirely under the cloak of roses and bushes. 'Comes in handy for me, don't you think?'

She could now hear a new sonata. It was time to dance with Wilkin. Picking through another part of the bush, she wondered what would be going on inside.

'Do you want to dance with me instead?' he asked.

'Huh?'

'You've had your first dance. Let me have the second with you?' His eyes were bright and filled with a glint that promised fun. 'Besides, there is no one here, and it would be a waste of perfect music if we don't,' he added. He stretched out his hand to her.

Ella wondered how he never hesitated to speak his mind. He seemed a thousand times better than the secretive wolf of a person called Wilkin. He took her hands in his. Heart pounding as his hands almost made contact with her ribcage, they started dancing. It was her very first dance with someone who wasn't her father. In Yovaria, it was forbidden for a girl to dance with any other man until she was of age.

It is beautiful, and I am eighteen, she thought rebelliously.

She placed her hand gently on his broad shoulder, hoping he would take the lead as soon as possible, and he did. Each move more thrilling than the previous one, every turn was laced with passion. Ella's eyes couldn't leave his. Her pounding heart threatened to break through her ribcage. There was something strangely familiar about his embrace, like she'd been in his arms before. But she couldn't have.

As her emotions heightened, the roses around began budding. Each note led to an intense crest. As soon as the violinists plucked the last musical note, the rose petals fell sparingly on the floor, covering it in soft red. Their arms wrapped around each other for a split second after the final note. Eyes locked on each other.

'Well, that wasn't bad. Was it?' Edmund broke the ambience.

'No, this is the best part of the evening, Edmund,' she said, whispering his name softly.

'Why?'

'Because I had my first dance with you.

Somehow, though, it didn't feel like the first time at all, she thought.

CHAPTER 3

Ella wished the music hadn't stopped. The roses never failed to respond to her *touch of life*. Except that it wasn't the touch they responded to now, it was the *force of bliss* that came from her happiness. She hoped the boy before her never left, because he was the one responsible for it.

'You are someone who harbours no evil intentions, but why did you get in here by climbing the wall?' She prayed for an answer that would confirm her suspicion. The suspicion that he was a Gilmore but didn't despise the Desouzas.

'At one point or the other, every man embraces that dream of having a beautiful dance with someone as beautiful as yourself,' he replied.

Oh, dear Aphrodite, please don't make it known to him that I am blushing, she prayed.

Edmund wanted to ask if there was any chance that they might meet again, but she was tongue-tied from the intriguing affection she felt for him and so she couldn't move.

'ELLA,' a voice called.

'Someone is probably looking for you,' he said, cursing himself under his breath for being less of a man because he hadn't told her everything he was feeling.

'I need to go. I'm sorry, I …'

'It is fine. I must have overstayed my welcome.'

Ella wanted to scream that he was the best thing that had ever happened to her in her boring life. She tried to beg him to stay. She tried to tell him that things didn't seem the way they were, that he was welcome whenever he wished to show his face.

'No, no, you have … have not. You are always well …' Her stutter was incoherent. 'You are the best thing that has happened to me in a long while. If God is to be so kind as to give us another chance to meet, I want it.'

Edmund grasped her hand gently. 'Then I shall pray for that day every day of my life from today.' *Sophie! What of Sophie?* his mind yelled, but he ignored it.

She used the *touch of life* to reveal the hidden door and hastily ran out, leaving the door closed so no one would find the Gilmore boy as he tried to leave the same way he had come. She found Nurse Marcie a few feet away from the rose garden, glad the short pale woman hadn't noticed her departure from the hidden door.

'Where have you been? My lady requires your presence,' she said.

Ella nodded and made her way to the mansion. She turned around by the doorstep to see Marcie suspiciously inspect the garden, looking for answers Ella hadn't given and had been sure to conceal with all her might.

* *

Their eyes focused intently on the busy crowd socialising across the banquet hall. They were searching, hunting for the bigwig-nobody who was to marry their daughter or at least win her heart. Lord Desouza and his wife kept looking for Wilkin.

'Have you found him?' he asked one of his servants.

'We're yet to see him, my lord.' The hunched fellow bowed and retreated.

Lord Desouza heaved a fuming sigh. He was beginning to doubt Wilkin's integrity as a man. Perhaps he had been too hasty in promising his daughter to the man.

Just then, Wilkin ran into the room, panting and sweating like he had seen a ghost.

'You blue-blooded idiot! Where have you been? You missed her first dance.'

'Sir, they are here, they are here.' Wilkin gestured towards the entrance. 'We have visitors from Gilmore's hell. I am calling the guards.'

'That is not your call to make,' Lord Desouza cautioned, fuming. 'Why would we need guards on this lovely day? Today shouldn't be messier than you've made it. For the sake of my daughter, we will welcome them with loving arms.'

Two men walked through the main entrance; they expected their anticipation. Lord Desouza welcomed Gordon Gilmore with a wry smile. As much as he felt like sinking the sword from the wall-piece into Gordon's neck, he didn't show it.

'It would be rude on our part if we fail to give our regards to your daughter,' Gilmore, a tall man and of stout build, his hair a flaming red, started.

Wilkin's face strained. He shared the same inexplicable detest for the Gilmores. Their presence alone on the porch was infuriating.

Desouza looked into the coy eyes of the man before him. 'Of course, we are happy to welcome you. Do come in, we will serve you with the best of our wine.' Desouza signalled to a servant.

Gilmore and his brothers, all possessing the bodies of warriors and the same infamous red hair that came with being a Gilmore, walked in. They walked past Desouza to stand in the middle of the room. Although it seemed like they had no intention of making a scene, their very presence was an act, a pretense among veteran actors. 'I might be here to give my regards to your daughter, but—'

'If you're not, the very air you breathe is not welcomed here,' Desouza cut in.

'You and I know why I am here today, or has it skipped your mind?'

Desouza's face became even more riled up than before. 'You tell me,' he answered. One of his servants came with three glasses of wine. He held out the tray to the unwelcome guest. 'I hope it is worth my time and the risk of walking here without an invitation, Gordon,' Desouza added.

'We came with a message, Derrick, or a reminder.'

'You have the floor. Make it quick. Your irksome self is upsetting my guests.'

Gordon Gilmore shoved off the insult. Exchanging words with Lord Desouza in his own territory was a foolish thing to do. 'They will be twenty-one soon, the same age as those two. You remember, right?'

'It doesn't matter to me. Now is not the time to remind me of that night,' Desouza warned.

'We both saw them die, Derrick, and whoever killed them is still out there, probably plotting his next move. Isn't that of concern to you?'

'It has nothing to do with my daughter.'

'It has nothing to do with my son also, but it would be folly on your part if you fail to acknowledge that it has everything to do with us, Derrick.' Gilmore wasn't going to leave without dishing out his subtle jabs. He took a sip of the wine and returned the glass to the tray. He faked a smile after the release of his coy laughter. 'How about a piece of advice for old friendship's sake, Derrick?'

The once peaceful party was now sore. A dead silence had fallen across the room right from the moment Wilkin announced their arrival. It was excluded from today's programme, but the scenario amused the guest.

'Anticipate your opponent's move when moving each piece on your board, especially when you are the gamemaker or an audience.'

Desouza laughed. 'Visit some other time, old friend. Let us treat ourselves to a pleasurable game of chess.'

Gilmore thanked his sworn enemy for the drink and

walked out with his brothers the same way they arrived, except that the mumblings of the guests trailed after them.

~

'Your Highness, the royal priest would like to have a private audience with you,' the messenger said, holding out a letter.

Prince Kai took the letter and dismissed the messenger. Messages of grave importance were for his eyes alone. He read the squiggly writing once, reread it and read it one last time. Sometimes it was hard to decipher the older man's graffiti on paper, but he had to be sure of the message. He walked out of his room to the observatory. The knight guarding his room accompanied him with the dense but smooth steps of a man who had done this numerous times.

'It is okay, Fred. Just make sure no one comes in till I am out,' Prince Kai instructed at the gate of the observatory tower. The knight bowed and assumed the guard post, while Prince Kai walked into the observatory tower. Inside the temple were grey walls wrecked of age and long spiral steps leading to a dark room. He met the priest gazing at the stars.

'Is this necessary tonight, Linus? I had a busy day.'

'You should include this in your daily schedule, Your Highness. Each star represents each person in your empire,' the priest answered.

'Through the stars, you can see the goodness and evil in all, right?' he repeated the words that had been taught to him with ease. 'You can always send a report to me each day, or do you enjoy my company so?'

A happy curl found its way to a side of the priest's lips. 'Your Highness remembers. It is my honour.'

The prince walked to the edge of the observatory. He noticed the stars were bright for a day like this. It was perfect. However, a star on the side of the Virgo was even more brilliant. 'A hue of red today?' Kai asked. 'Virgo is starting to pull the star towards itself. It can either connect or collide. The bond between them should they meet can never break …' Kai recited.

'… But when they collide, they will destroy everything around them,' the old priest supplied.

'Virgo has found its star. What will it do to the other? Will it attract or repel? The intensity of the circumstance is severe.'

'Perfect, Your Highness! You have taken these lessons to heart.' The priest blazed with excitement. 'Those two are no ordinary individuals. One holds the lock, the other *the touch of life* – soft as rose petals, sharp as thorns. One will find the gem to break that lock.'

'It is all blurry. Can you locate these stars?' Kai asked.

The priest walked away from the observatory towards the door, and Kai followed swiftly behind. They descended the dusky, cold steps. 'I will send you a letter and other things you need.'

The prince groaned inwardly as he thought, *More of his squiggly writing.*

'The boy will come to me, Your Highness. When he does, I'll guide him,' Linus added.

'Okay, old man.'

Linus' crumbled face moulded into a stern look. The youthful yet ancient priest who wore a grey garment, black girdle and carried an ancient staff hated to be called *old*. 'Your Highness …'

Prince Kai smiled. He enjoyed watching his reaction.

'Be prepared, Your Highness. Your greatest foe is yet to come.'

'Is that from you or the stars?' Prince Kai joked, and walked away.

Edmund returned home and slumped on the couch in his room. The exhaustion and tension from his experience at the Desouza mansion lingered. Thankfully, his father wasn't back. He wondered where he would have gone and hoped they hadn't noticed his absence the entire evening, especially today when he had gone and done something that could get him into trouble. Lucky enough for him, Leofrick had found his cousin waiting at Canary Lane. He had warned him about the Gilmore's visit to the Desouza mansion. That was enough time for him to get home unnoticed.

So many thoughts preoccupied his mind, and Sophie wasn't one of them.

How could someone control nature? he thought.

He hoped she was okay and wondered when he

would be able to see her again. Deep in thought, he failed to notice Leofrick and Neal walk in.

Leofrick faked a cough. 'Hhmm … Hhmm.'

He jumped, his face a display of worry. 'How was it? What happened to Ella? Did she get into trouble because of me? What did Father say to—'

'One question at a time,' Neal cut in.

'For someone who spent the evening with the daughter of his father's sworn enemy, I feel thrilled. She acted pretty well, not in the least bit scared or surprised. She even …'

'Your father was there, Edmund. My father, too. And Uncle Yuno. They spoke to Derrick Desouza, and he offered them wine.'

'What was he doing there? He usually avoids standing by their side on every occasion, even during the prince's military session at the castle,' Edmund commented.

'Shouldn't you ask whether they got out alive or what message was strong enough to push him into Desouza's hades?'

'All right, then. I hope no one is dead. What did they talk about?' Edmund asked.

'We are not sure ourselves. It was about something that happened a long time ago. I couldn't make any sense of it,' Neal answered.

Edmund's furious but comical face got Leofrick laughing. 'Why did you raise my interest with such inept information?'

'That is the true world of adults, my son, complications in every possible way,' Leofrick said amidst laughter.

'I need to visit the temple.'

'What are you lads up to this time around?' Lady Gilmore interjected. She strolled in and rested on the door frame of Edmund's room.

'We were talking about general youthful happenings. Very general.' Neal supplied the blatant lie from his bag of tricks, but his demeanor at that moment gave it all away. He stood stiff like a rusty old tree.

Edmund saw his mother's suspicious eyes. He needed to act fast. 'Is Father home yet?' he asked.

'Not yet, Son. He is in the middle of something important, and he will be late.'

Something like a fight with the Desouzas? Edmund thought.

His mother turned to Neal and Leofrick. 'You two should be home now. You shouldn't keep your parents worried.' Neal and Leofrick walked towards the door, mouths sealed and too heavy to say goodbye. 'You should go to bed now. There's no need to await your father's return.'

Edmund slumped into the comfy sheets of his soft, king-sized bed.

CHAPTER 4

The Moonlight Festival was only a score and two days away, and everyone at the temple had so much to do, since this year's preparations were more considerable than those of the last.

Athena's Day was a day of celebration for the lads and maidens of Yovaria. They were to pray for protection from Fenrir's ghoul, a creature that was said to dwell in the forest. The last night of the festival fell on a full moon, a day on which no one dared to enter the forest, because Athena, their goddess, would be in a battle with Fenrir as a response to their prayers.

Three years ago, on that very night, there was an unfortunate occurrence. A lady had gotten into the forest somehow. The next day, her mutilated, gory body was found next to the olive tree in front of the temple. As a result, the emperor ordered that the security around the forest should be tighter than before. This decree, against the priest's values and wishes, allowed the soldiers to participate in the festival.

Edmund hadn't visited the temple in a long while. He still didn't feel the need to do so, but no youth in Yovaria could ignore Athena's call.

He prayed in silence. *Please give me the courage to protect the one I think I love.*

Linus, the priest, sprinkled some herb-infused water from a glass on the altar onto his head, while Ed remained on his knees. A sign of blessing. 'I haven't seen you in a long while, Edmund,' he began after Edmund finished his prayer.

'Busy trying to win the heart of Lady Sophie?' Linus added. For some reason unknown to everyone in Yovaria, all the lads and maidens loved Linus. They found comfort in him and trusted him with their secrets, and in return, the priest never betrayed that trust. They respected him both as a messenger of the gods and a friend.

'Not Sophie, but Ella,' Edmund replied.

'Ella of what house?'

'You know already, old man.'

Linus, wondering why everyone was so insistent on calling him an old man, said, 'I don't think I know—'

'Ella of the Desouza house,' Edmund cut in.

'It is too early to be a drunk, son.' Everyone knew the Gilmores and Desouzas were sworn enemies and would continue to be so for years to come.

'I haven't had any wine, old man.'

'You young ones bask in the delight of disorder.'

'You can't control who you fall in love with, old man.'

'But you can control your desires,' Linus countered.

'You know she can control roses. Not just roses, bushes and plants in general … maybe trees too, but how is that possible? Royal guards are hundred percent *humans*, right? Her father is the emperor's royal commander, and his wife is human too, there's just no way …'

'How do you know this?'

'I saw it with my own eyes, or maybe she wanted me to see it.'

Linus smiled. 'You know nothing. Come, sit, and let us talk.'

** *

'Why do you find it hard having an interest in what young maidens of your age like?' Marcie asked while helping her tie the laces of her nightgown.

Like every young soul, she hated unnecessary comparison. She had been reprimanded over and over by her parents for sneaking out of her own party. Sometimes Marcie had a way of bringing her back to reality.

Edmund, she thought. Ever since that day, she had prayed each day to see him. Anywhere, somewhere, even in her dreams and before the next full moon.

'I almost forgot. I got you something.' Marcie fumbled under the bed and pulled out a box. She handed it to Ella and waited for her to open it.

Ella took it out. A supple red hood.

'Thought it would look lovely on you.'

'It is beautiful. Thank you,' Ella answered swiftly and absentmindedly, then resumed her daydream about Edmund.

Nurse Marcie watched her for a dozen seconds. 'Goodness, what kind of girl goes into her thoughts while speaking? You have so much to learn. How long do you want to keep Lord Wilkin waiting? He cares for you, you know.'

Ella snapped out of her thoughts as soon as she heard Marcie speaking. She took her seat on the edge of the bed beside Nurse Marcie. 'I want you to promise never to leave me when my ill-fated life begins.'

Marcie picked up her hand tenderly, burying it warmly in hers as she stroked her fingers gently. 'I promise, but never say you have an unfortunate life. Did Lord Wilkin say something to you that night?' a concerned Marcie enquired.

'No, not him. Someone else stole my heart.'

'And who might that be?'

Ella hesitated. 'First, promise me that you will accept whomever I choose to love.'

'Ella, dear, I have always placed your happiness above anything else since the day you were born. Yet I shall reaffirm that promise to you. I will accept your decision no matter the circumstance. Now, who is he?'

'He caught my eye long before the first dance. No, from the very moment he entered the mansion. His warm gaze melts all distress. I feel safe in his arms, and every day I pray that we cross paths once again.'

'You speak so highly of someone you met for one night. He is from which household? Is he better than Sir Wilkin in any way?'

'He is better in every way. But to Mother, Father, you and everyone else, he is—'

'Marcie! Marcie!' Lady Desouza called from the drawing room.

'Dear me, I forgot her tea. Wash your face and undo your hair for the night, would you? It will take me half an hour to get supper ready,' she said hastily, walking out of Ella's room.

Perfect timing, Ella thought. She walked to her dressing table and undid her pins and ribbons.

Something hit the window … She jolted in fear.

It hit the window again …

This time she was sure it was someone, not something. She hastily grabbed a thick wooden hairbrush from her dressing table to serve as her weapon. She felt the rush of wind flow into her bedroom. The intruder had successfully opened the window. Curtains flying, tension rising, she could see the human-shaped shadow.

A figure hid behind the curtain. Ella instinctively lunged forward to hit it with the brush. It held her hand mid-air, and the brush fell out of her hands. Her heart skipped. She was about to scream when the figure covered her mouth as her trembling hands clutched her chest.

'Sorry to frighten you, miss …'

Her stare was crowded with disbelief, mouth open in shock.

'Aren't you going to say something?' Edmund asked. 'I am always climbing over something to see you. Like how I'll climb over every obstacle just to get to you.'

'I am not happy that you are here,' she said.

Edmund's face revealed a mixture of shock and hurt.

'No, I mean words are too empty to describe how I feel seeing you here, but it is too dangerous. What were you thinking?' she quickly rephrased, hating that she had put such an agonised expression on his face.

'That once your nurse accepts me, I will be one step closer.'

'You were listening? How could ... how long were you outside my window?'

'Not too long. A gentleman knows when the time is right. Hanging onto a tree as if your life depends on it can be fun sometimes, and I needed to give you these things today.' He took out a sack from the right corner of his belt.

'How often do you illegally climb over people's walls?'

'You're making it sound like a crime. I do it only when I need to see a pretty girl like yourself.'

'It is a crime, and from your words, it is not wrong of me to guess that you do this for other girls too.'

'A woman, only once. Consider me wanted, if climbing into your room is felonious.'

'Who was that?' Ella's eyes were now green with jealousy.

'My mother.'

'Oh.' She blushed. 'Why would you go through that stress when you can just walk in through the door?'

'So that I could make the second woman I love jealous.' Edmund took her hand and pulled her closer.

Ella couldn't hold it in any longer. She giggled like a

toddler. 'You're different. Every time my mother talks to me, it is always about the Duke of Kroukhesta. I was never allowed to do what I want. That was why I needed to get away from everything at the rose pavilion.'

'I guess the duke didn't get that far with you.'

Ella laughed. 'We aren't engaged, and we can never be. My heart belongs to someone else.'

'And I am that person, right?' He handed her a fan.

She accepted it. The texture of the fabric startled her. It had the same feeling as a rose petal. She would have sworn he made it from roses, but was that even possible? She felt flustered. 'I don't know what to say.'

'The first would be thank you, and the second would be yes.'

'Yes?' Ella was confused.

'Would you go to the Moonlight Festival with me?'

'Yes?' Ella asked, still confused.

'Okay, that settles it.'

'Oh, you tricked me. I want to, but you and I know why no one can see us together.'

'That is why I have this. My second gift.' Edmund held out a pair of masks from the bag. They were wrapped in silk. Just as she was about to unwrap them, she heard Nurse Marcie's footsteps.

'Quick, you have to go.' In a split second, she hid the mask beneath her gown just as Edmund hopped through the window.

He held onto the frame and placed his legs on the tree outside. 'Ah, I forgot something!'

'Wha—'

He pulled at the nape of her neck, bringing her closer to him, and kissed her. Those soft lips of hers moved in response. Ella felt an inexplicable yet delicious bliss for the first time in her life. Not too long after that, Edmund jumped down the tree, leaving her flustered and hungry for more, her face radiant as the morning sun.

'What are you doing?' Nurse Marcie had walked in without her noticing. Ella turned swiftly in a bid to act normal, but her smile betrayed her. 'That smile, I haven't seen that in a long while. What is going on?'

She wanted to spill it all out. She tried to tell her about her first kiss, how it felt, how she was feeling … something she had never felt before. But she turned to enjoy the sight of the silver crescent and hoped for the eclipse to arrive faster.

Sir Wilkin stood by the window in his manor, in a town east of Yovaria. A town called Kroukhesta. He had just arrived from the royal palace, where he'd executed his official duke duties. Exhaustion weighed him down as usual.

'Sir, we have little time before we welcome the full moon,' Wilkin's advisor, Raoul, reminded him. Raoul pushed up his glasses as he continued scribbling on a long piece of parchment he held.

Wilkin sighed, and a wave of worry and fatigue swept over him. Raoul's voice meant more work, more talk. 'How many days left?'

'Three days, sir.'

Three days! It is all moving too fast, he thought. 'Anything left to do? I need to clear my duties before going to bed. I am to leave on the morrow at sunrise.'

'Nothing much, my lord, except for engagement gift preparations for the Desouza princess tomorrow.'

I still don't know why he calls her princess.

'Aha, the gift.' He acted surprised. Wilkin had no intention of giving it to her. Custom and culture made it mandatory if he ever wanted to marry her. It was the second gift. 'Dust and polish the imperial emerald necklace.'

Raoul rolled up the parchment, dipped in a bow and walked out, coming back almost immediately.

'Why are you still here?'

'I don't know, sir.'

'Then get out!' Wilkin raged. 'And don't allow anyone in tonight,' the Duke warned as Raoul made his exit.

Wilkin felt the sudden chill in the air. *He is here*, he thought, feeling the tell-tale signs of the mysterious arrival.

'There is no need to be so uptight with your subordinates, Bodolf. I rule over the entire Fenrir clan, and that includes you, my devoted shadow,' Leofrick, the god who hid in plain sight as a human among the other humans, spoke from one part of the room. Doors and walls were no obstacles for the god of mischief.

Wilkin felt indifferent about his unsolicited guest, but he had no choice but to welcome him. No force could ever break the *shadow law*. A shiver ran up his spine, and he pulled his robe closer to his body. Leofrick could be creepy sometimes.

'My utmost greetings, Master Loki. I prefer to be called Wilkin, not Bodolf.'

Loki smirked. 'Why? I named you Bodolf, remember?'

'I know, but the name ties me to an invisible chain.'

'Yes, you are bound to me. You have no choice; you are just a shadow. Shadows have no feelings. Consider yourself lucky. Most shadows have no pleasant rapport with their masters ... gods. We are a proud kind.'

'With all due respect, proud master, I have pressing matters needing my attention. This gab adds to my exhaustion.' Wilkin made his way to the door.

The door slammed shut, causing Wilkin to freeze. A ringing sensation sounded in his ears. Realising his mistake, he turned and knelt submissively, never daring to meet the gaze of his master, Loki, who was in his mystic form. No shadow ever remained alive once he or she set eyes on their master's real state.

'My sincere apologies, Master Loki. I have overstepped my boundaries,' Wilkin begged.

Loki returned to his human form, Leofrick, reaching towards Wilkin to hold his face. A shot of horror raced up and down his spine. Sweat beads rolled from his petrified forehead down to his neck. 'Let me make one thing clear, Bodolf. You have no say over your life, no say over your destiny. You are my shadow. You'll do as I always say whether it is pleasing to you or not.'

'Yes, my lord.'

Leofrick stepped back. 'Now, let's talk about your engagement.'

'Wh-what about it, my lord?'

'What gift do you intend to give her?'

'A necklace of immense value, my lord.'

'You will do no such thing. Remember your resolution?'

What resolution? Wilkin thought.

'Humans. Your thoughts are as fleeting as your life. Remember the item you stole after the slaughter?'

Flashes of gory images filled Wilkin's head. Never could he forget that night, except for the face on the carcass.

'You are to hand it over to her as a gift,' Leofrick instructed.

On this, Wilkin could agree with Leofrick. The time was right to hand it over to Ella. 'Yes, my lord, but I wish to know what you have in mind, master. This plan has me in the dark. It can only lead to distrust,' Wilkin added.

'I don't need you to trust me. I am your master.'

'Then I can choose not to go with your advice?' Wilkin probed. He knew what he asked for could lead to rage from him, but he felt like doing so all the same.

'You can choose whatever you like,' Leofrick retorted.

'Can you at least tell me how to fix it? It has remained broken since that night.'

'You are asking the wrong person.' Leofrick walked towards the window. 'Ask the person currently sitting on the Yovarian throne. The owner hides beneath his nose.'

A strong gale gushed in through the window, causing the chandelier to sing and the curtains to dance to its tune. The doors bolted open to reveal a frantic Raoul rushing in with a few guards. 'We heard a disturbing noise, sir. Are you okay?'

'There is a purple chest placed underneath the closet floor. Get it for me. It has been stored away for too long. It is time it returned to the rightful owner's blood.'

Derrick Desouza sat at the dining table. He had risen from bed early today, maybe because he was having breakfast with the Duke of Kroukhesta, and sharing breakfast included severe political discussion.

Lady Desouza walked in with a bouquet of fresh flowers, followed by two servants holding trays of tagenites – pancakes topped with honey and cheese – a loaf of white bread, yoghurt and pomegranates, too. They set the food on the table while Lady Desouza replaced the flowers in the vase with the fresh ones.

'Why is Ella yet to be here?' Sir Desouza asked impatiently.

Lady Desouza helped herself to the table, sitting beside her husband as expected. 'I was with her some moments ago, and she will be here any minute. Here she is.' She gestured at their daughter.

I thought it was a notable event. Why was I forced to wear a palla? I can't remember if my mum has ever worn one, Ella thought. People wore a palla over a dress, and it slightly covered the head. 'Today must be very significant. It is the first time I have ever worn my palla, you know,' she said, breaking the odd silence.

'Of course it is. I will be announcing the occasion soon enough,' Derrick replied.

'Is he here?' Lady Desouza asked a servant who had walked in.

'Yes, the duke has arrived, Lady Desouza.'

Is he here? No-one ever mentioned that I would be meeting him, Ella thought, bewildered.

The curtains were pushed back to reveal the entrance of their expected guest. The duke walked gallantly to the dining table.

'Welcome, Sir Wilkin. I am glad you'll be joining us today.'

'I am happy to be here. To do whatever I can for my in-laws and to gaze at the stunning face of my wife-to-be.' He smiled at Ella.

Ella was generous enough to return his repulsive smile.

'Sit! Let's feast,' Lady Desouza ordered.

As soon as he took his seat, the maids scurried to serve him. After taking a few bites from the bread, he spoke. 'My apologies, Sir Desouza, my ears are itching for this news.'

'You are to take my daughter's hand in marriage on the day after the morrow.'

Ella dropped the silverware in her hand. Sir Desouza's face was unreadable. She turned to her mother, her only hope. 'It is too soon. Mother, you said we would talk about this.'

'Yes, I did, and we are.'

'It is an honour, sir. It is my dream to wed the most elegant lady in the kingdom, but I pray thee, that you allow us to tarry for a while. I will be on grave official duties on the day after the morrow.'

'Very well, then. We shall keep it at that. A simple but sophisticated wedding with few friends and family is just right. What do you think, Wilkin?' Derrick said, remaining straight-faced. Several times Ella had wondered if he ever had emotions.

'That is perfect.' Wilkin smiled. He walked up to Ella.

Now is not the time to display cheap chivalry. I swear on Athena's name, I could kill you, she thought as he approached.

Wilkin revealed an item wrapped in clover leaves. 'A gift for my future wife.'

Her irritation swelled like yeast in bread. Everyone at the table felt it.

'Don't just stare at him. Accept it gracefully,' Lady Desouza scolded.

'Thank you,' she answered spiritlessly, opening it to find a circlet.

'Oh, it is beautiful, Sir Wilkin. A perfect combination with the wedding dress,' Lady Desouza exclaimed. 'The small green leaves flawlessly carve into the gleaming silver,' she added.

The circlet was beautiful all right. It was the only good thing that came from Wilkin, but why rose leaves? she wondered. He had no idea about her magick, or did he? A flicker of energy left her immediately; it touched her fingers.

Her father clapped. 'Now that is done, have your seat and let's celebrate. Wine!' Derrick signalled to a servant, who scurried over with a tray of four majestic glasses. 'In three days, two will become one. My people will be your people and your people, my people. The wedding will be held in the temple in the eyes of few, and rituals will commence after the full-moon festival.

To a blissful marriage!' he bellowed as he raised his glass.

'A blissful marriage,' they all chorused, except Ella.

'You can leave the room, Ella. The duke and I have so much to talk about,' Sir Desouza commanded.

Ella furiously pushed the chair backwards with her buttocks. The loud screech of the chair against the floor wailed beneath her. Nurse Marcie walked behind her to her room.

Priest Linus locked the doors of the temple's storage. All preparations from his end were complete; there was just one thing left to do. Ever since he met Prince Kai concerning the star, he had felt the need to take drastic action before leaving on royal order.

'Send a message to the prince now,' he said to one of the temple's attendants. They only noticed the stars connecting, but there was more to it.

Just as his aide was leaving, he met Prince Kai on his way.

'Is he the one who writes your messages?' the prince asked, gesturing to the aide.

'That is Yemini. He does all the writing,' Linus answered.

Kai whispered into the ears of the older man, 'Get another. He saves you the trouble, but he has horrible writing. I am here, I realized that it was best to meet you one last time before you leave Yovaria. We should expect you two days before the Moonlight Festival.'

'Yes. We need to make plans here and now. There are pressing issues we need to address.'

'Issues …?'

They started strolling together.

'Both stars will regain memories of past lives. Not good memories, Prince Kai. Visions will reveal themselves in bits.'

'How can we deal with this?'

'Patience, Your Highness. I haven't said anything yet. There is no way we can help them through this ordeal. We can only offer support after these occurrences. I have appointed someone trustworthy to be in charge of the Desouza daughter. The Gilmore lad will need your help.'

'It is a strange thing, looking at the reincarnation of my brother and doing nothing about it. I still remember how shocked I was when Loki told me Edmund is reborn of my dead brother.' Yemini walked in with a jug of honey and milk. The priest poured a cup and offered it to the prince, who took a sip. 'I am happy to do this without being asked, although I have no idea how I can be of help. Mother forbade me to speak about the death of Vaughan years back. I know little of it and can't fathom the missing link.'

'Let us place Her Majesty aside for a while. Her rage against the Duke of Kroukhesta controls her gloomy soul. Remember the map I sent through you to the Gilmore lad?'

'Yes, I will hand it over on the morrow.'

'Good. Vaughan left a final note and an amulet behind. I was able to get it beneath a tree close to the

River Thames before it got into the wrong hands. Never speak of it to him nor hand it over until he is ready.'

'Yes, but don't I deserve to know the contents of this letter? I am his brother.'

'When the time is right, Son,' Linus answered.

'One more thing. Never mention to them that they will receive vile visions. Let it remain as visions to them, not memories.'

CHAPTER 6

'My Lord, Edmund Gilmore is here,' a servant announced.

'Let him in.'

Edmund walked in slowly, admiring the royal library as he did so. 'Hello, my lord,' he greeted with a deep bow. 'I am here at your request, Your Highness.'

Kai looked up from the book he was reading. 'I assume that you are aware of the upcoming Moonlight Festival.'

'Yes, Your Highness. Even the rats of Yovaria are getting prepared.'

'The time is upon us. The wolves are excited as the day draws near. We are fortunate to witness another blood moon.'

'Yes, Your Highness.'

'Have a seat.' The prince offered him a chair adjacent to the majestic reading table in the imperial office. 'Wine? Milk?'

'Milk,' Edmund replied. He would have asked for

nothing, but it would be rude of him to decline a royal order.

Prince Kai handed Edmund a scroll. 'You can open it. That is the most and only help you can get from me.'

'Help? From what? For what?' Edmund wanted to ask.

Edmund walked to the table and opened it as he took a seat. It was a large map with rusty old tears at the edges. There, an image of a wide river stretched out across its age-stricken pages. Edmund traced his finger down the river. As he did this, the deep blue of the river turned a bright red. Edmund was startled so much that he looked for the prince for confirmation of what he saw.

Kai nodded for him to continue.

Edmund traced the river to the end of the map, and a sun appeared.

'Perfect, that sun is your destination,' Kai announced, as though he had found a treasure.

'What is this place?' a bemused Edmund enquired.

'I can't say. I have never been there myself.'

Edmund's eyes popped out from their sockets. *A creepy map and a bizarre destination. What a wonderful way to begin the day,* he thought. 'How many days will it take us to get there?' he asked calmly.

'Three days. Seven days at most if it rains.'

'I have no idea how I can leave home for that long without going unnoticed. My father isn't gracious with permissions.' Edmund poured out his worries to the only person who could take care of them while he tucked the scroll into his belt.

'I will get you out of Yovaria, so leave your father to me,' Kai assured him. 'Rest well.'

Edmund bowed and walked towards the door. Just when he was about to leave, Kai beckoned him once more before summoning Knight Fred into the room.

'Any questions, Edmund?'

Why me? What am I going to do when I get there? Does the creepy map have magic? Why is this important to you? What is going on? It is all too fast. All these were the thoughts that ran through Edmund's mind. Still, he could not question the Prince of Yovaria. Doing so would mean he was being impudent towards the Royal Crown.

'No questions, Your Highness,' he answered, although he was drowning in his thoughts.

'Is the Duke of Kroukhesta here?' Kai asked Fred.

'Yes, my lord. He awaits your presence in the imperial gallery,' the knight answered.

Edmund took a bow and exited the room, a little intimidated by the knight's huge form and gruff tone. Everyone in Yovaria was scared of the loyal knight, not just because he was a mountain of a man but also because of the long, jagged scar that ran along his left cheek which no one knew how he had gotten.

Kai nodded. *It is time to move a piece on the chessboard. His opponent was already on the attack,* he thought with a smirk as he watched Edmund leave.

**

Ella's fretfulness lingered on for a while. The news had hit her like a warring mace. She was pacing around in her room when Marcie walked in with a bowl of scented water and a towel to place on the bedside stool.

'Ella, dear, I know how worried you are, but pacing about isn't going to help. Take a seat. I will wash your face, and we can talk about it.' Marcie remained the only gentle person who understood Ella. 'Why are you against this alliance? Is it because of the special person you met the other day?' she added while squeezing the soaked towel.

'Help me. What do I do? I need to talk to …' Ella hesitated. She couldn't say his name, not in front of Nurse Marcie.

'Talk to whom?' Marcie, as sensitive as she was, couldn't let the unfinished sentence go, but Ella refused to speak. 'Talk to whom, dear? Your engagement is tonight. Ever since you were born, I have promised to put your feelings above everything else, and I am in no way ready to break that vow.'

'Edmund, Edmund Gilmore,' Ella blurted out. 'He is the one person I should have never met, but I did. I know you will be mad at me for this, but it doesn't matter now, I have no regrets. I will be married off to someone I barely know and have no feeling of love whatsoever for.'

Nurse Marcie took her by the hand and led her to the dressing table. Ella felt the weight of her secret roll off her shoulders even though she didn't yet know what to expect.

'What made you think that I would be mad at you? I have known you since you were brought into this world, Ella. You would never do anything to hurt the ones you love. You wouldn't even step on a flower bed for fear of crushing or hurting the flowers.' Marcie stroked her hair gently. 'I know you've not been able to tell your parents because you love them, and you don't want to upset them,' Marcie added.

Ella's face brightened up. 'Do you think I will be able to get out of this predicament?'

Marcie straightened her back while she removed her palla. 'Put your trust in *Elpis*. She gives hope to those who need it.' That wasn't the answer Ella wished for, but it brought her relief and hope. 'I can relay any message from you to Edmund. It is the least I can do for you.'

Ella smiled. Marcie was a blessing. 'Thank you so much. Can you pass me the parchment, quill and ink? I need to write a letter to him as soon as possible.'

'I will get them from the study after you've washed your face.'

Ella rolled up her sleeves and wiped her face with the towel, looking into the mirror. *That's right. I should tell Edmund about the wedding at the temple,* she thought. *Maybe he will be able to think of something before it happens.*

'I knew I would find you here.' Edmund walked into the Faded Tavern. He had been looking for Leofrick all over town and had finally found him. Sighing, he chastised himself for not starting there in the first place.

Leofrick was in the company of drunk companions

who were laughing at the smallest possible occurrence. To Leofrick, the tavern was a place of music, dancing and much laughter, not just a place to get mugs of beer and colourful cocktails like most people did.

'Edmund! My pal. My brother from another mother. To what honour do I owe this visit?' a tipsy Leofrick called out.

'I never knew that my presence could be an honourable thing. May I talk to you in private?' Edmund requested, crossing his arms.

'My my! What is the name of Pandora could it be? The curiosity tickles me to the foot.' Leofrick punched his left foot. There was a barrel of laughs from his companion.

'All right, pal. I know you are having the best time of your life, and I am happy for you, but I won't be around for a while, and I really need to ask you for a favour.'

Leofrick picked up the urgency in Edmund's voice. 'How far is the journey?' he asked soberly.

'Far out from the forest.'

'When are you planning to leave?'

'At dawn.'

Leofrick nodded. Now was time to get serious. He excused himself from his drunken companions. He and Edmund walked out of the tavern. As they walked towards their horses, they noticed a woman standing beside Edmund's horse, her back to them.

Ella? Ella? That must be Ella, he thought.

Edmund touched the figure by the shoulder. It turned to reveal a face that wasn't Ella's.

'You must be Edmund Gilmore.'

'Yes, madam,' Edmund replied. He remembered her. She was the one who gave that little introduction about Ella during the dance.

Marcie removed the hood of her black cloak to reveal her wrinkled yet so beautiful face. 'I have with me a letter from Elizabeth Desouza to you. It contains her innermost feelings, good and bad. I need to know yours. If you have any.'

'My feelings are pure, just like my love for her. Nothing else,' Edmund replied.

The nurse took out a scroll tied with a pink ribbon and held out her palm. 'Swear by the goddess Athena that you would never hurt her in any way.'

Edmund placed his palm on hers. 'I swear by Athena and the seven gods of this world that I would never hurt her in any way nor feed her to the evil claws of this world.'

'Then make haste, my child. As you need to save her from the hands of someone else. Someone higher than you, of course. If your love is true, then there is nothing stronger than that. She is to become a bride to someone other than yourself tonight at the temple of Athena.'

It hit Edmund harder than a truckload of barrels. 'At what hour is the ceremony?' he asked hastily.

'Hour you say, but it is by the minute. It took me the night to get here by horse. You should be there by sunrise. The wedding is an hour before sundown.' Marcie handed him the letter.

Edmund collected the letter hastily. 'Get on your horse, Leofrick.' He scanned through the letter, his eyes moving through the words quickly. Just as the woman had told him, Ella was getting married to a noble. Not just any noble; it was the Duke of Kroukhesta. He rolled up the paper and tucked it into the pouch on his belt. He jolted the horse, and it replied with an aggressive neigh.

'Lady, can you pass on this message to her in case we tarry for long?' Edmund requested.

'For Ella's sake, I shall do so.'

'Please tell her that her wish is mine and I will be with her tomorrow. Not as the wall-climbing Gilmore boy but as her husband.'

Marcie smiled. *Young love. Always beautiful and brave. Ella has found the right person*, she thought. 'Very well, I will relay the message. She will be happy to hear that,' she answered. *Do you have a plan? Will you swoop in and drag her from the altar?* she wanted to ask, but watching Edmund's anger and determination over the news he had just received erased her questions.

'Thank you,' the lad answered, and off he went. He galloped frantically on his black horse, and Leofrick raced behind him on his.

'Pal, you've got a lot of explaining to do. What is it that I have missed?' Leofrick called from behind.

'I shall feed your itching ears later on. First, we need to get to the temple at the speed of Hermes' magical sandals.'

Kai arrived at the swan gazebo where Wilkin awaited him. He watched as Wilkin bowed after seeing him walking towards the railing. 'Get up, Bodolf. There is no use in offering pretentious respect,' the prince said.

Wilkin smirked and stood up. Just like the prince, he, too, had no time for dramatic displays.

'That is right, and it is expected of you, Your Highness. Even though I have known you all your life, you've always kept your distance ever since your family ascended to the throne.'

Kai's eyes turned cold within seconds. 'No matter the reason, orders are orders and you must carry them out. We end up with no choice but to obey. When our minds were full of pure youth, we learned this.'

'Which is why I am here, since I have business in the capital,' Bodolf confessed.

'I am thankful that you chose today. It makes the hunt easy.'

Wilkin laughed. 'Your passion for hunting hasn't faded one bit. I remember the times we used to do that together alongside your brother. I can recall the very first lesson you had from me and when you both managed to get hold of a cougar preying on a white-tailed deer. You were so joyful that His Highness chose to offer all of the creatures to the gods. We travelled around the country, displaying it as a royal offering to be offered in the Wistron Temple.'

Kai laughed. 'Yes, those blissful memories will remain evergreen.' Kai let his guard down.

'Why don't we try hunting again for old times' sake?' Wilkin asked.

'I would love to … with a friend and not someone I hold in contempt.'

'Everyone makes choices at one point. There is no such thing as good or bad,' Wilkin said, defending himself.

'But these choices affect others whether they are right or wrong,' the prince answered while he walked towards the knight guarding the entrance of the gazebo. Kai placed his warring fingers on his sword hilt. It had been a while since he'd pulled it out in actual battle. He closed his eyes to embrace his inclination.

'You can pull it out from its sheath. I won't move an inch. However, I had hoped you would want to know why I agreed to see you.' Bodolf wasn't pleading, but Kai smelt trepidation in his voice.

Good. Just what I needed. Kai held the sword tighter. 'I got the news that you needed to speak to me. A letter would have sufficed, Bodolf. Why did you come here?'

Kai asked, knowing that the hatred he felt for Wilkin would always remain.

'I did mention that today is my special day. I am going to have an alliance with a particular someone.'

Kai's eyes almost popped out from their sockets. 'You don't even know if your wife still lives. I hope you haven't forgotten that her disappearance twenty years ago still holds a string of hope, even though the queen proclaimed her dead. Now you want to take a new wife?'

'Dear Prince. It seems to me that you don't know me well enough. I have never had emotions for anyone. On the other hand, she had an attachment to almost everyone and anyone, especially that red-haired girl. Memories of that night still fill my head. When the river turned red, the girl fell asleep by the riverbank. My wife was foolish enough to leave with her.'

'Are you saying that you contributed to her death?'

'Yes, I am. If you want to put it bluntly.'

'You are admitting that you're a killer?'

'Yes, and I know you can't get me punished without the king's seal.'

'Fine, but why your daughter? She was your blood. Your blood, yet you refer to her as that red-haired girl?' Kai asked confusedly. He was taken aback by Bodolf's inhuman nature.

'It is a curse Loki placed on the Fenrir clan. That girl was turning twenty-one soon.'

Kai emitted a frustrated sigh. 'You say that, and yet you are getting married to that gentle Desouza soul. Do you intend to keep the woman childless her whole life?'

'Your ignorance amuses me, my prince. I am obsessed with power, and I already have all that human life could afford. I do not need an offspring, I desire something more supreme.' Bodolf walked up to the prince. He forced the prince's hand and sword back into its sheath and whispered in his ear. 'What I want is a complete circlet. After years of research on how to break my curse, I am this close, except that I need someone of elven blood to put the circlet back together.'

'Elven blood?'

'Yes, my little prince. They control poison, which is the very essence of the gem.'

'The stone can neutralize poison?' Kai's inquisitive glare became even more pronounced.

'Close. It soaks in poison like a sponge, natural and cursed alike, and modifies its properties.'

'Have you been able to find someone with dripping magick strong enough to manipulate that stone?'

'Yes.'

Who can handle such magick in all of Yovaria? Kai thought. Wilkin was up to something, and he couldn't get a complete grip on it. 'What is your deal? Why are you telling me this? You know I won't stay quiet.'

'You can sing like a canary or be dumb like a mute. It changes nothing. You can do anything but be reminded that whatever move you take will break you. The bond that ties the royal family to the kingdom and throne will snap like a withering twig.'

Don't think you have me pinned against the wall, Kai thought.

'She is strong but naive, just like you, and unmindful

of her magick. She's my future bride – Elizabeth of the house of Desouza,' Wilkin deadpanned.

Kai was taken aback. He took a few wavering steps backwards and collided with a breastplate placed at one end of the gazebo for aesthetic purposes. The relic brass fell onto the ground with a booming thud, filling the silent room with a crash.

The knight ran into the room, sword unsheathed and shield at arm's length. 'You have overstayed your welcome, Sir Wilkin. Protect what is left of your honour by leaving now.'

Wilkin frowned. 'Ah, the royal dog. I would much prefer a local coyote. Put away the sword. If I wanted him dead, you couldn't stop me. Imagine how infuriating it would sound in the ears of every Yovarian that the royal house in all its splendour is full of shady secrets. Disturbing, right?' He gauged the position of the sun.

Kai cursed silently, knowing he had to keep all he knew about Wilkin to himself if he wished to protect his family.

'I need to get going. My engagement shouldn't commence with bad impressions about me.' He made his way to the entrance. 'Look after the prince, royal dog. We don't want anything stirring up the palace. Well, at least not yet,' Wilkin called out while leaving.

Fred made sure he was out of the gazebo completely before speaking. 'Your Highness, are you all right? Can I send for some water?'

'I am fine, Fred.' Kai straightened up, took a deep breath and faced Fred. 'Check through the mortality records. Go as far back as twenty years ago. I need all the information you can get from all possible deaths within that period.'

Fred bowed. 'Is there anything in particular Your Highness wishes to know?' he asked.

'Yes, all deaths connected in any way to the royal family. Find out from anyone. Keep Edmund Gilmore completely out of this.'

'Yes, Your Highness,' the knight replied.

'Keep me updated to the very last about your findings. Leave no book of record untouched,' Kai added.

The knight nodded. 'If you need anything else, Your Highness, do not hesitate to send for me. Remember, I will lay down my life for you just as you once did for me.' He fell to his knees and at Kai's stiff nod, he rose to leave the room.

Kai beckoned to one of the royal servants who was watering the flower beds in the garden at a distance. He asked him to run to the stables and pass on the message to the stable boy to prepare two horses.

He leaned against the pillar and closed his eyes. His need to discover the truth had never been so strong.

The carriage stopped at the back entrance of the temple, and the horseman got off quickly to open the door. She stepped out, holding her dress with one hand and the other stretched out to the horseman for support. The blinding sun shone on them with no mercy.

I hope she managed to get it across, she thought.

She felt a chill as her feet touched the ground. For reasons bizarre to her, the sun was blazing but the ground was cold. The widespread myth of the Yovarian Kingdom hit her. It was believed that if one felt a sudden cold before any life-changing event, whatever one was about to do would work against such a person.

Then she quelled her fear in a fit of soft giggles. The myth wasn't a curse at the moment; it was a blessing. Her anticipation at the prospect of the day ending badly rose a notch. She just knew that all would be well and something would surely happen to stop the engagement.

A lady draped in a flowing red dress walked out of the gate. Her hair tied in a high bun with thick dark strands dangling across her face. Ella watched her with keen eyes and noticed her bare feet tapping loudly against the floor with each stride she took.

The lady came close and peered into Ella's eyes with no respect for her personal space. Ella jolted back awkwardly. 'You do look like a Virgo, except the hair,' said the lady, her teeth surprisingly silver.

'Uhmm, okay. Who are you?'

The lady took some steps back and straightened with great poise. 'My name is Cafelle. I am the priestess of Athena. I am only accessible when there is a royal celebration.'

'I beg of you to accept my apologies. My rough naiveté made me impolite.'

'It's fine. You are not expected to know much, but what you should know is that I'll be the one at the helm of your engagement tonight. Your dress seems perfect already,' the priestess added.

Ella curtsied. 'I brought my palla. My mother said I'd be needing it today.'

'Ah, yes, that is good. It will save us a lot of trouble. Can I assume you know about the bath ritual?'

'Yes, Priestess.'

'Well, then we shall begin preparations right away. I believe your parents are on their way here.' The priestess gestured towards the two girls who looked the same age as Ella as they walked forward, waiting for orders. 'The girls will get you ready. You two should make sure she is ready for the ceremony later. For now, I want you to teach her the basic rituals and practices required of her as a wife.'

Ella was led into the temple by the two girls. Her feet hesitated at first, resulting in slow, sluggish paces towards the temple entrance.

Cafelle noticed her hesitation and shook her head. Of course, a girl like her wouldn't want to marry someone like Sir Bodolf Wilkin. She knew she was in love with Edmund. She had seen the star, and Linus had told her. 'Something on your mind?' she asked.

'I am fine, Priestess, and ready for tonight,' Ella answered without batting an eyelid. She increased her pace in a bid to act normal, while the two maidens scurried behind.

The priestess watched her leave. 'Such is this maiden's fate that she is yet to realize what is, however, to come,' she mumbled. The priestess knew that Ella's marriage had been decided long before the blameless baby appeared on Earth, and love couldn't affect destiny.

Another carriage arrived at the temple. Lady Desouza stepped out, filling the air with her elegance.

'Welcome, Lady Desouza. You are as elegant as your daughter, even at this age,' Cafelle greeted.

Lady Desouza curtsied, her eyes flitting left and right. 'Your daughter arrived some moments ago, and she is in the temple as we speak,' Cafelle said reassuringly.

'Ah, that's good. I need to get going, engagement preparations are needed still.'

'What intention do you have as regards this marriage? Are you using this to hide your husband's mistake?'

'My intentions are known to my family and me,' Lady Desouza said with as much defence as she could muster. 'All I know is that I do not wish for her to go through what I have experienced. She shouldn't be caught up in the tangles of the past. I will do anything to keep her away from that family.'

'You've pushed her into the claws of deceit itself in your bid to protect her.'

'Lord Wilkin promised to give her a normal life. That is all she needs.'

'Vain promises from the lord of deceit. You are so engrossed in the past that you fail to see what lies ahead in your daughter's future.'

'Whenever I see her each morning, I remember the light that appeared when I found out I was pregnant with her. I was happy yet scared. My husband saw those two take their final breaths, and the words of an elf never go unfulfilled. My fear grows stronger as the full moon comes upon us,' Lady Desouza confessed.

The priestess tried to make sense of Lady Desouza's words. Maybe things weren't as they had thought after all. 'You said your husband heard the final words of the elven queen. What did she say?' Cafelle enquired.

'She swore over her dying body that her soul and that of her dying comrades would appear before their killers and seek revenge.'

Cafelle pondered for a brief moment. 'Did she or anyone else mention a name? The name of the killer.'

'No. The killer had fled the scene, leaving them to die before Sir Gilmore and my husband arrived.'

'I share your worries, Lady Desouza. You want all to be well before the next full moon ...'

'Not just any full moon. I fear the blood moon. The red-haired girl and her lover died during the last blood moon. I will be damned if something similar repeats itself.'

'It will never,' Cafelle said vehemently. 'Not under my watch. I share your fear, and I will do all I can to ensure the engagement runs smoothly.'

'Thank you, Priestess,' Lady Desouza said. She was happy to find someone who shared her feelings.

CHAPTER 8

'You can get into the bath now, my lady,' one of the priestess' maidens said.

Ella placed her palla at the edge of the bath and sat beside it. The statue of the goddess stared at her from a few feet away. The yellow lamps lit around the room warmed her. One of the maidens placed a plate of grapes beside her and started putting her hair into a bun. The maiden arranged several stalks of lotus buds through the bun. Ella felt a surge of heaviness press down her hair.

'Must I wear that in my hair? It is heavy,' she cried.

The assistant continued attaching them. 'Yes, you must. It signifies your purity of heart to the goddess and shows that you are ready to accept the burden that comes with marriage,' she answered abrasively.

The burden of marriage? Yes, it was a burden, and with Wilkin, it could become an affliction, Ella thought.

The assistant then closed the curtains, leaving only a bit of light shining at her through the window behind the statue. The crescent moon revealed itself hiding behind the clouds and the image reflected in the bathwater. She stared at the water, scooped some into her hands as she pretended to gather up the moonlight.

'You can go in now, my lady,' the maiden called from behind.

Ella glared at her. 'It is okay for me to do this alone, right?' Tense silence ensued in the room. 'I shall call you if I require your presence,' she added, trying to embody her mother's elegance and grace.

The girls looked at each other for a brief second, speculating on what to do before one of them finally placed a small golden bell near the bath. 'We shall wait for you behind those doors. Ring the bell to call our attention,' the one who'd tied Ella's hair into a bun said. The girls took cautious steps out.

Something was in the dark. She could hear the sound of shuffling feet. 'Who's there?'

'Shush … There is no cause for alarm.' It was Nurse Marcie.

'You've returned. How was it? Did you see him? What did he say?' she asked in impatient whispers.

Marcie smiled. 'Too many questions, my dear.'

'Do tell me if it is good or bad. Nurse, my itching ears desire satisfying reports.'

Marcie's eyes were exhausted. 'Ella, dear, I am worn out. Can I take a little rest and quench my thirst before I speak?'

'Yes, yes, please sit. I am so sorry, but delaying this heightens my uncertainty.'

'Edmund is someone I can accept as your husband,

even though that decision has no ties to me whatsoever. Yet I snuck into a temple and hid behind the shadows to do his bidding.' Marcie sat beside Ella on the patio leading to the bath. An apple from the basket the girls had left was in her hand. She took a tiny bite and chewed silently. 'Where is my lady?'

'Mother? Why would I require her presence at this dire moment? If I were to confide in her and not you, I would be in Wilkin's bed already.'

'Calm down, child. I just wanted to be sure that no one is eavesdropping.'

'I am sorry. She is with the priestess.'

'Good. Edmund has promised that he will make you his wife before dawn. He had it all planned out with Priest Linus long before you conceived a somewhat similar idea.'

Ella's face lit up. This was good news. 'Thank you, Nurse.'

'We have no time to keep on exchanging gratitude. Hurry up with the preparations, because my lady will be surprised to see you in a dress still.'

Ella slipped out of her shoes and removed her clothes all in one action. Marcie placed what was left of the food basket beside her.

'I need to meet with the priestess to help with preparations. Keep yourself soaked for another half hour, then begin to learn the rituals.'

'Okay,' Ella answered, already daydreaming about her engagement with Edmund Gilmore.

∽

The nurse walked out of the bathing room and instructed the girls to go in.

'Where did you come from?' asked one of them. Shock was written all over both their faces.

'I am Marcie. Ella's nurse. There is no cause for alarm.'

'How … how … how did …'

'Be a dear and lead me to the priestess' room, will you?' Marcie interrupted the girl's stutter with her head held high and her face betraying nothing suspicious.

'It is the first door to your left from the hallway,' the other girl answered. She was the more composed one.

Marcie left their presence and ventured into the hallway. She reached the priestess' room, but just as she was about to knock, she heard voices coming from behind the mahogany door. Even though it would be immoral of her to eavesdrop on matters that she wasn't invited to, her curiosity overruled her sense of morality.

Sir Desouza was in the temple, just like Lady Desouza. She could hear their voices whispering behind the door, as well as another's voice. Suddenly, Linus opened the door, causing Marcie to hide quickly behind the door even though she hadn't anticipated his footsteps. She watched as Lady Desouza and Sir Desouza followed behind him as they discussed securing the perimeter.

'How long are you going to hide behind that door?'

Marcie revealed herself and stood by the doorway as she recognized the priestess' voice. Something must have given her presence away. The priestess sat with her back to the door and was pouring a new cup of tea as a maiden carried away a tray of empty chinas.

'My apologies, but I wish to speak to you about an urgent matter. However, I need you to give me your word that this stays between us.'

'You have my word, Nurse Marcie.'

Marcie entered the dimly lit room. It had a huge candle on the table and a few torches hinged on the walls. 'It is concerning Elizabeth.'

'Yes, I know. I've seen it happen.'

Marcie was puzzled. 'Seen what, if I may ask?'

'Seen you back then refusing to stick your nose where it belongs.'

'I am sorry, but I am ...' she stuttered as she wondered how the priestess knew her name without seeing her and what she meant by 'refusing to stick her nose where it belongs.'

The priestess pulled out one of the torches on the wall as she stood up and turned around to reveal her face. 'Did you miss me?'

Marcie stared at her, mouth agape and eyes wide with shock. It couldn't be. 'You? You lived?' Marcie staggered.

Marcie's shock intensified Cafelle's confidence. 'Now, let's take it slow, shall we? I have made the necessary preparations for what will happen before dawn tomorrow.' Cafelle walked towards Marcie, reveling in the nurse's shock with every step that she took. 'I believe you have full knowledge of what I mean.'

Of course, Marcie knew what she meant. She had made preparations for what was yet to happen. A move like this one could only guarantee the certainty of the morrow.

The nurse had never thought that those who set things in motion twenty years ago would be back on this day to watch a tragedy unfold once more.

CHAPTER 9

Edmund and Leofrick arrived at the temple in the middle of the night. Edmund was treading a narrow road towards the temple when he suddenly stopped Leofrick.

'Why? What's wrong?'

Edmund gestured towards the main gate entrance. Soldiers were stationed at the east gates. It would be hard to get in the usual way. The idea of sneaking into a place of worship didn't go down well with him.

Leofrick could tell what was running through his mind. 'Thinking of how we are going to get in?'

'Yes, somewhere far from the main gate. The back gate is the next choice, but they wouldn't be witless enough to leave it unguarded.'

'Why not sneak in?'

'It is a temple. We can't just climb over like we usually do.'

'It's okay. Everyone knows that the royal guards are the most gullible set of soldiers.'

'And how do you intend to deal with it if you're caught?'

'I have my methods, pal. Just as you have yours. Get yourself in, and do what needs to be done.'

Edmund knew he was right. He had to get to Ella before sunrise. He looked around to find an opening and noticed a high tree near a window, which thankfully was near the room to the main altar. It was pretty far from the gates, and it was the only spot without guards. Sneaking into the temple was forbidden, but it wasn't actually in the law. It was in the heart of every Yovarian. No one would expect him to climb up a tree to get into the temple.

Athena, please forgive me.

He prayed silently.

When Leofrick saw that Edmund was out of sight, he vanished into thin air to appear in the main altar room of the temple. The dingy room was poorly lit with a single lamp in front of Athena's statue.

'It's been a while, Athena,' Leofrick articulated softly. 'You have never left that place since then,' he added.

Silence greeted him once more. 'I know you don't want me here, so I will make it brief. You know better than anyone that these two must become one at all costs. I will keep my shadow at bay, and you should protect those who believe in you.'

In an instant, other torches in the room lit at once. He walked towards an open window and vanished at the same time Edmund yanked the door open.

'Ella.' It came to her like a whisper.

She stirred. Were those voices from the gods?

'Ella, wake up!'

Her eyes flew wide open. She could recognize that voice even in her dream. 'Edmund?'

'Where are you?'

'I am right here.'

'Where?'

'Find me.'

Edmund laughed slightly. 'Now is not the time for games. You didn't give locating your fiancé in this darkness a single thought.'

Ella blushed. 'We are yet to be married.'

'We will upon the hour.' Edmund's voice dripped with fierce determination.

Ella traced the voice to the ledge on the roof. There, she could see him sitting. 'What is it with you and climbing?'

'It makes me access the situation without interrupting,' he answered. He jumped down, walked up to her and hugged her. 'I am sorry I didn't arrive sooner than this. I had no idea the temple would be even more heavily guarded than the palace.' He inhaled her scent of violet flowers.

'It is better late than never. Besides, I thought I was going to be alone today, but I ended up ...' She trailed off as she stared into his eyes. Even in the night, his eyes were charming as ever. Her heart skipped, and all thoughts of Wilkin vanished.

He breached the gap of personal space between them, and Ella leaned in with her eyes closed. Edmund pressed a quick kiss to her cheek. That wasn't what she wanted, but it made her blush still. Edmund could tell what she wanted. She hit him lightly. Her lover flashed that smile that never failed to melt her heart.

For some reason, she trusted him as if she had known him a long time. Never mind the fact that this was the third time she had met him. Suddenly, distant memories flashed across her mind as he played with her fingers.

Images of a red-haired girl and a boy sitting on top of a tree whispering adoringly into each other's ears flashed before her eyes.

Ella heard a name in the distance.

She could feel the boy pulling the girl closer and trying to hide with her beneath the leaves and branches. She trembled with fear, but he played with her fingers beneath the camouflage the same way Edmund was doing.

Ella looked into the eyes that melted all her defences. They were deep brown, like that of the boy in her memories.

Someone interrupted their tiny moment of bliss. Ella and Edmund flinched as the door burst open so suddenly that Edmund hadn't had enough time to hide. The figure dashed into the room like it was being chased.

'Ella, dear, why are you …? You! You shouldn't see a bride before the ceremony,' Nurse Marcie said with a smile. 'Leave now. She needs her time,' Marcie ordered sternly.

Edmund walked towards the door and took one last

glance at Ella before walking out. It was the first time he'd entered a room through the window and left through the door.

'Edmund Gilmore, I presume?'

'Yes.'

Cafelle studied his face for a brief moment. 'You are changing, too, albeit slower than Elizabeth.'

Edmund stepped back. Something didn't feel right. 'Do I know you? When did we meet?'

'We never have, but we meet again.'

Her words made no sense to him, and he wondered if she was crazy. 'Where did we meet initially?'

'I can't say.' She walked towards the shimmering pool of water with a bunch of stalked lotus. She opened each flower and let them into the water. After placing the last one, she watched them float. 'How did you get in?'

'I can't say,' Edmund retorted.

'Do you love her?'

'Nothing in this world and the next can replace the feelings I have for her.'

'You are young, Edmund. You are at that stage where the feelings of love and hate brew tremendously. She sparks the flame in your heart, but she can consume you in it. You may never know when it dries out.'

'The flame is eternal. I can feel it. I am changing, too. I am a different person when I am around her.'

'Even honey could be poisonous.'

'I am fine with the poison as long as it remains sweet.'

'Good. I hope you'll stay by her side until the end.'

The side door shrieked open and Ella walked in.

She was draped in a lovely yellow dress as bright as a sunflower. The darkness dissolved at the sight of his breathtaking lover.

Hair tied in a half updo with an array of lotus flowers and pins holding it in place, loosely wrapped palla gathered at the waist running like a stream within the morning mist and flowing till it reached the floor. A diamond necklace sat on her neck, glittering like an arc formed by several shooting stars.

For the very first time, Edmund hated the wedding process.

Getting into that pool in a dress as pretty as this will only taint her beauty, he thought.

The temple maidens followed behind like the rear tyres of a cart. They were littering the floor with rose petals. Ella was controlling them. He knew, because the flowers didn't hit the ground, they were floating on air. As soon as she reached the pool of water at the altar, they dropped all at once to the ground.

Edmund's eyes couldn't leave her. For the very first time, he was experiencing a new shade of beauty, a new spectrum of heaven.

'Get into the pool, young man.' The priestess' voice pulled him out of his fantasies and back to reality.

Edmund yanked his shoes off and stepped into the pool. The angry frost of water accepted him. With locked eyes, they smiled lovingly at each other, but behind those pure eyes was fear.

Fear of the unknown.

Cafelle wrapped their hands together. 'In Athena's presence, we join thee to be as one soul, one body and one spirit until the cold hands of death break thee away.' Then she began the conjugal ritual.

Ella joined her while Edmund stood in the freezing water surrounded by lotus, watching and doing nothing. The females always performed the Yovarian nuptial ceremony.

Following this ritual was the most anticipated segment – the vows.

'Seeing you jump down from the garden wall melted away all my defences.' Her voice shook with both excitement and fear.

'And when I saw your hair tangled within the thorns, I knew we were meant for each other.' Edmund's voice tore through the fear.

'Together forever, against all odds.' They said it together. A sentence they had never practised but which found its way to their mouths.

They sealed it with a kiss.

Immediately after joining the young couple, Cafelle lost consciousness briefly. 'Take your palla and leave,' she said as soon as she came to. 'Go straight to Priest Linus. Take your husband to the front entrance,' Cafelle warned.

CHAPTER 10

Ella dashed out with Edmund, but they parted ways at the entrance. She made her way to the minuscule altar dedicated to the god Apollo. She found Linus in the middle of his evening prayers.

'Greetings, Priest. I received your message.'

'Ah, you are right on time, dear child. I sent for you because there are things you have no knowledge of. However, swear by Athena that it will be kept a secret.'

This was getting serious. Ella walked to the altar, closed her eyes and stretched out her palm to receive the holy offering. Linus placed a rose on her trembling hands instead.

'You knew?' Ella asked, surprised.

Linus smiled. If only she knew that he could read the star of every Yovarian and he had read hers, too. 'I know a lot about your gift and your new husband. I told Cafelle to persuade your mother to tell you the truth about your birth, but I'm guessing she never did.'

'Mother? She never told me anything of the sort, but

she knew of my powers. She considered it a curse,' Ella cried. The feeling of betrayal crept slowly into her heart.

'She is right, though. This is something that should never be revealed to anyone. However, calling it a curse is an exaggeration.'

'What is the truth concerning my birth? I have always felt they were hiding something.'

'Right before you were born, Lord Desouza received an order from the queen. She desired to gain control over the elves, lamia and the fairies.'

The rustle of the olive tree outside the window arrested her attention. She smiled. 'I know the queen, and she would have wanted to use them as a force against humankind. Wasn't there a peace treaty among all creatures in the universe?'

Linus was surprised at her political understanding. It shouldn't be surprising; she was a Desouza after all. 'Yes, but things went south between Yovaria and the neighbouring kingdoms. The emperor wanted to increase the military power of the country. He decided to capture these creatures and use them for his bidding. Only those who knew the ancient sealing technique could take on that mission.'

'This technique, can it be reversed? Were those creatures captured? Can they be released? What does that have to do with …' Ella froze. An epiphany fell on her like an avalanche.

'Yes, Ella, the blood of the floral maiden runs through your veins. You are no human. You are an elf, you have …'

'Ella, leave right now!' Lady Desouza's voice cut through the room like a sword piercing a stack of hay. She walked in with her hands fisted by her side as the wind whipped her blue gown back and forth.

Ella hesitated. Linus nodded to her to leave, but she remained still. It was time to take hold of something in her life.

'Yes, child. It is high time you left. Confide in the gods and have no fear. You will get all the answers you need.'

'Thank you.' She bowed. She wanted to hug him and go on about how she felt her parents were hiding things from her. How he had been accommodating and how just a few sentences he had said changed her life. A void had been filled. 'I will prepare myself for tonight, Mother,' she assured her mother before leaving.

Lady Desouza's eyes watched patiently until her daughter closed the door behind her. 'I presume that she knows nothing.'

'She knows nothing yet, Angela. You have to give her enough information before she can begin to comprehend the whole thing,' Linus answered. A priest couldn't lie, but nothing was stopping him from merely speaking half of the truth.

They heard a loud, abrupt clang outside the temple. Lady Desouza rushed out, and Linus scurried behind.

The two family heads, Lord Derrick Desouza and Sir Gordon Gilmore, had drawn their swords.

~

Edmund was behind his father. Thank the gods that Leofrick had found him on time. He couldn't imagine being caught in this frenzy. Only the clang of their sword had broken the previous silence.

'Did you think hiding would alter the future?' Gordon's harsh voice reverberated through his son's ears. Sir Gordon Gilmore was always loud whenever he was angry, and this was a brawl between two angry men.

'You have no right to tell me what is wrong or right, Gordon!' Lord Desouza bellowed back, his voice even louder. Although the distance between them wasn't more than three inches, they yelled at each other like barking dogs.

'You know very well what would happen if the royal family knew about Elizabeth. You bawling, uncharitable dog betrayed our friendship.'

Edmund noticed the shade of his father's face turn bright red.

'I have sworn to keep my family safe from my mistakes. If this is the price, let it be.' Desouza tightened his grip on the sword.

Sir Gordon walked forward. He drew his sword. 'That day, I had no choice. Her Highness possesses the Mirror of Truth. She is bound to know the truth, one way or the other.'

Prince Kai walked up behind Gordon. 'I thought today was to be a marital experience. This is such a rare sight. A public duel in the abode of the gods?' He looked at both family heads and shook his head pitifully. 'Sheath your swords this instance!' he commanded.

They reluctantly replaced their swords.

Kai turned to Gilmore. 'Yes, there is a mirror, but it is not the Mirror of Truth. It has no magical elements. The queen probably blackmailed you with your secrets and asked you to betray others. I know my mother.'

Gilmore pressed his lips tighter than before. His face was even brighter now. 'I will settle this with her,' he retorted. 'A private audience with you, Your Highness?' Sir Gilmore requested.

'When should that be?'

'After the morrow. When the dark wind of this occurrence is long gone.'

Kai's face hardened. 'Let it be as you wish,' he answered. 'I presume that you both have forgotten my instructions. I warned that if any one or both of you drew your sword against each other, someone else would raise your heirs.' His eyes caught Edmund's, and they reminded him of himself.

Sir Gilmore and Desouza stepped forward like two lads being reprimanded by their father.

'I wouldn't want to see your son-in-law leave the kingdom without Athena's blessings on their marriage,' Kai added.

Wilkin, who had been standing calmly, finally spoke up. 'Your Highness, I have a bride waiting inside the temple.' In an instant, he pulled out his sword and drifted towards Edmund. 'So it will be best if we finish things right here and now.'

Edmund, aware of the impending danger, took a few steps back and dodged the attack aimed towards him. He grabbed his father's sword and took a stance. 'I doubt you'll be alive to make her your bride.' His voice dripped with anger.

Kai noticed the slyness rousing behind Wilkin's eyes. This was the perfect opportunity to send Edmund outside Yovaria. 'Get the hourglass.' He signalled to Fred just as Gilmore and Desouza wondered why he was suddenly egging on a fight when he had stopped one between them. 'I am sure you know the implication of this?' He didn't wait for a response. 'Begin!' Kai yelled as he turned the hourglass. 'There shall be no interruptions or assistance,' he added.

CHAPTER 11

Edmund took a defensive stance as he waited patiently for the right time to launch an attack. This wasn't a battle to be won, even though understanding the tactics of the enemy was key to eliminating him. However, this was the only way he could leave without raising any suspicion from anyone.

He pushed his father's incessant chatters behind him just as the duke launched another attack. Their swords kissed violently. Edmund was quick to dodge that strike, and he responded with a kick. Wilkin retreated.

The duke launched another attack, but this time he swerved left. Edmund countered with a block, but the force had sent him to the ground. Wilkin was the only person he could see. The air changed; he was in another realm.

Was the duke using illusions?

'Surprised to find yourself in another realm? You wanted a taste of my power, now savour it.' Wilkin had expected Edmund to wait for his attack, and he did.

That was enough time for him to bring the battle to the lad. He leapt into the air, sword above his head.

Edmund was quick enough to hold out his sword to defend himself. Wilkin was surprisingly strong. The young lad was pushed backwards as he struggled to keep his grip on his sword.

However, Wilkin was an experienced swordsman. He sliced Edmund twice; a quick one on the arm and chest.

Edmund squeezed his eyes shut for a split second. Writhing in pain, he opened them quickly and braced himself for another attack, but he found himself in another realm. This time, he was on an isolated island, and he could hear strong waves crashing against the rocks.

Edmund couldn't see much. His only source of light was the moon. Like a chameleon, the colour of the moon changed with each passing cloud. The eye-stinging wind swayed him slightly. He was two inches from falling off the cliff.

Wilkin laughed maniacally. 'Too much for you? I am just getting started.' Wilkin launched another attack as he put all of his weight into the wielding of his sword.

Edmund tried once again to block the attack, but his opponent had the upper hand. Wilkin's sword was at his throat in the blink of an eye, then it went slashing down at Edmund's shoulder. The pain sent Edmund to his knees.

'It is a pity you can't go further,' Wilkin jeered. 'I wonder how Gilmore will feel when he sees his son losing within minutes?' he added. This was the final blow. Wilkin held the sword high towards Edmund before brutally plunging it down.

Edmund had read his move. He stared at the sword and wondered if this was going to be the end.

Then it stopped … Wilkin had frozen, just like everything else around him.

He stood up in disbelief. Someone was behind him, and he turned around to look.

'What are you doing? You have no time to remain numb.' The man behind him was standing. No, he wasn't, his feet weren't touching the ground, or he had no feet. The brown cloak he wore covered all of him. Only his hands and a faceless head peeped through the cloak. A faint light glowed above him like a halo.

Edmund was terrified. 'Who are you? What did you do? You need to reverse this now. I need to fight him.'

'You are not strong yet.' His voice sounded godlike, just like his appearance. 'You have so much to learn. For now, turn your weakness into strength,' he added. 'Listen to the voice. That voice. Can you hear it?'

As if fighting in another realm wasn't enough, an eerie man was telling him to listen to voices. 'I don't have time for this.'

The mysterious man moved closer. Edmund felt every strand of hair at his nape rise as a sudden chill overtook him. 'Time, time, haven't you noticed it break?'

Edmund stepped back. It couldn't be. The man couldn't possibly be right, for only the gods could do such a thing. He observed again, and truly, time had stopped.

Then he heard a faint voice calling out to him.

'Do you hear it?' the man asked.

'Yes, I do, but I can't make sense of it. Is it time speaking?'

'No, boy. You have felt the touch of life. Your magick, it beckons. The man behind you is no man, he is a werewolf.' He gestured at a frozen Wilkin.

Edmund closed his eyes, trying to take it all in. How could he have magick when he was merely human? If he was magick, he needed to tap into that cryptic provision. It was too much to handle. 'He is a werewolf? He has magick as well? But he didn't stop time,' Edmund soliloquized.

'That may be me. It could be you also, but one thing is certain. I am a concealed part of yourself.'

'No, I am you.'

'Come in, Gordon.'

Queen Adela, adorned in a burgundy-red dress, was seated on her throne, fiddling with her ruby ring. A maid walked in with a silver tray filled with cards. The queen took the cards and tucked them in her dress sleeve before waving the maid off. She showed no interest in welcoming Sir Gilmore as he walked towards her and bowed.

'I am here for the prince, Your Majesty.'

'He has his hands full. I am to meet with you instead. Although I have no interest in solving family problems of common men like yourself, royalty performs royal duties.' She replaced the ring onto her index finger as she stared at him with disgust.

'At the prince's command, I shall relay my message. I presume that you know of the she-elf you trapped many years ago?'

'That is no news to me. It was foolish of her to meddle in things that weren't her concern. I only did what had to be done.' Adela paused to caress the ring with her right finger. It was apparent it meant more to her than a ring. 'The Pack in the Broken Woods would have found the gem if I didn't step in. I have no regrets,' she added.

'Permitting the death of someone under the pretence of protecting the gem was never the right step to take.'

'The death of one to save the lives of many? Gordon, it is a pity that those two lost their lives,' she simply said with indifference.

'They were at the wrong place at the wrong time …'

'What about the Desouza girl? What business does my son have with her?'

A sharp knock came between them. The queen signalled to one of the guards to open the door. It was Desouza.

'Why are you here, Derrick?' Gilmore bellowed with anger.

'To break my oath. My daughter's life is on the line. My duty as a father comes first.'

'Was the girl the cause of my first son's death?' Gilmore yearned for the truth. Nothing could stop him.

'Her Majesty is in the best position to answer. Sir Vaughan could never have hurt the red-haired servant.

He protected her until the end.' Desouza was going all out. He was ready to reveal the secrets.

'He died protecting her?' Gilmore asked.

'No, he chose death so that he could be with her in the afterlife. The elf Her Majesty wanted us to capture sacrificed her life to preserve the memories of those two.'

Adela knew nothing was going to stop Desouza from spilling the beans except killing him. A faint sound from a bird – *the vermillion flycatcher* – sitting on the windowsill caught her attention. She took out a deck of cards and held them out. Each card began floating in mid-air.

Closing her eyes, she gave one a gentle push on its tip. A hidden image revealed itself on the card. She held it out for Desouza and Gilmore to see. A pale-faced girl covered in mud donned a green dress and lay fast asleep on a bed of roses.

'Your Majesty! This is …'

Desouza interrupted. 'The she-elf. Vasilisa.'

'We can wake her, right? Only she knows the truth.' Gilmore's hunger for the truth ached to be satisfied.

A slight smile formed on the queen's face. She stared at the girl with deep, piercing eyes. 'Hearing her story would be greater torture than spending years in the Hidden card.'

The bird which had Leofrick's mischievous eyes chirped for a while and flew away.

CHAPTER 12

Edmund sighed. The sun was mocking him. His hands heated beneath the scorching sun as he walked through what felt like the realm of Hades. Last night's rain should have birthed a pleasant morning. Ever since he met himself, he had tried hard to freeze time or at least to call him out, but to no avail.

The Broken Woods is truly broken, he thought as he walked through the thick forest. He took out his goatskin and drank some ale, ignoring the tiny droplets that trickled down his face.

He wondered how Ella was doing back home. He missed her and was worried about leaving her among the wolves, especially now that he knew what Wilkin truly was. The look on her face when she saw him bruised and battered after the duel flashed through his eyes. He had been banished from the capital after that at Wilkin's request. Since he had won the battle, his request had been granted.

Freezing time was the only way he'd been able to

save his life. He had lost because he was weak, not because he'd planned to lose. He couldn't keep up with the immeasurable strength of the duke.

He took out the map and held it in the direction of the rising sun. He had tried to find his exact location but to no avail. It slowly dawned on him that he was lost. There was no stopping. He had to continue his journey, only three days left. He needed to be at the Moonlight Festival.

It was getting dark. Reading from an age-stricken faded map was useless. He found a large tree and sat underneath it. Being banished should give him time to hone the powers the hooded man had told him he possessed and come up with solutions, but it wasn't as easy as he thought.

He thought once more about Ella and how she must be feeling sad and alone, and the urge to turn back and sneak into the capital rose within him.

He placed the sack he'd brought with him against the tree. The rustle of the leaves beckoned to him. It was getting stronger. He pulled out a dagger from his waist and was ready to pounce on whatever was coming out.

'Who is there? What do you want?' he yelled, voice coated in trepidation.

'If you keep yelling in here, you won't make it out alive,' the voice answered.

Edmund placed the dagger back into its sheath. 'Must you always make a scene?'

Leofrick walked out from hiding. 'You are getting better, pal. You didn't think I was a ghost this time.'

Edmund smiled. Something he hadn't done since he got banished from the capital.

'I should have acted scarier than before,' he added.

'What are you doing here? Don't tell me you came looking for me.'

'You are right. I am here of my own accord, not for you.' Leofrick saw the pendant hanging around his waist. 'You still have it? Good.'

'Does it matter?' Edmund asked.

'Maybe. I don't know.'

'I have been travelling for days, how is it that you are here?'

'I tricked Hermes and stole his wings,' Leofrick joked.

'What? I am exhausted. I have no time for jokes.'

'The priest sent me to tell you that you are too much of a nuthead to do this alone.'

'Did he say I am a nuthead?'

'Are you? You have been love drunk ever since you climbed those grapevines. This is the longest we have spoken to each other.'

'What a subtle way to put things across.' Leofrick's appearance wasn't as helpful as Edmund thought it would be, at least for the few minutes he had been here.

'At least I can talk some sense into you now. The priest wanted you to have this.' Leofrick handed him a piece of rolled parchment.

'What is it?'

'I don't know and sincerely don't care. He said I should tell you these words; inside the waterfall, reflection gives the key to Thavma Gi. Oh yes, I think it sounded something like that.'

'Thavma Gi? The same one in the stories of old?'

'Maybe? I don't know if it may be the same. I have done the priest's bidding. Time to leave.'

'Wait, aren't you forgetting something?'

'Oh, right. Here, drink.' Leofrick threw a small vial at him.

Edmund drank it without giving it any thought. It's sour-bitter taste cut through his tongue. He stopped to stare at the bottle; it was filled with thick dark-red liquid. 'What is this?'

'It is Adam's ale. Drink up.'

He opened it and continued drinking. His face cringed, and he felt numb. He grabbed his neck and started coughing.

'You'll be fine, pal. This is the only way to wake you up from your dream world.'

Edmund's eyes were heavy. His head began spinning and he collapsed and stopped moving.

Leofrick placed his palm on the lad's forehead. 'Good. He is fast asleep. Now to find Hermes, he must be going nuts looking for his shoes.'

A seraphic man appeared before him. 'I knew you would find me.' Hermes leaned against a tree and crossed his legs. 'You went through the hassle of making a potion with pitcher flower this bitter?'

'The pitcher is supposed to be sweet in the real world.'

'Don't play dumb, Leofrick. No, not in any world. You will remain Loki to me in whatever realm we find ourselves.'

Leofrick smiled. He looked at the sleeping Edmund. 'Until the rise of the Fenrir clan, I will remain Leofrick in the real world.'

'Need I remind you that you must be dead in the real world before your wolves come to live.'

'That is not it, Hermes. They are asleep like this lad. Only when they come to me and seek forgiveness will they have a chance at life,' Leofrick explained.

Hermes walked closer. 'How long do you intend to hide?'

'Until everything is back in place.'

'He thinks of you as a good friend. How do you intend to deal with your betrayal against him?'

'That doesn't mean a thing. I don't care if he finds out.'

'I never wished to be a pawn in your game. Hand over my shoes,' Hermes demanded, and left with his shoes.

Leofrick held the pendant hanging around Edmund's belt. 'This is the least I can do to make up for my shadow's mistake.'

She heard a knock at the door. Ella ran towards it, and the guard followed. Only Lady Desouza had visited her for the last couple of days. Her visits were not worthwhile; she only taught her how to act like a lady, smile and walk. She wasn't allowed to eat more than a serving. Girls were not to gain weight before the wedding. Well, before the wedding they were all aware of.

However, much to her relief, it wasn't her mother that passed through those doors; it was Cafelle. She felt the urge to hug the priestess, but she restrained herself. Her mother could be watching her from a distance.

'Why are you here?' she asked defensively with her arms crossed across her chest. Just because she was glad to see someone other than her mother didn't mean she wanted to look needy or weak.

Cafelle handed her a wooden woven basket. 'Don't act all grown up. She is not here.'

Ella relaxed. She took off her ribbon to let her hair

loose. 'So we can talk without inhibitions, right?' Ella asked. Her eyes glimmered with curiosity. Ella took out the fruit cake and dried fish from the basket.

Would this be the right time to tell her? Cafelle thought. No. She erased the thought as soon as it formed. 'Follow me,' she ordered Ella.

The guard made to go with them, but when Cafelle gave him a fierce look, he immediately fell back into the seat and waited behind.

Ella and the priestess walked to the garden. Roses of every colour were littered around. Cafelle plucked ten fragrant peach roses and handed them to a nearby maid who was tending to some bright purple roses. 'Weave a *dreamcatcher* with these roses and make use of swan feathers.'

The maid bowed slightly and left.

The priestess walked to a swing and took a seat beside Ella, who was swallowing some of the dried fish. 'Have you ever wondered why they bloom around you?'

'No, I don't know why. Maybe because it has something to do with me being an elf.' Ella still found it hard to believe.

'Elizabeth, every action is a product of a force, even magick. Each spell you cast can never be effective without your blood.'

Ella was amazed at the new information. 'Have I been making use of spells all this time?'

'Yes, unconsciously, though. Only Vasilisa, the sole elf in the entire elven clan during her time, could do what you do. Maybe she gave you her magick.'

'Who is Vasi …?'

'Vasilisa,' Cafelle cut in.

'You said maybe she gave … Does it mean I am human?'

'You were born to human parents, Ella. It is safe to say that you are human, nothing more, nothing less. However, she met Orichamaru, the person who gave her a purpose. She was just like you, a little bit older and loved roses too. Helen, the goddess, would have been her only beauty rival if she was human. The elven blood in her drew her so close to nature that she spent the more significant part of her life wandering in the Broken Woods. Every creature in there felt her touch. She was a symbol of true peace to elves and other creatures. They even named her *Aranyani* – the shadow of the goddess.

'The dying wish of the Queen of Elves was for Vasilisa to succeed her. But things changed when Vasilisa met a girl on the brink of insanity in the woods. The sounds of birds and the falling leaves scared the girl. The girl attacked her. She screamed at Vasilisa for being the reason for her daughter's death in the future. A member of the then royal family saved her by sedating the girl with a lethal dose, or so Vasilisa had thought, but it was her powers that sent a rose thorn to her neck. Vasilisa learned that the girl was the cursed sibyl Cassandra. The girl whose prophecies would never be heard.'

'Cassandra! That name rings a bell.' Ella thought for a moment. 'Sir Wilkin's late wife was a sibyl? I should have expected more from someone as hideous as him,' she added. A sibyl was a creature with immense magical power who prophesied but had mental instability. They were a clan formerly from the Yovarian elven clan.

The priestess paused for a moment, looked down, and forced a smile. 'She was a cursed sibyl. No matter what she said or did, no one would ever believe her. It was her fate to go insane. That is beside the point, Vasilisa is our focus. After she met with Cassandra, she spent a long time developing a spell with a man. A spell that was so strong it could subdue the magick and emotions of others. The Darkest Rose spell.'

'Who was the man?' Ella enquired.

'King Alphonse, Cassandra's uncle. He couldn't hate himself less for her death. Wilkin was to marry Cassandra.'

'Always getting hooked up with one person or the other.'

The priestess laughed. 'Cassandra would have known from the start that this would happen …'

The maid who'd left the room with the roses returned with the *dreamcatcher*. She handed it over to the priestess.

Cafelle hung the dreamcatcher on the bark of a tree. 'It would be good if you can hear the rest from her mouth directly.'

Ella was puzzled. 'This is a story from two decades ago, she should be long gone by now. How is that possible?'

'She is very much alive. You'll learn your very first magick spell – *dreamcatcher*. Let us visit her.'

He could hear the rush of water flowing from the rocks. As he got closer, the whisper of the wind against the trees engulfed him. Droplets of water fell on his tired face from the leaves on the trees. A whiff of sweet caramel scent drifted through his nose. He looked further, and what he initially thought to be a creek was actually a waterfall.

Edmund bent down to scoop a handful of crystal-like water. It felt like velvet in his hands. He took out the map and tried making sense of it. It didn't show anything, and Edmund felt like something was missing or had been missing.

To his left, a strange mark on the ground called his attention. They were white circles heavy with symbols, symbols that were fading away. As he slowly approached the centre of the circles, a howl pierced the air.

A wolf emerged from the shadows, and Edmund

immediately clenched his dagger, ready to pounce. 'Who is there?' His voice went shrill with fear.

It was definitely a wolf he had seen, but instead, a woman ran out from behind the trees. With tattered clothes and bleeding feet, it was clear that she was the hunted.

She began calling out to someone. In a split second, she was on the ground, not dead, but shaking the life into someone he knew was dead.

'Virgo. Virgo, dear. Wake up,' the lady cried. 'Virgo, wake up, wake up.'

Edmund moved a little closer. She didn't notice his presence. Trickles of red liquid flowed into the river.

'I should never have trusted him. His vain promises beguiled me. Look at me, okay?'

Edmund stepped closer, his curiosity making him restless. He froze at the sight of the two lifeless figures. A girl and a boy clinging to each other as if their lives depended on it. The girl's hair a bright red, even brighter than that of the Gilmores. A rare colour for a Yovarian.

The boy clutched something in his fist – something that even his death hadn't taken away from him. Edmund was close enough to see what he held now, and his eyes almost popped out of their sockets. It was a pendant similar to the one he had, but inked in blood. Quickly he brought his out to compare, and it was the spitting image of his.

The lady lifted the girl and placed her by the river-bank. She walked back to the boy and whispered into his dead ears, 'I will keep an eye on Wilkin till the day you rise to fulfil your destiny.' Tears streaming down her weary eyes, she lifted him and placed him by the riverbank also. She pushed them in it.

Something hit Edmund from behind suddenly. He turned to see a turtle taking steps backwards to charge at him once more. Edmund picked the little thing up and was about to place it aside when someone yanked at him from behind. He fell into the water before he could react.

In the water, he saw the images of the dead boy and girl and that of the lady again floating away. The current pulled him deeper so fiercely that he prayed he wasn't going to be the third dead body. He gasped for breath, his legs numb and skin pale. The light got dimmer.

Was he slipping away like those two?

He landed.

'Is he breathing, sir?' the blue-eyed man with dark-blue webbed feet enquired.

'Not yet. His neck wasn't slit completely, what a tough one,' a man with silver hair answered. He took off his glasses and beckoned to Kain for another lily root. Kain walked out of the room. The silver-haired man placed his palm on Ed's forehead; it was still too cold.

Kain walked in with a long root and an age-stricken book. The rusty object had the letter 'A' written boldly on its spine. He handed the root over and sat down beside Edmund to read the book.

The silver-haired man squeezed the roots, allowing a few drops into Edmund's mouth. 'Haven't I told you to give the patient all your attention? Do away with that book!'

Kain glared at him for a split second, shrugged, and continued reading. The air was stiff. 'I have …'

A scowl forming on Edmund's face interrupted them. He had started to stir. 'Humm … mmm … hmm …'

Kain raised his left brow. 'It seems the lad has a dream.'

'Hush, Kain. His pain lingers, he needs rest. Why don't you burn a message to Loki that he is fine and will be leaving soon.'

'I can use the floga dust?' Kain couldn't believe his ears. His master had never allowed him. Even though nothing was exceptional about the dust, it could teleport a body into extinction if misused. Besides, it was an expensive item. Kain smiled at the thought that he and his master had reached that level of trust.

'Place that book over there before leaving,' the silver-haired man called out, but Kain was halfway across the room already. Once again, Proteus called him back, urgently this time, causing Kain to walk back up to him. 'Do not say a word about his past, do you understand?'

Kain mockingly placed a hand on his chest. 'You really put that in a way that stabs my heart. It would have been better to just tell me to forget the colour of my blood.'

Proteus scowled at him for not taking their conversation seriously. 'Do you want His Majesty to find out that a human has entered the waters of Thavma Gi again?'

'King Varuna has always controlled the waters. I would know that better than anyone, don't you think?' said Kain, insulted at Proteus' lack of confidence in him.

'No, you should not know. I know very well that you lost your family due to His Majesty's new laws at the time. Thavma Gi was sealed, and only a true blood could enter the place. This means that the human you brought has no chances of going in.'

'And why won't he? I am a true blood, aren't I?' Kain said.

'Yes, and for that reason, I need you to stay hidden. His Majesty should never find you, Kain.'

Kain remained silent as his jaw tightened with anger.

'Kain, do you understand?' Proteus pressed, needing a definite assurance.

Kain opened a box instead and took out a blue ring. He held it tight in his hand and closed his eyes, seeing all the things he had once seen before leaving the room to send the message to Loki.

Edmund opened his eyes slowly. His cold body took a while to adjust to the warmth of the room. Was it a room? Something was crawling up his arm. He tried moving it but couldn't.

'Ah, your reflexes are fine. That must have made you a little uncomfortable, it is a healing conch. Here, have some tea.'

For some reason not known to him, Edmund's lips

parted. He took in the hot, bland liquid the queer man called tea.

'Here are your clothes. I couldn't save others, and they were beyond repair. Those beings sure did a number on you. What is left of your belongings are there.' He pointed to a stool at one end.

At first, it was hard to process, and as seconds passed, it became even harder. Edmund couldn't say what happened. Why was he here? Who was this? His hands. Edmund took the clothes from him. Apart from his silver-hair, his fingers were thin and longer than usual, a bit red too.

The severely injured lad took another sip from the tea. Yes, it was bland but useful. 'Edmund Gilmore.'

Edmund put on the black outfit and the dark-green seaweed belt that came with it. It was the replacement he had gotten from the man, and he was surprised that it was an expensive upper-class leather. 'Yes, sir. What is this place? The water suddenly swallowed me that last—'

'Kappa dragged you in,' the man answered, adding more confusion. 'They are small frilly creatures with an insatiable hunger. Try not to look away from the crystal.'

'Then who brought me here?' he asked once again.

The silver-haired man pointed to the turtle behind him. 'He helped you,' the man added.

'How can that thing pull me?'

'That "thing" has the strength of two carriage horses. I know you have a lot on your mind, but we have limited time. Not everyone can stop time, you know.'

Another bombshell. As if things weren't bizarre enough.

'Kain will take you to the gate,' the man said.

Edmund tried coming up with questions that would keep his mind still, but he shook them off as soon as they appeared.

'You aren't strange to an occurrence of this nature. Still, I will provide some answers to that worried mind of yours.' He pulled a stool closer to himself and took a seat. 'First, you are on the outskirts of Thavma Gi.' The older man hesitated, then he continued. 'Well, that is all you need to know.'

'Who are you?'

The man stood up at once with such royal gusto and imperial bravado. 'I am Proteus of Knatth, the legendary healer of Thavma Gi, the greatest physician in all of—'

'When is the other person returning?' Edmund drowned the self-acclaimed ignoble's introduction, damping his spirit.

'Just about now,' the old man retorted. The anger in his reply was clear enough.

'I am sorry, Proteus of Knatth.' He noticed the curl on the older man's lips.

The young lad placed the conch that had been resting on his arm on a side table. The healer pulled a switch on the left, and the door opened. It was a large hole with thin layers of semi-fluid shelling the entrance.

'Why is the door covered in such a manner?' Edmund was quick to ask.

Proteus heaved a disappointing sigh. He had been used displays of absurdity by humans but not to this level. 'You are on another level of cluelessness,' he replied. 'Have you noticed that you can breathe in here? Yes? Because it is dry even though we are in the water,' he sarcastically added.

'We are in the water?'

'No, no, no, we are in a hot boiling volcano which will explode anytime soon.'

'Really? It is cold in here, shouldn't it be hot?'

The healer squeezed his head with his hands in disappointment. 'Well, I understand. Not many humans have been opportune to be here. The thought of jumping into a waterfall holding onto the belief that you would get to Thavma Gi is ridiculously dangerous.'

Ed nodded and looked at the door once more. A seal was dancing around, and his eyes sparkled with excitement.

'Get in here, Kain!'

The seal came towards them. It placed its head through the door and changed into a human. Ed's spark of excitement transformed into terror.

'Take him to the gate,' Proteus instructed.

'What are you?' Edmund asked. He was staring at the webbed feet and hands the creature now had.

'Here, have some lily roots.' The seal-man handed some queer-looking plants over to Edmund.

Edmund refused it. 'You haven't told me what you are.'

'Oh me? I am a selkie. A seal, that's all. The transformation power is from the cave. Now, eat this.' He stretched out the roots one more time.

'Why?'

'You will need it to breathe under water.'

'I am an excellent swimmer, you know.'

'Sure, a very good one saved by the turtle,' Kain jeered.

'That was no ordinary turtle—'

'We have no time for this, Kain,' Proteus cut in. 'Removing the limiter will be our only option now,' the physician added.

'The king's pet will swim here in no time if we do that.'

'Yes, I know. We should be long gone before that happens. The responsibility on this young lad's shoulders is too heavy for him to bear alone.'

'Well, if it is going to get you in trouble, then—' started Edmund.

'Shut it!' the master and his servant chorused.

Kain walked to one corner of the cave and returned with a belt. He tied it firmly around himself. 'Hold on tight. No matter what happens, never let go,' he instructed, and exchanged glances with Proteus. 'One, two, three ...' Kain yanked out his bracelet. All at once, Ed could feel his body slicing through the water speedily.

A siren blew up noisily behind.

CHAPTER 15

Cafelle placed a candle beside the *dreamcatcher* and lit it.

Ella was in her palla, and silk gloves covered her hands. She was standing outside, staring at the priestess through the window. The end of the palla was pinned to the centre of her hair bun in elven style. The young lady wanted to speak to Vasilisa as an elf, not as a human. It was her way of embracing her true self, the one her parents had tried so hard to hide from her. Her glow was soft against the moonlight.

'Come in.' Cafelle beckoned to her and Ella walked in. 'Come closer, stand on the left side of the candle. This spell does not require candlelight, but it will help you concentrate.'

Ella faced the flame. It was dancing in the wind.

'Look closely and focus on who you wish to see. Do it with all of your heart. A small break in your thinking may get you somewhere else.'

'How do I know what Vasilisa looks like?'

'Think about her very existence. The very essence of her, focusing on your motive for meeting her. Submit to your thoughts and allow them to push you into it. Do not fight or resist. You will feel the connection. When it is time, say the spell; your name and *Oneiroi syllepsis.*'

Ella nodded eagerly like a toddler. She closed her eyes and thought hard about that one person trapped in another realm for decades. Sending her thoughts to one image or idea wasn't new to her. She always did it in her leisure time. Gradually, a picture began to form. It was that of a girl on a bed of roses.

A drop of hot tears trickled down her cheeks. Quickly, she opened her eyes. She couldn't be crying now. There wasn't any candle, nor a dreamcatcher flower. She wasn't even in the room anymore.

Cafelle was amazed. Virgo herself had come to Ella's aid. She had come to stop the darkness from spreading. Ella was sought to be with her on a transcendental level.

'Say it now. The spell.' Ella could feel the urgency in Cafelle's voice. 'And never forget the path you tread. That is the only way back.'

'Elizabeth Desouza, Oneiro syllipsa.'

Something began pulling her. She began fighting back.

The priestess panicked. 'Do not resist it. Allow it to absorb you,' she warned.

She couldn't stay calm. There was no way she could remain calm. Ella wasn't in control of her body anymore. The connection had been stronger than she could handle. Seeing that she couldn't help it anymore,

Cafelle placed her index finger on the flower petals. There was a break and a snap at the same time.

Ella fell. Two maids came running.

Cafelle bent down to examine Ella's body. *She got in. She is in. I pray she keeps it together,* Cafelle thought.

They placed her in a comfortable position. One of the maids was about to remove her gloves when the priestess stopped her.

'Do not remove or add anything to her,' she warned.

Be safe, my daughter. You died once at the wolf's hands. Such will only repeat itself over my dead body.

It was gradually coming to an end. No, it wasn't. The light had been so bright that shutting her eyes wouldn't do anything. She felt like she might go blind after the experience.

Ella felt herself slowing down. The light was so intense, she felt herself being pushed back a little. The sun was so harsh and bright that she had to squeeze her eyes shut.

After a moment, she realized she had already stopped. A large door was in front of her. She had to take a few steps back to see the top of the door. The door was so intricately carved, and she could see designs cutting it more as each second passed. There was no way to open the door ... just a knocker. The door gave her a very fearful yet lonely feeling.

Ella took a step back in doubt, and turned around to

see a long path behind. Ella figured that it might be her way home.

She wondered if that could be the right door. It didn't feel like an elf was on the other side fighting to live. Ella looked around to see if there were any others.

'Guess I have no choice,' she muttered before she knocked on the door.

It opened slowly, but a powerful gust of wind rushed through the door, bringing some fallen leaves and loose soil with it. Ella gathered her dress and stepped into the unknown place, which looked like a forest.

Ella walked around in curiosity, calling Vasilisa's name. After a long time, she got so exhausted that she sat on a big round stone, stroking a wild rabbit that was munching on a radish.

Looking for Vasilisa was taking forever. She sighed. She was getting worried about Edmund as well, as she had not heard from him since he had been banished. He had promised her he would break off her painful engagement.

She picked up the rabbit and held it up to her face as she sighed again, staring at the rabbit. 'I want to see him. I want to see if he is all right, but I guess I have to trust him, right? And focus on finding Vasilisa.' The rabbit bent one of its long ears.

'Vasilisa? Did I hear you correctly? Did you mention the name Vasilisa?' Ella heard a deep and solid voice.

Ella looked surprised. 'You talk?' she asked.

'There is no way a rabbit can talk, foolish girl.'

'I know, and yet you are. Aren't you?'

'For the love of Pandora, turn around. You came to

another's dreams, and you do not even know how to follow the directions of sound? And put that rabbit down, it looks like it has seen Medusa herself.'

Ella put it down as it quickly scurried off. Ella turned around to see a man sitting on a white horse. His clothes looked tattered and his face had a prominent scar. Whatever caused that scar had made such a deep wound and clearly he hadn't been able to treat it appropriately. The man on his horse was towering over her and she had to crane her neck to see him clearly.

Ella stood up, flustered, brushed her dress and bowed. 'Oh, my apologies, sir. I did not think there was anyone else here in this place. I have been walking around for quite some time looking for someone, and as you can see it has been quite unfruitful. I was looking for ...' Ella paused and asked, 'Sorry, but you are?'

The man turned his horse around. 'Who I am matters not. You mentioned the name Vasilisa. No one casually mentions her name around here. This is my dream world, and with the dream guardians gone, anyone can come and go.' The horse started moving as he looked over his shoulder. 'Why are you just standing there? Are you not going to follow?' He then went into the woods.

Ella ran behind and caught up with the slow-walking horse. She had to climb over roots sprouting from the ground and push past branches that hindered her path to catch up with him. Now she knew why his clothes were in such horrible condition.

She walked alongside the horse for a long time, hoping that the man would say something to break the cold silence, as it was far too quiet and awkward for her to handle. Ella ended up floundering, as her legs were no longer listening to her. Soon the horse stopped. They were no longer in the middle of a thick jungle. Ella looked up and was awestruck.

They had ended up at the edge of a cliff.

Ella could not believe what she was seeing. The cliff she was standing on had a steep drop. The fog below was so thick that she could not see half the distance to the bottom. What was even more astounding was that the cliff was round and hollow. She could walk around the cliff, with the fog looking like the smoke from a witch's cauldron, and it was not a volcano, as it was quite cold and the mud at the top of the cliff was wet.

'What is this?' Ella asked curiously.

'Looks like there is a lot of shudder mudder here, right? Nope, it is just an abyss. Every person's dream world has one. Fall into your own, and you die. In the real world, we call it dying in your sleep. Here, we call it the Abyss.'

'Wait, you said this is your dream world. Then what happens if someone like me falls here?'

'You will get trapped in my dream world instead. Each dream world is different and unique, created with the person's deepest secrets. To many people, their dreams are a place to escape from reality, but playing around in another's dreams is dangerous. Which brings back to me asking you.' The man looked at Ella with his dagger eyes and asked, 'Why are you here?'

'I did not come here looking for you. I was looking for Vasilisa, whom you seem to know, so could you let me know how to get there?' she asked with a quiver in her voice.

'That name you keep calling is not someone many know about. As we were walking before, the feeling was similar to what I felt before from her. She was just so like you. Vasilisa used every ounce of energy to protect someone I could not. She did more than what she should have done.'

'My deepest apologies for your loss, sir. But may I ask who she was trying to protect? She might be someone who has the solution to how to defeat …'

'Me, perhaps?'

Ella froze. Her knees went weak; she knew that voice.

They turned around to see two pairs of yellow eyes staring among the bushes. One of the wolves ran and attacked Ella. Ella screamed, only to be saved by the scarred man.

'You have come again, Wilkin. Later than I expected. I thought you would be here an hour ago.'

Wilkin stepped out, looked at Ella and beckoned for the wolves that had been hiding among the trees to reveal themselves. He then turned to the wolf beside him and said, 'Don't kill him yet, Roukan. He is yet to tell me what I need.'

The wolf transformed into his human form, with thick brown hair running down his spine. Ella could not believe what she was seeing.

Roukan glared at Ella with his yellow eyes. The wolf behind Wilkin transformed and said, 'Lower your eyes, Roukan, for she is our leader's betrothed.'

Ella managed to regain her lost legs. She looked at Wilkin and said, 'It seems that there is one person who knows how to behave.'

'That is correct. It looks like only my advisor knows the rules of society. Well done, Raoul,' he said to the man-wolf behind him, and bowed. Wilkin then turned to Roukan. 'Step back, Roukan. We do not have enough time.'

'Yes, my lord,' he said, and he bowed.

'Let me interrupt for a moment. We have other plans at sunset. It would be best to finish things up earlier today,' said Raoul as he pushed back the long, hanging sleeves of his coat.

'Now, getting back to business, Your Majesty.' He bowed to the man protecting Ella. Ella's eyes clouded over the scarred man, who lowered his sword.

The man looked at Ella for a second, his eyes trying to tell her who he was before turning to look at Wilkin, and snapped.

Was he the king? I had no idea that the royal family was involved in this. Why did the priestess not tell me? pondered Ella.

'Do not think that today is any different, Wilkin. I will not tell you where Vasilisa is. Ever since you murdered your wife twenty years ago, I knew that you were not someone I would place my trust in. I gave my niece Cassandra to you with my full heart when you said you would keep her happy. You knew of her weakness, and instead of protecting her, you took advantage of it. You ended up killing her for your selfish gain.'

Wilkin's eyes were now full of fury. He pulled out

his locket and held it, facing it down to the earth as he walked towards Ella. 'You do not talk about Cassandra in front of me!' he growled menacingly.

Ella was gripped with fear. She knew then that the man on the white horse must be King Alphonse, whom Cafelle told her about. She did not know why, but she felt like she had seen this before. Ella felt dizzy, trying to balance herself by holding onto a tree. She heard someone call her name, but she could not recognize the voice. It was too far away.

The king panicked. He wanted to go to her, but he was still fighting against Roukan. It was not easy to go towards Wilkin either, as he was protected by his advisor, who was well known to be much stronger than Wilkin himself. He tried calling out to Ella, but she was already hallucinating.

Ella felt her surroundings disappear. She could see another vision, much like the one she had seen when Edmund played with her fingers.

The same red-haired girl suddenly became paler, and her lips were barely there. Then with one step forward, she crumpled like a puppet suddenly released of its strings. All she could see was the sky and a familiar shadow, which made her shiver in fear. She noticed a locket falling on the girl.

The last thing she heard was someone calling out her name just before she fainted.

'Oh my my,' exclaimed Wilkin, who was standing above Ella. 'She reminds me of that crazy red-haired servant I had all those years ago. Passed out within mere seconds of releasing my limiter. It looks like she is not that useful as well. What a pity, I thought she would have made a lovely bride.' He bent down and transformed just his hands to that of his wolf form. 'All that is left now is handling her parents as they mourn the loss of their precious little girl.'

The king knew what was next. He used every ounce of his strength to fight back. He knew Wilkin was going to throw her into the Abyss. Wilkin had already lifted Ella by her neck. Trying to figure out how to force his hands to change back to their human form was difficult enough, and Wilkin's magick wasn't as powerful as he wished it to be.

Roukan was still going strong, but his movements had reduced considerably in strength to before.

The king could easily predict his motions now, as compared to the swiftness of his movements earlier. The king quickly slit the wolf's stomach as he pounced on him. Roukan was now bleeding and in pain. He took a step back and was about to jump again when the king retrieved a card from his pocket and slammed the wolf down, pressing down the card on its forehead. The wolf then changed back to his human form and was absorbed into the card.

The king mounted his horse and raced towards Wilkin. He aimed an arrow at him and shot. Within a split second, Wilkin had turned his head and was seeing the arrow fly towards him. He dodged it easily.

He turned to the king and growled menacingly, as though he was the definition of death itself, 'You can't choose how it ends, Your Majesty. The only one who chooses the ending is me. I will do what it takes to find out what it is. Even if it means I need to kill someone to know.' He continued to walk towards the Abyss and held Ella over it. Ella was dangling dangerously, with her hair over her face. The scarf, which was once pinned to her hair, now fell around her neck.

The king aimed and shot another arrow, but this time Raoul used his quick speed and caught it. He turned to Wilkin. 'Sir, may I get rid of him for you? He is getting in the way too much now,' he said.

Wilkin just nodded. This was enough for Raoul to throw the arrow straight at the king. The force was so strong that it pierced through the king's hand and got stuck to a tree quite a distance behind him.

The king was shocked, quickly pulling out the arrow. His hand was now bleeding, painting the grass red with each drop that fell. He looked up to see Wilkin slightly turning around and smirking before letting Ella go. The king's eyes flashed at Wilkin with anger and resentment. He could no longer command his legs to run. As he tried to stand up, Raoul used his speed and was in front of the king in a split second.

'Stand up, and my aim will be to your heart this time,' said Raoul, with a dagger inches away from the king's chest.

'That's all you care about, isn't it, Wilkin? You killed someone again! Just because they do not tell you something, it does not validate your deed. You will pay for this, Wilkin. Mark my words.'

Suddenly, Raoul yelled, 'Lord Wilkin, in the woods!' He turned around and threw the dagger into the forest.

A red-hooded figure, face hidden, stepped out.

CHAPTER 16

From the tiny frame of the hooded figure, one could tell it was a female hidden behind the red cloak. Just as her hand gripped the dagger tightly, Raoul approached her but was halted by Wilkin.

'Don't take any step further! The king should not escape,' said Wilkin to Raoul before turning to face the hooded figure. 'Who in the name of Hades are you?' he added.

She ignored him and returned her gaze to the king and bowed. Without warning, she rose and flung her dagger straight to the locket around Wilkin's neck. The force sliced the locket that held his magick in half, and he fell unconscious to the ground.

His advisor stared at her with hateful eyes, ready to devour her.

'You have no chance against me. The longer he lies in that state, the harder it becomes for him to leave the dream world. You don't want him stuck here, do you?'

She tilted her head to the side in a manner that said she wasn't in the least bit intimidated.

Raoul scowled; he detested her for being right. He took out the bottle of Adam's ale and poured some in Wilkin's mouth. Both of them slowly became translucent. They were falling deeper into sleep.

'You should never have done that. He was the one who killed the girl; he doesn't belong here,' the king said to the hooded figure.

'The girl is not dead, Your Majesty. Let your mind be at ease. I will get her out, so you can leave now.'

'Who are you?'

'Haven't we met before? Yes, we have met before, and at the same time, we haven't. My apologies, Your Majesty.' She took down the hood of her cloak and applied pressure to his wound.

Alphonse's face twisted in pain. 'What do you mean? Do I know you?' he managed to say.

'You can always reach me in your memories only if you look deeper in your mind, Your Highness, but it would be better if they were left hidden.' She handed him a small vial. 'Drink this. It should send you back.'

'What will happen to you? This is my world, remember?'

'Do not worry about me. My work here isn't done. I'll follow the child to the Abyss. I failed her once. I won't do it again,' she said.

It dawned slowly on Alphonse that she already knew what had happened years ago. 'You know more of me than my ... my ... se ...' the king trailed off sleepily; the vial was already working.

'I saw it all happen. The laughter they shared on that tree lingers still in my head. Vasilisa's sacrifice for us all drove me here, and I remember how the queen picked the card in the woods and left in so much rage.'

'Are you Vasilisa? I thought Vasilisa was asleep for decades, never to be awakened. Didn't you stay in the shadows to protect your clan? Who are you?' The king tried hard to fight the sleepiness, but the vial was too powerful, and so he drifted into sleep.

She walked to the door of the Abyss and gave him a last look. She turned around as the wind blew her hair wildly, and she pulled her hood back up. 'It was a pleasure meeting you once more, Uncle,' she whispered before walking away.

Edmund squeezed his eyes shut just as a gush of sand blew across his face.

'They are catching up!' Kain warned as they both ran like their lives depended on it, which they did.

Edmund had realized that also. The sandstorms were more violent than their sea counterparts. Edmund saw Kain's seal cut through the water like a tail. Kain was hurt but was pushing through it. The young lad wanted to pretend like he'd never seen what happened. Then he saw it advancing as the army of the dead in full speed. It was the biggest sandstorm, brewing away in the distance. Kain wasn't going to last.

'Kain!' he bellowed.

'I know I can't make it, but I need you to do something for me.'

'Come on, you fool. I am not leaving you behind.'

'Take the pendant around my neck. It is hard to do anything with these webbed fingers of mine.'

Edmund took off the alluring locket that had a dark-blue gem in the golden ring that encircled it. 'It's yours. I don't think it is right for me to hold onto it.'

'It is yours now. It has been yours forever.'

'I don't understand.'

'The final memories of Vaughan Petyer, former Prince of Yovaria, are in it.'

'What would I do with the dead prince's memories?'

'You will find that out on your own. The storm approaches and I am running out of time. The air bubble is getting weak. I will help you get to the entrance of the cave.'

The storm was upon them. Edmund put on the chain hastily.

Kain sped up one last time. He pulled Edmund's hand. Edmund knew immediately what he was going to do. 'No, please don't.'

'Look upfront, Edmund.'

They were approaching a cave already while standing strong against every wave. The cave was dry, and it had the same entrance as that of Proteus' cave. 'Is this it?'

Kain let go of Edmund and aimed directly for the cave.

'You're seriously leaving me?' Edmund screamed. A

stream of bubbles fell into the water while he struggled to reach dry land.

Kain was gone.

Rocks and flowing streams of water welcomed Edmund. He saw a door and just stared at it, wondering how he could get in.

He stared into the dark cave and moved close enough for him to see someone at a distance. The figure hovered above the waters in the cave, then it came at him with great speed. Startled, Edmund took quick steps backwards.

'You have no ounce of magick. This is not a place for you, little child. Why are you here?'

'Why I'm here is not something I'm particularly interested in telling a stranger. I am here on a quest for Prince Kai,' he managed to say boldly.

'Oh, the lad has got courage.' The creature laughed, and Edmund noticed that he was a selkie, too, like Kain, although his form was much more divine than that of Kain's and he donned Eastern clothes.

'Kai, you say?' the man asked, then his eyes landed on the blue gem around Edmund's neck. 'You? You … No, it can't be. It is impossible,' he muttered to himself. He walked closer to Edmund, who began to feel uncomfortable. The man touched the chain with his webbed fingers.

'Uhm … Well, at least respect my personal space, but one thing is sure. I must go through that door.'

'What is your name?' he asked.

'Edmund Gilmore, the son of King Alphonse of the western royal guards,' he lied.

The man bowed. 'My apologies, sire. I am Evian, a subject of King Varuna, ruler of the deep sea.'

'It's okay,' Edmund replied audaciously. *This must be how royalties feel,* he thought.

'My job is to guard the Thavma Gi entrance and no one, under my watch, is allowed to get in without the shadow code, but for you, I will make an exception,' he said.

'If you'll let me in, just do so now.'

Evian stretched out his hands to pull a conch from thin air. He handed it over to Edmund. 'Whisper your name into it, sire.'

Edmund did.

Evian passed the conch through the door and a thin layer of liquid melted into the door. In an instant the walls became mirrors, and several reflections flickered here and there. 'Fascinating, right? This is Thavma Gi. A shadow recognizes his master's mirror. You need to find the right one.'

'I am no one's shadow, and I am not here for any god. I need the gem, nothing else.'

Evian chuckled. 'The tree of life can only accept those with magick. It wouldn't be easy to—'

'Make it happen.'

'My apologies, sire.' He passed the conch back to Edmund. 'That will be your shadow code for now. You can use it to get into Thavma Gi anytime.'

Edmund, still confused but not wanting to show it, thanked Evian and walked in.

'You were there, weren't you?' Kain asked just as Edmund went out of sight. He had been hiding somewhere in the cave and had managed to evade the stormy seas.

Evian could see the injuries on his tail. 'A few decades ago, six eyes saw the two lovers sink to the bottom of the sea. Only the girl was murdered, but the boy followed her in death. What a strong bond.'

'Your memories don't fail.'

'My memories are blurry and distinct. I remember slipping in and out of their bodies and trying to keep them in a gem. However, the gem broke into two; emotions that strong couldn't stay in one place. One stayed here, the other with the boy.'

'Proteus took it,' Kain answered. 'He asked me to keep it safe until it reached the rightful owner,' Kain added.

'The timing could not have been more perfect,' Evian said with a smile.

Kain returned the smile as the memory of that day flooded his mind.

He had been near Thavma Gi that day, swimming as a seal and circling around the same area, causing the sand on the seabed to disperse.

The sight of a drop of blood caught his attention. The colour of the blood was different from his own and emerged from under the seabed, causing a beautiful ripple in the waters, but contrasting to its beauty, the ripple was deadly. It was no different from a thorn of the nightshade.

The seal slowly transformed into its human form to reveal Kain, and he hovered above the ripple for a while before placing his feet in it, only to quickly be repelled.

As the ripple got stronger, he looked up and saw some humans falling in. He knew that it was going to alert the palace by binding itself into the blood of the humans falling. He was curious to know what kind of humans had met their ends in such a pitiful manner this time. At this point, he had lost count of the number of humans he had seen fall to the bottom, and every time, the bodies of those humans were taken to His Majesty King Varuna. Since the day his family had left him, he had noticed each time it happened.

'Watching dead humans is not a very good hobby, Kain,' said a man as he stepped out of the gates of Thavma Gi.

'Funny hearing that from the gatekeeper of Thavma Gi, Evian,' he said. 'What are you doing here, Evian?'

'That boy, he doesn't feel like a human.'

'Then what is he?'

'I can't tell for sure, but he may be a true blood,' said Evian.

They both turned to the ripple. Instead of the crimson of humans, a drop of blood the same colour as his own emerged from within the seabed. A dark blue, almost as mysterious as the existence of a true blood. The blue from the centre of the ripple slowly drifted towards them.

Kain quickly grabbed the dagger on the gatekeeper's coat and jumped up at a tremendous speed. He caught up with the blue ripple, cut his palm and stepped between the two humans and the ripple. He could almost feel a jolt of current running through his whole body.

'Selkie! What on earth are you doing? You are disrupting the domain of the ripple. His Majesty will find out about you now!' Evian yelled.

'If that boy is a true blood as you say, then His Majesty definitely cannot know about him.'

'But you need to have the same blood as that boy to be able to bind with the ripple. You are not a …' He trailed off as he saw the blood drip from Kain's palm as he held the girl over his shoulder and the boy by his wrist.

'How is that possible? All true bloods were traced and massacred by His Majesty a long time ago. The ones who still live are the ones who escaped the kingdom,' said Evian.

'I'll explain later. Help me bring these two out.'

Evian swam up and helped to carry the girl. As they laid them down, a green gem fell on top of the girl. Almost immediately, the gem changed colour to something much darker.

Kain touched it. 'It is pretty hot for something in water.'

'Selkie, this girl is too cold for someone who died just moments ago,' said the gatekeeper.

Suddenly, a bright light shone from the gem that was once green, causing it to shake wildly like it was about to shatter. Instead, as soon as the light vanished, the gem was split into two separate gems, one yellow and one blue.

Kain touched the blue gem on the boy. As the heat on the gem dissipated, Kain caught a glimpse of the boy's past. *This boy really … hid his own identity to die with the girl. Had he removed his limiter, he could have healed in the waters,* thought Kain. Then again, it was thanks to that limiter that the gem was able to split neatly into two instead of breaking.

'What do we do now, Kain?' asked Evian. 'We can't just leave them here.'

'There may be a way to hide these two,' said Kain. 'Bring me to the entrance of Thavma Gi. We will send them on their journey to their next life.'

'Hey, hey. I am not allowed to force open the gates, even though I am the gatekeeper.'

'Don't worry,' said Evian as he picked up the gems. 'This boy will have no problem opening the gates for the both of them.'

'Then the gems? Won't it be best to let them bring their own memories into their afterlife?'

Kain pondered for a while. 'Obviously. We will let them hold onto what is theirs.' *Just not yet,* he thought as he felt the palace guards getting close.

CHAPTER 17

Edmund strode in with his mouth wide open. His reflections in the mirrors were not staring back at him. It was as though each reflection of himself was a different version or character altogether. He tried to turn away from the mirrors several times, as some of them cried out for him to stop looking at himself.

How am I not supposed to look at myself? he thought, pulling his hair in frustration.

'It appears someone is getting angry,' said one of the reflections.

'I'm not angry!' Edmund lashed out. His reflections became quiet.

Then one of them said, 'Yes, the lad is definitely angry.' He then started laughing. A few other reflections joined in the cackle.

Edmund's muscles grew tense, and he clenched his jaw. He then looked around and realized something he hadn't seen before. He had been walking for quite some time already, and there seemed not to be an end to the road.

The reflections of him were already driving him crazy. He did not want to get lost amidst that. So he sat down and dipped his hands into the stream.

As soon as he did that, he saw an image of a boy writing something on a piece of paper, crumpling it up and then placing it on a hollow tree. That boy then turned around and looked at the trail of blood flowing into the river. Edmund could not figure out whose blood it was, but he could tell that the boy was in deep sorrow, as his eyes were filled with tears.

Edmund suddenly felt as though he was being yanked deeper into the vision. He saw the same boy peeping through a wide gate and his eyes glued to a lady being killed by a creature that was half wolf-half man, and the sight shocked him.

The boy stood dead still with his hands cupping his mouth, trying to be as quiet as possible to not attract the wolf's attention. However, that did not stop the wolf from turning around to see the boy watching it devour the woman.

Edmund's face turned deathly pale. He knew that face, there was no way he could forget the look in the creature's eyes as his bloodthirsty nature rose to its peak.

It was Bodolf Wilkin … and he had killed someone.

Edmund, now more than ever, wanted to get out of this vision, but there was a part of him that wanted to see it through to the end. He knew Wilkin was far from a good person and that he had harmed many countless times, but he didn't know that he'd actually killed someone.

Wilkin turned and took one step towards the boy, but the boy's reflexes were faster. He ran straight into the woods. He kept looking back, feeling the muscles of his heart tighten with incredible force, sending gushes of blood down his veins in a single movement. He failed to notice a tree in front of him and bumped into it.

The boy fell. Edmund knew that he could hear the sound of Wilkin getting closer, as he was crawling back in fear. He did not notice a hand slide up his shoulder. He turned around, shivering, and saw a lady smiling at him from behind. Her long silver hair was shining against the sunlight, and her green dress blended in with the surroundings.

Edmund noticed that the lady's circlet looked familiar. It was too similar to the one he'd seen at Ella's bedside that night at the temple. The one difference was the presence of a green gem on the one the silver-haired lady wore.

Suddenly, the gem flickered brightly as sunlight shone on it.

Dark-red roses began to grow around the lady and the boy. The boy's eyes grew with fright, but he reckoned she was better than the werewolf chasing after him. 'Wh-wh-what are ...'

The lady covered his mouth and plucked a thorn

from the bush to prick him. 'I'm sorry, Sir Vaughan, but I cannot allow any harm to befall you. Her Majesty sensed you were in possible danger and has ordered me to assist you in getting out of this, because you are young and cannot fight a werewolf.'

She then stood up, with Vaughan, who was slowly losing consciousness, leaning against her chest. The lady stroked his hair for a while, then plucked out a rose. She brought it close to her nose, enjoying the gentle scent it released. 'It's a pity, isn't it? Such beautiful flowers and I'll have to use it on someone I do not wish to. I'll leave if you do, Sir Wilkin.'

A wolf ran out from the darkness of the woods. At its last pounce, it transformed into a young man in his early twenties. Edmund was trying to figure out if the vision he was having was that of Wilkin's past or the boy's final memories …

'Give me the boy, Vasilisa, and I'll leave,' a younger Wilkin said, straightening out his clothes.

'You want something from my clan, and this boy has nothing to do with it.'

'He has seen too much. I will, in any way, make sure he does not ruin my plans with his childish curiosity.'

'If you wish to harm the boy, you will have to go through me first, and you and I both know you possess no such ability to do that.' She then crushed the rose, which let out fumes of black smoke.

The smoke was so strong that Edmund started coughing. He started to suffocate, and his vision was getting blurry. He was now desperate to get out of this vision.

Suddenly, he could feel someone pulling him. Within moments, Edmund found himself sitting on a boat on the river of Thavma Gi, moving forward, with the boat rider humming.

'Don't touch the stream here, boy. You're really lucky that I got you out of there. Can't imagine seeing a lad lost in his own past. Such a touching scene.'

'What happened? What do you mean by "his own past"? I did not see myself or anyone I know in there. They were a bunch of other people. The last thing I remember is dipping my feet for a while, and I could see this lady with long hair and a boy and ...'

'Ain't interested, so stop talking for a while, will you? This stream is connected to Lethe, which is part of the underworld. You see visions at the beginning of the stream, but as you move closer to the end of the river, you slowly lose yourself in your own memories. Yes, your memories. There might be things which you may have forgotten before. It's fine, people forget memories all the time, but most times remembering them is the last thing they want. So just don't touch it or drink it or do anything with it. I had a hell of a time getting you out, the way you were panting just now was worse than looking at Cerberus.'

Edmund sighed, exhausted, but could not wrap his head around what he saw. He may not believe what he just saw, but he realized one thing. He and Ella's fight against Wilkin had more untold reasons than they ever imagined. 'Where are you taking me?' asked Edmund.

'To the centre of this place. There is no better way of

finding your way around this place than getting a leaf from the Tree of Life.'

Edmund's head was now spinning. He felt like his head would explode from all the information. 'Say that again?' He briefly remembered Evian saying something similar.

'The Tree of Life! The name says it all, doesn't it? The tree that holds the life of Thavma Gi itself. It does just that, although the leaves of the tree can direct you to the right location of the mirror. Location, mind you, not into the mirror itself. That part, you will have to find out for yourself.'

Edmund pushed back his hair, which was still a bit wet from the earlier ordeal, held the locket around his neck and stared at the deep blue of the gem. He lowered his head, feeling tired and a bit worried. He was starting to regret the quest Prince Kai had given him.

'Now, don't look so glum, boy. The first time is always the hardest, you've just got to try and push yourself a little. Look! The river is getting wider. That means we are just about reaching the centre of this place soon.'

Ella could not see a thing at first. The blackness rushed by in a blur.

It had been almost half a minute since she had been thrown down by the vile hands of Wilkin. Ella knew the pain was coming. It went by fast, yet slow, almost suspended.

Her eyes fluttered open, drawing into small slits. The walls of the Abyss were a queer shade of lilac, constantly dripping. Her eyes grew as she stared at the walls. A teardrop rolled down her face, but her hands were too beaten up to wipe it away.

The Abyss was showing her what she wanted to see the most. She could see Edmund on a boat, lost in thought. It was fairly dark, with candlelight against the cave walls. His pushed back wet hair was gorgeous, but his eyes were filled with a lonely sorrow.

Ella reached out her hand towards him; she felt another teardrop against her cheek as she realized how close yet so far away he was. For all she knew, it might have been an illusion. Maybe even something Wilkin was doing to cause her more pain than she already felt.

Suddenly, the image changed.

She could now see the red-haired girl and a boy sinking into the waters. The water looked like there was red dye flowing into it, causing a ripple. Ella figured out that it was blood, and it belonged to the girl. The boy, who was holding her hand, closed her lifeless eyes, kissed her probably for the last time, and closed his eyes as well. His other hand was clasped tight, as if holding something.

They then sunk to the bottom and fell to the riverbed. The boy's clasped hand loosened and a green gem floated out. Thick smoke engulfed the gem and it split into two.

The vision then changed to reveal the surface of the waters. She saw Wilkin looking over the riverbank into the waters.

He must have done something, Ella thought.

Wilkin turned back and picked up something off the floor. He then handed it to one of his men and said, 'Look after it well, for it shall be given to Vasilisa's chosen floral maiden.'

Ella could not see the man, as he was obscured by Wilkin's back. The man took it and asked,

'Will everything be all right, sir? The girl is dead, and Vasilisa is well hidden with your wife.'

'As the Queen of Elves, she will neither die, nor will she die without someone to look after her people. Worry not, for I will definitely take control of elven magick. It is only a matter of time.'

Wilkin then walked away, and Ella could not believe what the man had in his hands.

It was the circlet Wilkin had given her as an engagement gift. The bastard was using her even more than she had imagined.

Ella's tearful eyes were now filled with rage. She screamed.

Suddenly, the vision faded away and she found herself falling fast. Somehow, her body could feel that she was reaching the bottom soon. She clenched her fist and squeezed her eyes shut, hoping it would end soon.

Ella, amid her anger, did not realize that her clenched fists were releasing rose petals to the bottom. As she landed, she fell onto a bed of roses. Her head was on the lap of a lady, who had managed to hold her tight enough to prevent a strong impact.

'She sure is knocked out cold,' said the priestess as Ella landed gracefully in front of Vasilisa, who was stroking the girl's hair.

Vasilisa did not look up. 'She is the one who I gave my magic to, is she not? She looks just like Virgo, Cassandra.'

The priestess knelt in front of them and said, 'Do not call me Cassandra anymore. Cassandra died that night alongside Virgo. No one knows that I still live. I was right in front of my uncle. I shot an arrow at my husband. None of them recognized me, not that I expected them to. My husband killed my uncle, and I covered it up to protect the royal family.'

'Everyone might have forgotten you, but I have never forgotten you, Cassandra. I was the only one who believed you that day you came to me asking for help. I failed to help you and caused you so much pain and suffering … Not just you.' She looked back down at Ella. 'Even this girl is in pain because of my weakness.'

The priestess stood up and turned her head away from Vasilisa. 'Yes. It is and always will be your doing. You broke my family, even after everything I told you.' She glared at Vasilisa with hateful eyes. 'I will always hate you for that,' she added.

'I know, and I do not ask for forgiveness. I only ask for a solution,' said Vasilisa.

'I'll give you the solution for taking revenge, my revenge, on my husband, but I will not give you the solution for mending our trust.'

'Very well, Cassandra,' said Vasilisa. 'Then, I shall assume that it is time to wake her up.' She walked to a small pond and scooped some water, sprinkling it on Ella's face. Ella stirred but failed to wake.

'Why is she not waking up? Is she awake already in the real world? This is not her dream world, so she cannot be dead just by falling into the Abyss,' said the panicked priestess.

'That's because she overused her powers in a short time. Her sudden burst of anger was probably the first time for her.'

The priestess sighed. 'All right, I've been here long enough. I only came to do two things.' She then took out two small vials tied to her belt. She took one and gave it to Vasilisa, who took it and tied it around her belt.

'Pitcher juice?'

'Yes. It will work on her.'

'What's the second thing?'

'Teach her your magick.'

'Of course, there is no other reason for her to be here.'

'No, not just elven magick … I mean your own magick. The one you created to fight against Wilkin to save Her Majesty's son, Vaughan.'

Vasilisa was shocked. 'That is no ordinary spell, Cassandra! She is too young and has barely learned the basics. On top of that, she is not even a full elf. She is half-human, and if not done properly, can affect her human self.'

'I know, but right now she has no choice. If you see Virgo in Ella, then Vaughan is also Edmund. That boy has gone to Thavma Gi to learn of his shadow code, but he will also regain his lost memories, and when he does, he will recognize the spell. He will be able to assist her. From the day I died at the hands of my werewolf husband, I saw a vision before I woke up – a vision of a girl wielding your magick against someone. At the time, I did not believe myself, for I never knew who that girl was, but when she walked into the temple the other day, I realized that she is Virgo's reborn. You, the Queen of Elves, chose her. Train her till she is at least half as good as you. That is the only thing you can do right now, by making things right. I'll heal Ella before I leave.'

Vasilisa did not know what to say. The priestess looked at her and realized she needed more time to think about it, especially since this was their first meeting in a long time. She also noticed that Ella was waking up.

She walked towards Vasilisa, took her hands and said, 'Do not hesitate, Vasilisa. The other elves are waiting for your return. They have lived long enough without a ruler. You need to go back to them. Defeating the one who put this curse on you is the only way you can go home. How long do you plan to sleep in the real world?'

CHAPTER 19

Queen Adela was getting more impatient by the second. The frown on her face reflected back at her in the glass of water she held just as she sipped from it. The king had still not awakened, and things were getting out of hand. Then again, it was not the first night without her husband. It had been nineteen years.

Does the guilt about his niece keep him in this sleep he cannot wake from? she thought.

The only way to awaken her husband was to at least prove to him it was not his fault that she died, but there was no way to rid him of that guilt. It was a futile battle with his inner self, and she knew that he had to figure things out on his own.

'Your Majesty! The king has risen!'

A maid burst into the queen's quarters. The queen was shell-shocked.

Now?! she thought. It was too sudden. She swiftly got up and ran towards the king's chambers.

The king had finally woken up, but he could barely keep his eyes open.

'Your Majesty, can you hear me? How are you feeling?' asked a man clad in white attire at his bedside.

'Who are you?' asked the king in a barely audible whisper.

The man stood up and poured some water in a goblet. 'I'm … I am a royal physician. Here, have some water,' he said, extending the goblet to the king.

The king took the cup. 'So the royal physician has been replaced.' He then came to realize that he had been asleep for a long time. 'How long have I been asleep?' he asked.

'Nineteen years,' said the physician.

'I see.' His eyes widened with shock. 'Is the queen on her way here right now?'

'Of course, Your Majesty. Word has been sent to her, she should arrive soon.'

'No! She cannot see me now. I have something to do first! Get me some parchment and quill. Quick!'

The physician grabbed some parchment from the side table and brought the ink closer to the king. The king quickly scribbled a long letter and handed it to the physician.

'Hide it quick! Do not let the queen see it. Write another copy of it and send it as soon as possible to Desouza and Gilmore. Tell them to refrain from moving until they receive my orders.'

The physician took the letter and quickly tucked it into his coat. 'Yes, Your Majesty, it shall be done immediately. I shall take my leave for now.' He bowed and left the room.

At the same time, the queen rushed in and looked at the king. She could not believe her eyes. 'You finally woke up.'

The king looked at her with eyes of sorrow. 'How have you been, my queen?'

'How do you think I have been? Leaving me alone with the responsibilities of the kingdom, knowing full well that I hadn't been in Yovaria long enough?'

'How are our children? They must have grown up now.'

'Don't act like you care about them. You abandoned them for nineteen years. You are nothing but a coward who chose to live with your guilt of not being able to protect one person, turning your back on your whole kingdom instead.'

The king sighed and remained silent for a while.

Queen Adela was frustrated with his silence. 'All right, now let's get down to business. Who has been visiting you? I bet your dream world had a lot going on compared to the real world.'

'The Duke of Kroukhesta, Sir Bodolf Wilkin.'

'Why would that man want to see you?' The queen was nervous. 'D-do you know something I don't?'

'Yes, Adela. I know where the Queen of Elves is trapped, and I am positive that you do, too.'

'W-what? How would I know such a ridiculous thing? What do you mean she is trapped?' she gasped and let out a choked cough, her round eyes betraying how shocked by his words she was.

'I think the one who needs to speak is you, don't you think? Since you trapped her, you are the only one who knows how to free her.'

The queen was shocked. 'You better not reveal this to anyone. I did it to protect you and our people.'

'No, Adela. You hurt them. Maybe not now, but you will soon.'

'What are you trying to say?'

'That the truth is already on the way to the people who need to hear it the most.'

'Alphonse, please don't tell me you …'

'Yes, Adela. Sir Derrick Desouza and Sir Gordon Gilmore need to know. They cannot be left in the dark any longer. I have already sent them the message.'

'They are better off not knowing anything. Why would you tell them anything about that night?'

'Because their children are already trying to find their lost memories …'

'And how do you know that? You were asleep the whole time.'

'The one who visited me was not only the Duke of Kroukhesta. Elizabeth Desouza visited me, too.'

'Vaughan …' Virgo called. The warmth of the sun flowing into their hideout caressed her smooth ivory skin.

'Hmm?' said Vaughan, laying his head on her lap with his eyes closed.

'The sun is going to set soon. Don't you think it is time to leave?' she asked as she ran her hands through his soft hair.

'It's fine. Let's just stay this way a bit longer.'

'Are you sure? People might begin to notice that we are missing.'

'Let them. They will never find this place.'

'How are you so sure?'

Vaughan opened his eyes and looked into hers, which were staring back at him with a few strands of her bright-red hair hanging over her face, obscuring his vision of her beautiful face. He pushed them behind her ears and said, 'I told you that I am a shadow, didn't I? I put a time barrier around this place, a power I got from my god, Chronos. With my magick, I can cast a spell to make time stop if I want to. Right now, no one knows that we are here.'

'Really? So we can just stay here all day? And not get caught?'

Vaughan smiled. 'Yes, my love. Besides, we are sitting in a treehouse hidden among the trees. There is no way we will get caught, even without my powers.'

'That's nice,' said Virgo.

'You seem to have a liking for this a bit too much. Or is it just me you like?'

Vaughan sat up, and Virgo took his hands into hers. 'I like both you and the fact that I can stay with you for as long as I want.' She sighed. 'If only this could really last forever, with no strings attached to our lives.'

Vaughan looked at her worried expression and asked, 'Hey, has something been bothering you? You seemed lost in thoughts the whole day today.'

Virgo thought for a moment and shook her head. 'You are right. I did have something on my mind today, but not anymore.'

'Why is that?'

'Because the person right in front of me is you,' she said as she came closer to him and kissed him. Vaughan pulled her in for a hug and laid his head on her lap once again.

She then pulled away. 'Vaughan?'

'Hmm?'

'Promise me you will never leave me alone.'

'Virgo, it is something I would do even without you asking.'

'I know, but just promise me so that I can feel at ease.'

Vaughan sat up and held her face, saying, 'I promise, Virgo, that I will never leave you alone. I swear it.'

He pulled her in his arms again as the wind blew, rustling the fallen leaves.

CHAPTER 20

Edmund jolted awake suddenly.

Was that a dream? he thought.

It had felt too real. He was lying down on the boat when he saw a few leaves falling from the top of the underground cave. As he reached out to catch one, it disappeared.

'It must have been quite a vivid dream,' said the boatman.

'Yes, though it was a bit too familiar,' said Edmund.

'Well, either way, you are awake now, so all is good. We have reached the centre already. Look!' He pointed to the end of the river.

The end of the river stood by a small piece of land with a huge tree standing strong in the middle. As they reached the land, the boatman got off the boat and anchored it. Edmund then jumped out and looked around.

It seemed that it was not something he could take in with one breath, but he noticed something odd. Around the tree was not the end for one river but five. 'How are there five rivers here? Where do they lead?'

'Don't worry about that, they are the least of your concerns. How about you do what you need to do first? I cannot be of help to you every time.'

'Really? Because to the best of my memories, you've only helped me once, and that was when I fell into the river.'

'Right, your memories are all muddled up. I forgot. Okay, start by finding your leaf and following it to your mirror. Put your hand into that mirror, holding the leaf. Wait till you feel something. If the leaf is taken away from you, then that means you have been permitted to enter the mirror. If not, you will receive something.'

Edmund looked at the tree. There were probably millions of leaves as it was. 'How am I ever to find a single leaf from all this?'

'Boy! Do I have to tell you every little thing? Figure it out yourself. The one who dropped you off at the entrance should have given you a hint.'

'A hint?' Edmund took out the gem. *This is all I got, though*, he thought.

'Okay, well then. I'm leaving; I have wasted too much time with you already. Oh and when you're done, just drop the leaf in the river. It will find its way back to the tree.'

'Wait! I still have to ask ...' Edmund turned to see that he was already gone. Even the boat was no longer docked. He sighed, turning back to the tree and ruffled through the branches. He pulled a random leaf, and that leaf just turned to dust. He noticed that a new leaf had grown in that spot. He pulled another leaf, and the same thing happened again.

Edmund walked around the tree. It was so huge that it would take a while just to walk around it once, but he also knew that he was left with no choice but to walk around it, hoping to find clues.

As he walked, he saw another man holding up his shellcode. He said some words and waited for a while. To Edmund's amazement, a leaf fell from the tree and landed on the shell. He then turned towards Edmund, smiled and bowed, then walked away towards the mirrors.

Edmund reached out for the shell he'd got at the entrance and held it up. He tried to recall the words the man had said.

'Mudento Presi.'

Nothing happened.

'Modunto Piresi.'

Nothing happened again.

Edmund closed his eyes tight and tried to think back to figure out the right words. An image of Vaughan flooded his head as he saw the boy standing in front of the tree as well. Edmund opened his eyes and was relieved.

'Mudentro Piressi.'

A leaf finally fell from above, falling lightly on top of the shell, but it did not stop there. He suddenly had the urge to start walking. It felt as though the leaf had a mind of its own, pulling him somewhere.

He started walking back into the riverbank where he'd come from and was welcomed by his numerous reflections again. Still, this time he was not frustrated. He was elated. Within a matter of time, he was standing in front of a mirror. It was comparatively smaller than most of the other mirrors he'd seen along the way, and he wondered if that mirror was really his.

It was nested among other large mirrors and was just the size of his face. It was placed rather low; therefore, one had to bend for it to be reached.

Edmund looked into the mirror. The reflection looked back at him and smiled.

'You found me.'

Edmund snickered at his reflection. 'How did I find myself? I am you.'

'Really? Then how is it that we are speaking to each other?'

'Are you some kind of inner thoughts or something?'

The reflection shrugged. 'Not really, but I guess you could think of it like that.'

The reflection stopped moving on its own. Edmund remembered what the boatman said and held the leaf, slowly putting his hand in. It felt like he was sticking his hand in the water, a cold feeling, yet not wet. After a few seconds, he removed his hand. On his hand were the leaf and a box.

Edmund dropped the leaf in the river. The leaf floated upstream in the direction of the tree. *It really does go back there*, he thought.

He opened the box and found a letter. It was written in red, probably with the leaves of the mignonette tree. Considering how it faded, it must have been quite some time since it was written. He picked up the letter and found a stone inside. It looked extremely similar to the one Kain had given him. He picked up the stone and kept it in his waist pouch.

He was about to read the letter when he heard a voice.

'Edmund! Hurry!'

He turned around to see Kain, all tattered up, running at full speed towards him. 'Kain, what are you doing here?'

'There's no time. Hurry! They found out that you are here!'

He pulled Edmund and fled. 'Just run a bit longer. The gatekeeper is trying to fend them off, but he is not strong enough. I need to get you to the surface before they find you. They are already at the entrance.'

'Um … Kain? How do I get to the surface? I'm several feet underwater, and I cannot breathe in water to start with.'

'Just walk through the waterfall. You will reach the top. Oh and Edmund …?'

'What is it?' asked Edmund.

'Nothing, just be careful, okay? Be safe. Protect her, at least this time.'

'Her? You mean Ella? How do you know her?'

'I do not know of anyone by the name Ella, but since she is the first one you thought of when I said to protect her, that means that you really are the late prince.'

Edmund's eyes grew wide. 'What …'

'Sorry, let's catch up another time.' He pulled Edmund by the collar into the waterfall. As he came out the other side, Edmund was gone and he was back to his seal form.

Be safe, Edmund, because if you aren't, the one who led you and your lover to your death in your past life will repeat his actions again. It will not only lead to another tragedy but to something greater this time. That is why Proteus and I were trying to keep your coming to Thavma Gi a secret. Well, then again. This does not concern you, at least not yet. I'll see you again when the time is right.

The wind was still for quite some time. Vasilisa had been seated next to the bed for the past two days, with Ella still not awake. Well, not exactly a bed, more like a large flat rock covered in rose petals.

Ella was not completely awake yet, just as she was not in the real world either, according to the news received from the priestess. So she was probably in a temporary sleep coma. She should awaken any time soon ... She'd better.

Vasilisa had a lot to say to her, and time was not on their side. She looked up, but instead of the sky, it was a black hollow space. Even though the surroundings were lit, it was still dark.

'Mmm ...' Ella stirred.

Vasilisa ran to Ella and sat by her bedside. 'Ella, how do you feel?'

Ella's eyes fluttered open. She looked at Vasilisa and asked, 'Who are you?'

'We are meeting for the first time.'

Ella looked around. 'Where am I?'

'What is the last thing you remember?'

'The king … then the wolves … Wilkin … Then I was falling down somewhere, I saw Edmund. How could I see Edmund? Then I saw Wilkin … He killed someone. Wilkin killed someone! A girl! She had red hair.'

Vasilisa took her hands. 'Ella, calm down. I will explain everything to you. Cassandra sent you to me so that you can learn of your past.'

'Who is Cassandra? And who are you? Where am I?' asked Ella, confused.

'That's right. You do not know Cassandra. You probably know her as Cafelle, the priestess.'

'The priestess …? She is Cassandra?'

'Yes, Ella. She is Cassandra, the cursed sibyl, and I am Vasilisa. The Queen of Elves, and the one who gave you your powers, although it was a sudden, impulsive decision.' She stood up and picked up a goblet, filling it with some water at a small fountain a small distance away. She then handed it to Ella. 'Here, drink this. It will help you remember the memories of your past life, although its effects will be rather slow.'

Ella drank it. *It's sweet*, she thought.

'Ella, look up,' said Vasilisa. Ella looked up to see a large, hollow hole. She could vaguely remember those lilac walls.

'That's where I fell through, isn't it?'

'Yes. That is the Abyss. You are lucky that you didn't touch those walls.'

Ella closed her eyes and took a deep breath.

'I know it is a lot to take in, so why don't we take things easy? Let me start by telling you a story.'

'A story …?'

'Yes. A story about a very dark occurrence, dating twenty years back. I will also tell you the way to defeat Wilkin, for only I know. The time has come for you to know as well.'

Back in the real world, within the Broken Woods, Leofrick rode towards the waterfall and fast. He had received word from Prince Kai about the lifting of Edmund's ban, but it was too soon. He was yet to pass on some very important information to Sir Wilkin, which for his friend was good news no doubt, but he was still a god who had to look after his own shadow.

Furthermore, there were only a few days left.

He quickly reached the riverside, realizing that Edmund had not left Thavma Gi yet. He got off his horse and walked up to a large tree, which had a large hollow hole. Leofrick sighed and dug his hand in.

'What in the heavens are you doing, Loki?'

Leofrick continued fumbling in the tree. 'Funny, I'm pretty sure the heavens' intersect is a lot higher than that.' He turned around to see Hermes sitting on a large rock near the river.

'Looks like you have to take back your words, Loki. The heavens, which you look down on, sent you a message.' He then took off his sandals and dipped his feet in the river. The kappa was keeping a distance away this time, but Hermes could see them lurking beneath the surface, looking for their next prey.

'And what have the great heavens sent me this time? I am hoping it is not a family reunion of some sort.'

Hermes sighed. It looked like the task was going to take a while. He stood up and put his sandals back on.

'Why are you here today, Hermes? I know that you have come here not as a friend, but as a messenger. Just pass on the message and go. I would rather have a friend around right now. At least four hands are better than two when it comes to looking for lost things.'

'You're right. I am here as a messenger, not your friend. However, I wish to give you some advice as your friend.'

'What is it?'

'Don't let the innocent die again, Loki. You say you will help your human friend, but deep down, I can see that you still have a soft spot for your shadow and his pack. You already protected your shadow once. Let him protect himself this time.'

Leofrick sighed. He knew that Hermes was right. He wanted to save Edmund from dying again but did not want Wilkin to get hurt again. 'What message were you sent to deliver to me?'

Hermes opened his right palm, facing up. A scroll appeared, which he handed to Leofrick.

Leofrick read the words aloud. 'As you protect your shadow, I shall protect mine. Cronus.' Leofrick was dumbfounded. Edmund got the one thing which could have saved his shadow.

'Don't try to trick the human boy into giving it to you, Loki.'

'First of all, he is not human. He is a shadow. Furthermore, I do not want to see Bodolf get hurt.'

'I do not wish for the two stars to collide again, reborn and living through the same story over and over again. There is no torture worse than that,' said Hermes.

'Why would you care about that?'

'We are deities, Loki. If we don't care, no one else will.'

Just then, the waterfall created a ripple at the side, opening up slowly. Edmund was reaching the surface.

Hermes said, 'Seems to me that he has completed his quest. Time for me to leave then.' He then left, leaving behind a swift, passing wind.

Leofrick smiled.

Yes, he has, he thought. He was glad that Edmund was safe.

As the waterfall opened apart, Edmund walked out, fully wet but with a blissful glow on his face. He looked up and saw Leofrick. 'Leo, I did it. I found a way to save Ella,' he gushed.

'Ed, can I ask you something?' Leofrick asked.

'Sure, but since when do you ask for my permission before asking something?'

'Good point.' Leofrick shrugged. 'You said you found a way to save Ella, right? What are we saving her from, then?'

'Not what, but who. Our enemy is the Duke of Kroukhesta, Sir Bodolf Wilkin.'

Leofrick looked at Edmund's eyes. They were full of rage just at the mention of Wilkin's name. 'Why is he our enemy?'

'Because if we don't stop him, he will continue killing people like he always has been. We can't let a wild beast roam around Yovaria, don't you think?'

Leofrick realized that Edmund was right. He would be unable to protect Wilkin again. Still, if there was one thing he could do, it would be to prevent this vicious cycle from repeating itself all over. 'Let's get going then. I could ask you to tell me the whole story now, but Prince Kai has lifted your ban and wishes to see you. I'll do you a favour by making you say it once.' He winked.

Deep down, he knew that he was thankful.

'Your Majesty, lunch will be served immediately,' said the palace cook.

The queen nodded. The cook turned on her heel and was about to run off when she stopped in her tracks. She turned around and asked carefully, 'Will His Majesty be joining you for lunch today, my lady?'

The queen glared sharply at her. 'No! He is far too unwell to get out of bed just yet. Bring his food to his chambers.'

'You seem to have underestimated me, my queen,' said King Alphonse as he walked in with a limp.

Servants rushed in to help, but the king shrugged them away.

'Your Majesty, you are far too weak to be up and running yet.'

'I did not get out of bed to worry about my kingdom. I have realized that you and my children have done a job well done.'

'Why are you out then?' questioned the queen.

'To keep an eye on you,' said the king bluntly.

They looked at each other for a moment. All the maids and servants could feel the air grow heavier, with a strong, dense tension among them.

The king broke the silence by speaking first. 'Well, then. I do wonder what's for lunch today,' he exclaimed as he sat on the far end of the table. The cook bowed and ran back to the kitchen. The queen grunted and sat at the other end. 'May I know when I can meet my children? I have not seen them since I woke up. They must be so grown up now.'

Plates were placed in front of them, and the glasses turned and filled with wine. 'Lukan has gone with the priest to the kingdom of Amrita. To take part in the ordeals of seeking the princess' hand in marriage.'

'Yes. The Princess of Amrita should be of age to be wedded by now. What about Kai?' He then took a sip of wine.

'He has focused on his studies quite a lot these last few years, has a lot of interest in astronomy especially.'

A covered tray of food was placed on the table. The curtains were then closed, and the candles were lit. The ambience was solemn yet enchanting. The main cook then revealed a sumptuous dish of fried rice with a healthy addition of vegetables and assorted meat. The cook placed some of the rice on a serving plate and handed them to the other cooks as they served them on their plates.

'Where's the card, my queen?'

The queen paused for a moment but continued on with cutting the meat. 'That girl is the reason why Vaughan is dead. I am not handing her to anyone, especially to you, since you care about your sibyl niece more.'

'You know that it was not Vasilisa's fault, right?'

'No, it is her fault through and through. She believed Cassandra's words, words which no one else believed.'

'She wanted to give hope, and let's be honest, Cassandra's words were not all lies. There was a little truth buried in them, which we found only after she died.'

Queen Adela put down her spoon and dipped her hands in the rose-scented water bowl. She then wiped them with a towel. A maid scurried in and replaced the main dish with a dessert of orange cake. The maid then poured some custard over it, covering the cake with another layer of sweetness.

The queen was about to pick up the dessert spoon when the prince walked in. 'If you are here for your lunch, then you do realize that you need to work a lot more on your tardiness, Son,' said the queen.

The prince replied, 'I am here for dessert, Mother, as I heard that today's dessert is my favourite. I am well aware that I am neither tardy, nor am I unaware of the rules we have in our family.' He then turned to his father, the king, and bowed on one knee. 'It is good to see you well, Father. My deepest apologies for not looking for you earlier.'

The king held his son's shoulders and stood him up, standing up himself. 'You really have grown so much, Kai,' he remarked, letting out a deep breath. 'I feel deep regret for not being able to see you all these years.'

'I understand, Father. I am aware that you were in deep sorrow and regret all these years, and I also know the reason behind your sorrow.'

The king was surprised. 'I see. How much do you know, Son?' he questioned.

'I know that the reason behind the death of my brother was murder and that the murderer is someone the royal family is hiding.'

The queen dropped her spoon in shock. The king looked at his wife across the table and asked the prince, 'And who, Kai, is our family hiding?'

'I will let you know once my suspicions are proven to be true, Father. I am meeting the son of the Gilmores later this afternoon, and that will give me some long-awaited answers.'

Son of the Gilmores, the king thought. *So he was the one that girl who'd visited him in his dream world – Elizabeth – was in love with.*

The prince sat down at the table. When the cake was served, he took a small bite and savoured the sweet taste. 'Ah!' he exclaimed. 'I forgot to mention one more thing I found.' He then signalled for Knight Fred to come in. Fred and another servant came in, each holding a large painting, draped and covered with a satin cloth.

'What is that, Kai?' voiced the queen, pointing to the larger of the two paintings. Her voice was quivering, and she was starting to feel anxious. She rubbed her sweaty palms discreetly against her dress and hoped that no one noticed the sweat that was starting to gather on her forehead. If they noticed how nervous she was, there was no doubt they would begin to feel suspicious, and she could not afford that.

'Oh, that? That is a portrait of Edmund Gilmore, Mother, and something was so familiar about it that I had to show you,' he responded coldly. He removed the drapes of the first portrait, and then removed the drapes of the other painting to show a family portrait of the royal family painted a long time ago. 'This is our family portrait taken when I was very young. I did not know that we had this family picture in the first place.' He then walked to the other painting. 'Now take a look at the next one,' he added. 'This is Vaughan's portrait, a few days before his death. What do you see missing?'

'Just tell us, Kai,' bellowed King Alphonse.

'The pendant tied to his sword, it was not an ordinary one, was it?' asked Kai. 'I did some research on the symbols painted on the pendant. What I found out was rather shocking.'

The queen was visibly shaking, and she was pretty sure by now they had noticed her quivering lips and sweaty face. The words refused to form in her mouth, leaving her choked and unable to defend herself.

The prince was able to confirm his suspicions that the queen was hiding something.

The king's expression, however, did not change. 'And what does it mean, Kai?' asked the king.

'It means that it was a protection charm, Mother ...' said the prince, looking at the queen '... A protection charm from Thavma Gi. The reason why he died was that he did not have it with him that day.'

While the king remained stoic – never once did his face betray his emotions – the queen rose up suddenly. She pushed the chair back; the sound of it scraping against the ground pierced through her ears. Her mouth felt heavy, as though a ball of cotton had been forced into it. The goblet that held the red cherry wine she had been drinking earlier tipped on the table, staining the tablecloth with wine.

'Now, Mother, may I have that pendant?'

CHAPTER 22

'No, Ella. You're getting it wrong again. You need to clasp your hands together to gather your thoughts. Only then will you be able to control the growth of the roses. Look, you have only made half the roses bloom.'

Ella sat on the ground, tired of the almost five days of magick practice. She had managed to learn how to ripen fruits and turn spring leaves into something from autumn and other small spells. However, literally growing something was quite challenging, because every time she failed the spell, she lost a lot of energy. She managed to improve her energy control, but it was still not good enough.

Vasilisa noticed her disheartened expression. She sat beside Ella and laid her head on her shoulders.

Ella sighed and asked, 'How long did you take to learn all this? To learn how to stop Wilkin, you said it is advanced magick, but I don't think I will be able to learn in time.'

'Don't judge your strength yet. Your powers are almost similar to mine, so you will eventually be able to do it.'

'I don't know. I'm not able to gather my thoughts at all. Everything you told me about what happened twenty years ago, they feel so vivid, like I personally went through it all, and I'm worried about Edmund. Ever since I saw him on the walls while falling, I haven't set eyes on him.'

'You're worried, aren't you?'

'Yes, I am. I want to know where he is if he is doing something stupid if he is safe due to his banishment if he …' She paused.

'If he what?'

'… If he misses me.'

Vasilisa pondered. No wonder her magick was unstable and her emotions were too strong, not weak. She needed to control them, not gather them.

'Ella, do you want to talk to him?'

Ella was surprised. 'I can?'

'It is a spell similar to how you entered the king's dream world. It is possible to slip into the dreams of others through the Abyss. The difference is that what you did with the priestess was with your physical body, while this will be an illusion of yourself. I can't do that to myself, due to the queen's wrath, but you can.'

'Yes, please! Do tell me. Oh, that would be lovely!' Ella exclaimed, her eyes sparkling with delight at the thought of seeing Edmund after so long.

Vasilisa chuckled. 'Not now, Ella. Let the night fall.

Once he is asleep, I will personally create the door for you.'

Back at the Desouza mansion, Nurse Marcie had just finished with the distribution of chores to the other servants and maids. It was half past four, and she was free to do as she wished till six. She then decided to pay Ella a visit, maybe even bring her some of her favourite snacks. After knowing Ella's true heart and getting married to another, she could understand why she had not written a single letter to her parents.

She got changed and stepped out of the house, where she noticed the royal messenger galloping towards her, fast. The horse then stopped in front of the mansion.

She bowed and asked, 'May I ask what the purpose of this visit is?'

The messenger stepped down. 'I am here to pass on a message from His Majesty King Alphonse of our great kingdom, and would like to have an audience with the members of this household.'

'Ah! Of course! I will inform them right away,' she said, and scurried towards the house to see Lady Desouza standing at the door.

'There is no need to run, Marcie. I will bring him to the study myself. Derrick has been doing paperwork all day, and I doubt he will want to be disturbed.' She then turned towards the messenger.

'Do come in. Marcie, go see my daughter as you

originally wanted, in fact, stay the night with her. You do not have to prepare tea. I will get someone else to do it.'

'I will be back soon, my lady.' Nurse Marcie then bowed and left. After walking a distance away, she realized she had forgotten to bring along the snacks. She started walking towards the mansion when she heard a loud scream. Marcie was shocked.

She held her skirt and ran towards the mansion. Everything was suddenly quiet. Each step she took inside the house suddenly felt unfamiliar, with a strange nauseous smell. The horrible smell led her to the staircase, which was the way to the second story. She dropped her things in horror.

There was blood streaming down the stairs, and the howl of a wolf was heard, loud and clear.

Nurse Marcie silently gasped in horror, with her hands over her mouth. Her pulse sped up at an unbelievably shocking rate. 'Calm down,' she told herself.

She slowly retreated down the stairs, her back against the staircase wall. She gathered her breath, darted to the closest table and grabbed the candle. She tried to peek through the railing but suddenly came face to face with the wolf, causing her to fall backwards. Marcie froze.

Its fangs were sharp, dripping blood as it growled, peering right at her with its slit, green eyes. The wolf took its time walking down the stairs, stepping on the blood, and without dropping eye contact with what would seem like its next prey. Suddenly, there was another howl outside, and the wolf finally turned its head and ran for the door, leaving red footsteps behind him.

The shaken nurse quietly took off her shoes and ran up the stairs, slipping on the blood as she fled, causing her palms to get bloody. When she looked up, she saw a lifeless maid lying face down on the floor in front of the study. Her hair was completely messed up, revealing scars around her neck. Marcie crawled towards her.

'Sera … Oh dear gods, Sera. Come on, wake up. What happened to you?' She was whimpering softly while touching the still warm, lifeless body. She could barely hold back her tears of fear. She then turned her attention to the strangely quiet room. The door was half-open. She peered in, hoping there were no other wolves in there.

'It's okay. You can go in,' said a vaguely familiar voice.

Marcie's breath stopped. The air felt heavy, and her heart pounded loudly. Nurse Marcie whipped around. Her eyes, she was sure, could only be deceiving her.

Standing in front of her was the messenger she had met not long ago.

And his boots were covered in blood.

'Your shoes …' mumbled the nurse.

'My apologies, it seems to me there has been some confusion about our earlier encounter. Let me do you a favour and clarify that for you.' He unzipped his coat and revealed his royal messenger uniform. 'My name is …'

'I do not want to know your name, dog. I want to know if you were the one who killed her.'

The messenger closed his eyes and sighed. 'Yes, I did. I had no personal grudges against her, though. Poor thing just got in the way.'

'Got in the way?' The nurse glared at him in a fury, her eyes turning green. 'You may be a mutt, but I know about them more than anyone. You were here on some-one's orders. I know that. Where is that man?'

'So you do remember your task, Marcie. You were sent to this house twenty years ago, yet you chose to abandon your clan and live as a human. A great feat, no doubt ...'

'Don't make me ask again, mutt.' She then trans-formed her hands into claws, ran towards the man and wrapped her claws around his neck. 'Where is your master?'

The messenger did not flinch. 'You were once the pride of the Fenrir clan, Marcie. For a woman, you were exceptionally strong.'

'Flattery,' she spat. 'You disguise yourself well enough, hence I was unable to recognize you at the door earlier. That was my mistake.' She paused and realized she had not seen the owners of the mansion since then. 'Where are Derrick and Angela?'

'Why not let go of me and check the study? Your *master* is in there.'

She let go of him and hurried into the room. She found them both passed out, as if in a trance. Sir Desouza was seated on his chair in the study, while Lady Desouza was standing in front of the table. If they had been lying down, she would have thought they were dead. They looked as if they were staring at the same thing.

'How long have they been like this?' she asked, storming out of the room as she slammed the door shut behind her, but was blocked by the messenger. 'What do you think you're doing?' she demanded.

'I was about to ask the same thing. What are you planning to do?'

'I'll find that mutt leader of yours and break every bone in his body.'

'Then it looks like your search can wait. My lord is here.'

'Finally, I see these eyes again, Marcie,' said Sir Wilkin, leaning against the wall behind the messenger. He was holding an open locket, proving that Sir and Lady Desouza were in an illusion.

'Let me get straight to the point, Bodolf. Stop their illusion now. They are not your target.'

'No, that's where you are wrong, Marcie. I guess you being their nurse and serving humans all these years has changed you.'

'The part of you that never changed is beating around the bush. Your target is Elizabeth, just her. I don't remember you ever going after anyone else other than your target.'

Wilkin narrowed his eyes. 'Yes, you see, I have been really patient, waiting for you to do what you were assigned to do, but when I found out that this man has kept a secret from me, I realized that I have been deceived this whole time.'

Marcie questioned, 'What is this big secret they were hiding?'

'That night when we were chasing Vaughan, we were stopped by the Queen of Elves, Vasilisa. You probably remember that.'

Marcie nodded cautiously. That was the first time she had seen Sir Wilkin so weak in front of anyone, let alone a different species. Still, to the best of her knowledge, Vasilisa had been missing ever since.

'I know what you're thinking. That she has been missing since then.'

'Hasn't she? After that magick, I was the last one to leave the woods that day. She was so weak and frail that it would have been almost impossible to just run away or hide – at least not immediately.'

'She was able to do that spell because of her circlet.'

'The one you gave Ella.'

'Yes. Just the circlet alone absorbs negative energy, making the wearer bring out their worst emotions. I managed to get my hands on the circlet that night, by the river.'

'What exactly are you after? You sent me here to kill her, Wilkin. She was only a few months old, and she already had enemies she did not even know about.'

'The gem on the circlet … That's what I am after.'

Marcie looked at the frozen Desouzas again. 'All right. This has gone on long enough. Stop the illusion already.'

Wilkin snapped the locket shut. 'Fine. I stopped it. I did what you asked. Don't forget to do what I asked.'

'You still want me to kill her? Isn't she your future wife? Wait, make that your second wife.'

'No, no. Not kill her. I realized after meeting her in the dream world that killing her would get me nowhere. What I want is for you to find out where that gem is. The last person to set eyes on it was Vaughan, and the last person who saw Vaughan dying was Derrick Desouza. You have till the morning of the Moonlight Festival to find out.'

'What if I don't?'

'Then you will end up like that maid girl on the floor.'

'Is that why you did this to them? For defying you …?'

'They were so foolish that they decided to cover up his mistake by throwing their daughter at me, without knowing their action would only make her suffer, not happy. I merely used that to my advantage.'

The Desouzas started to stir. Lady Desouza was losing balance, and her legs were going weak and were about to fall. Thankfully, Nurse Marcie ran to her and placed her gently on the floor, making her more comfortable.

'Don't you think it's time for you to leave, Wilkin?'

'Of course, I shall take my leave. Don't worry about those two. They are not harmed, probably just shaken.' He then handed an object to the messenger. He asked him to go back to His Majesty's side to avoid any suspicion. The messenger bowed and left. Wilkin then pulled out a small vial from his belt and flung it at the nurse. 'Use that if they don't feel well. I did not control my illusion this time. Oh, and do me another favour, will you?'

Nurse Marcie did not reply but looked up at him.

'Do not tell my lovely fiancé that I was here today. She needs to finish what she started, even if it is a lifetime apart.'

It had been two days since Edmund and Leofrick left the Broken Woods. They had finally reached the inner gates of the castle where Knight Fred stood. He asked them to wait at the swan pavilion, as the prince was running late.

The two of them sat down, and Edmund suddenly remembered something. 'Leofrick, were you ever at the Broken Woods?' he asked out of curiosity.

'Pal. We met after a long time, and we have been travelling for the past two days. Of course I was in the woods. Don't turn me into a ghost again.'

Edmund shook his head. 'No, I meant when I was sleeping, did you give me something to drink?'

'You know, I'm starting to feel like you have gone a little delusional over the week.' Leofrick panicked for a second but managed to maintain his composure.

'Did you?' Edmund asked again.

'No, I did not, and let's push this ridiculous conversation aside, as the prince is here.' Leofrick stood up and bowed when he caught sight of Prince Kai walking towards them. Edmund followed.

'Welcome back, Edmund. You have worked hard,'

exclaimed the prince as he walked into the pavilion. He looked at his face more closely than the last time. *Looks exactly like Vaughan,* he thought.

'It has been a fruitful journey, Your Highness.'

'That's good to hear. Let's sit. I have a few things to say as well, but since you are probably tired from your journey, let's talk as we make our way to the guest quarters.'

'Very well then, I am going to tell a story now. It may also be a memory or someone's past, but this is a very crucial hint to know how to defeat Wilkin and the wolves.'

Leofrick's eyes involuntarily averted towards the sky. He was going to hurt Wilkin, he knew it, but it was too much for him to bear. However, his friend needed and trusted him, and he had no desire to break that.

The prince interrupted his thoughts. 'All right then, let's hear the story.'

Edmund pulled out the two things attached to his belt: the old letter and the box. Edmund started, 'At first, I saw a boy of royal status … The boy, Vaughan, was near Sir Bodolf Wilkin's mansion at Kroukhesta. He had been trying to sneak into their house, probably to meet Virgo, the daughter of Sir Wilkin and Lady Cassandra. He had been about to climb over the fence when he saw something he wished he never had. It was a scene that was probably etched into his mind until the end. Before him, a werewolf held a maid's neck and lifted her up. She was suffocating; Vaughan noticed that her face was going blue. So blue that it was almost pale. That did not stop the werewolf, however, from plunging his clawed hands into her chest. The girl's neck fell, and Vaughan realized she was dead. The werewolf pulled out her heart and threw the rest of the body away as though she was an unwanted leftover food. Vaughan was appalled. He could not move even an inch, afraid to attract its attention.

'The werewolf, being sensitive to even a bee's buzz from a mile away, could hear Vaughan's irregular breathing. It turned around, with blood sprayed across its face. The yellow eyes looked right at Vaughan, knowing full well that he had completely witnessed the murder. Yet, it continued its meal and transformed back into its human form. Vaughan was shocked to see the blood-stained face of Sir Wilkin right in front of the body.

'He ran, without looking back. Within moments, he could hear the panting of a pack of wolves chasing him, but he was too afraid to turn back.

'Everything I said just now is real,' said Edmund as he completed the first part of the story.

Prince Kai pondered and figured out that Vaughan was just at the wrong place at the wrong time.

Leofrick stood up and stretched. 'That was tiring. Let's rest for a while, shall we?'

Edmund strongly rejected the idea. 'I still have a lot to say. This is only the first part of what I saw.'

The prince cut in, 'Leofrick is right. I should have let you rest for a day at least before talking. I'll get the guest house cleared up.' He nodded to Knight Fred, who bowed and ran to make whatever preparations the room needed, while the rest continued to stand outside.

Edmund called out to Fred and asked him to wait. He then turned towards the prince and said hesitantly, 'Your Highness, I would like to visit Elizabeth Desouza instead. I'm afraid that she is still worried. She is not yet aware of the lifting of my banishment.'

'I can send a messenger or Fred to pass on the news. You can visit her in the morning.'

'Actually, I would like to see her now. Her temporary residence is near the temple, so it won't take long to get there.'

The prince smiled. 'Very well then, do as you please. But do return by noon, as we have to finish the rest of the vision and start planning before Wilkin makes his next move. We now know that he has been killing people, probably more people than we realized. What about you, Leofrick? Will you stay behind or go with him?'

Leofrick said, 'Neither. I would like to go home. I can't remember the last time I stepped foot in there. It will probably be covered in webs and hurling dust storms.'

'Do you really want to go home then? I doubt you will be able to sleep like that,' pondered Edmund.

Leofrick beamed. 'Probably not. I am actually looking forward to sparring with some spiders. Want to leave together?'

'Yes, we shall. Your Highness, we shall take our leave now.' They then bowed to Prince Kai and left.

The prince looked at them leaving. He then addressed Fred. 'Fred, keep an eye on him till tomorrow. Tell me if anything happens, only to me, not to anyone else.'

'Yes, Your Highness. I shall keep an eye on Edmund.'

'No, not Edmund, Leofrick is the one you need to follow.'

'Why him? Is there anything you suspect about him? He seemed genuinely worried about his friend.'

'He may be worried about his friend, but he seemed worried about something else as well, and I searched through all records of people around Edmund. That man Leofrick does not have a house.'

Marcie had finished scouting the rest of the mansion for other wolves and ended up finding maids and servants in hiding instead. She quickly got them to work, by laying the dead girl to rest properly, then fetching water from the well and starting dinner preparations early. She then went back to the Desouzas' sides and touched Sir Desouza's forehead.

Still hot, she thought. She could not imagine the amount of confusion they would experience when they got well. Hence, she thought that they should at least be comfortable.

Knowing that they were knocked out, she quietly carried them to their room and laid them on their bed. A maid scurried in with a jug of water and two cups and took her leave.

The nurse quickly grabbed the jug and began to pour the odourless white liquid she had been given by Wilkin in the jug. She was about to pour the whole thing in but quickly stopped. She thought it might be a good idea to try to ask a werewolf more about it, maybe try to make some of their own. She mixed half of it well with the fresh, clear water, and sprinkled the water over the Desouzas. Within minutes, they opened their eyes, though still drowsy.

'It's all right, sir. Please rest, I assure you that it is safe now,' she said.

Lady Desouza spoke first. 'Wh … where's Elizabeth? Wh … where's my daughter? Is she safe?' she mumbled. Her voice quivered. She could barely speak the words clearly, making it fairly hard for Marcie to decipher half of the contents, but she could understand the hidden question.

'She is safe for now, my lady,' she said carefully, not wanting to agitate her immediately.

'Wh … what? What do you mean by "for now"?' She started coughing. Nurse Marcie gave her a cup of water and tried to think of something else to say that would calm her down.

Sir Desouza, who had stirred not that long ago, responded instead. 'Nurse, you have to tell us what happened here after me and my wife fell into the illusion, but not now. We need to go to the Gilmores' at once.'

Lady Desouza looked at her husband in shock. 'Why would you want to go to the household you hate so much? Our daughter is in danger, Derrick. We made a mistake, and our child is probably suffering right now.'

'No, Angela. Our daughter will be safe for now. He

hypnotized me long after you. Wilkin is not who we thought he was, but if there is one thing I know about him, it is that if there is something he wants, he will do whatever it takes to get it. The only ones who know about what he wants are me and Sir Gordon Gilmore. This is a destructive relationship we share, and we have despised each other since then. Their son may be in much more danger than our daughter.'

Nurse Marcie continued. 'If you may permit me, my lady, to ease your worries, I will send a servant to pass on a message to the Gilmores. I will request them to come to Ella's place. I shall go to Ella's side immediately.'

Lady Desouza was quick to reject the idea, but Sir Desouza stopped her and told the nurse to leave and that they would follow soon.

The nurse left and closed the door behind her. She opened her worn, leather-bound bag and made sure that she had taken the red coat Edmund had given Ella.

She was going to save her from Wilkin's clasp no matter what. She refused to stand by and watch someone else suffer at his hands again.

Leofrick kept walking, with Knight Fred close on his tail. He went straight to the Faded Tavern, looked back to see if anyone was following, and went in once satisfied.

For someone who claimed to be headed home ... Although

I am pretty sure the night is going to be long, Fred thought. He knew that this watch was going to be a lot longer than he thought. Fred sighed, straightened his shirt and walked in, sitting at the table closest to the entrance, yet hidden by a pillar.

He saw Leofrick at the front of the counter whispering to a lady. The lady whispered back and poured him a glass. Leofrick pushed away the glass and sat down. He started talking to the lady, who was listening to him intently. Fred could not hear what they were saying, so he moved closer.

'… not awake yet. She is still with Vasilisa,' said Leofrick to the lady, completely sullen.

The lady thought for a moment and handed him a set of keys, directing him to the second floor of the place. 'I have been keeping an eye on Bodolf since the beginning, Loki, and I have been studying the flow of action between their past lives and their present. For which till now, I have not found much difference. Just one major truth Bodolf does not seem to know,' she said.

'I can make a few guesses.'

The lady hushed him up and looked around, hoping no one could hear the conversation. 'Watch what you say around here, Loki. There are simply too many humans and wolves in this area. Your wolf has completely made it hard for me to even walk out of this place without a pair of eyes constantly watching my every move.'

'Can't do anything about that … At least out of the many bad apples here, there is one good one today.'

Fred flinched. *He is not talking about me, is he?* He panicked. He tried to sneak away.

'Knight, freeze,' exclaimed Leofrick as he snapped his fingers. A pillar fell in front of Fred and he froze in fear. He turned around slowly, meeting eyes with Leofrick, who just smiled at him.

'How long did you—'

'How long did you think?'

Fred gulped. 'You're not going to let me go, are you?'

'No way. When you hear a story, it's best if you hear it till the end.' He then started to walk towards the stairs.

'Wait, don't we have to clean it up first?'

'Clean what?'

'The pillar or whatever that broke from somewhere. There might be people hurt and—'

'Oh, don't worry about it. Look behind you.'

Fred looked and realized that the place did not look like something had fallen a moment ago. He tried to move tables and chairs to see if there was any damage. He looked around the place and saw that everyone was looking at him, probably wondering what he was doing.

'See? Nothing happened. Stop imagining things and come along.'

Fred was still confused and his mind was blank, but he quickly followed, hoping to get some answers.

'What is this, Nisi?' Loki asked the lady. 'This place looks no different from when I was here last week.'

Fred scanned around the room, and his eyes stopped at a chest of drawers at the far end of the room. As he moved closer to it, he noticed something at the top. He swiped off a layer of dust. 'Leofrick, I think it may be better to hear her out first.'

'And why is that, Fred?'

'Because this drawer has the king's old seal on it. The one used before Her Majesty changed it when the king fell ill.'

'What?' He turned to look at the broken seal on the top drawer. He had always noticed it but had no idea that it belonged to the King of Yovaria, in other words, this room most likely belonged to King Alphonse, father of the prince.

And the prince was probably too young to even recognize it.

Fred opened the top drawer. Nothing much, other than a few documents covered in dust. The next drawer was filled with letters, many of which were still unopened.

He opened the third drawer and paused. He took out a photo and dusted it.

'What is it, Fred?' asked Leofrick.

'It seems to be a picture of the previous royal family, but something about this feels odd. It seems as though there was a third child in the family that I had no idea about.'

Leofrick took the framed photo. There was a boy around the age of five or six wearing a blue cloak, and the current queen was standing on one side of the child. On the other side of the boy stood the current king, who was still a young prince, but wearing a similar cloak in red. The resemblance the boy had with

Edmund was uncanny and the only one allowed to wear a blue cloak was the son of the heir to the throne.

'Do you have any idea who this is?' Leofrick asked Fred.

'Not sure exactly, but I am assuming it's a relative or someone.'

'You're wrong,' said Nisi. 'That boy is no relative. That's His Majesty's firstborn son.'

'The king had another son? How is it that no one knew?' asked Fred.

'It's because the queen herself buried that fact. There were rumours back then, on whether that boy was blood or illegitimate. The couple were not exactly very close, you know,' said Nisi.

'That doesn't explain why she would cover up his death,' said Leofrick.

Nisi said, 'I've stayed in Yovaria for a very long time, Leofrick, and I know enough to tell you this. The queen, she is one with many secrets, keeping them under a velvet blanket just so that she can sit comfortably on top of it.'

'So she played a part in the death of her son just to strengthen her position as the queen. Then how does no one remember it?'

Nisi said, 'I do not know, but the chances are very high.'

Suddenly, there was a loud scream on the first floor. Nisi ran out of the room to see what was going on. Fred put the framed photo back in the drawer and was about to run down to help, but was stopped by Leofrick.

'Don't you think it may be better for you to tell your prince about his dead brother first?' asked Leofrick.

Fred agreed. He took his leave, but before he could go out, he was stopped by Nisi.

'Fred, wait,' she said as she handed him another covered painting. 'Show this to the prince as well. He will be able to connect the dots.'

Queen Adela strolled into her chambers after completing the work together with the king, as he was still recovering. The sun was yet to set, so she took out her magick cards and laid them on the table. She put her palm over them and then took out the top card; Vasilisa's card was still locked. She put the card back on top of the others and flipped them over, then took the top four cards and kept the rest back inside.

'Boris!'

The werewolf messenger came in and bowed. The queen handed him the four cards. 'Here, take these and go to Rose Lane, towards the direction of the house close to the temple of Athena. You will find them there.'

'Yes, Your Majesty,' said the messenger as he took the cards. He bowed and turned to leave.

The queen stopped him. 'Your task is not to give these to them but to use them. Use it on them and give them back to me.' She then narrowed her eyes and stared right at him. 'Do you understand what I am saying here?'

The look on the messenger changed; he smirked slyly, his eyes glowing with mischief. He bowed. As he walked out, he saw Wilkin come in from the other door.

Wilkin walked in, noticing his pack member leave. Boris, the messenger, bowed as he walked out of the room. Wilkin then greeted the queen.

'This is rather sad. The last time we worked together, you had a family, with my husband's niece too. Now, you're alone.'

'I'm not worried about that at all, Your Majesty. My problems were because of my family. I just got rid of my problems.' He gave her a subtle piercing glace, stating that he knew that she had done the same before. She had gotten rid of the king's younger brother and her then-fiancé so that she could become the royal queen instead of the princess consort.

The queen did not notice the look Wilkin was giving her. 'Looks like that problem is trying to come around and bite you in the rear this time,' she said.

'I will make sure to get rid of it once and for all,' he replied. *Just like you did*, he thought.

'Yes, we shall do just that.' The queen then asked, 'Do you know which deity he is the shadow of?'

Wilkin paused for a moment. It was the one question he did not want to answer. If the queen realized that Edmund had become the shadow to Chronos, the same as her dead son, Vaughan, she might try to thwart his plans. 'From our last fight, I had a few hunches,' he said. 'Although I cannot say for sure, as he had just learnt of his magick. What I can say, however, is that he is not elemental.'

'If his powers are similar to—'

'It may not be, Your Majesty.'

'But it may be. Every magick has a weakness, Bodolf. If that boy has the same magick as Vaughan, it may put you at a disadvantage.'

'This is precisely why I chose to trust you. You do not hesitate to push away anyone who gets in your way. At times, you seem more like my sons than they.'

She then sat down. 'Let's get down to business, Wilkin. It seems that your fiancé is still with the queen elf in the dream world. She is getting stronger, and her strength will increase much more if she gets her hands on the peridot Edmund has right now.'

Wilkin shook his head. He did not think that Ella would be able to cause any major problems to his plan yet. 'Ella is still half-human. Her growth has its immediate limits. She may be capable, but she is still too young to drain me the way Vasilisa did.'

The queen was still cautious. 'But we still need to be careful. It may not be of much help, but I will make sure to separate those two on that day. I will summon him to my chambers and give him an order he cannot refuse. That should be enough time for you to get your hands on the peridot.'

'That would be of utmost convenience to me,' said Wilkin as he bowed. 'I would prefer not to fight against him. A shadow should never fight with another, no matter what. It is almost the same as two gods fighting each other.'

'Unlike your vulnerable daughter and my son, these two will have a lot of cleaning up to do after,' said the queen.

'The Moonlight Festival is a time of the year that all unmarried boys and girls look forward to, as it is a rare chance for them to set themselves free of the burden from their upcoming adult life and enjoy their youth for the last time. Ella had permission at first as well, but due to a miscalculation on my part, it may not be easy to get her out. Her parents will be more cautious about sending her out right now.'

'Oh, don't worry about that,' sneered the queen. 'I have already sent a member of your pack to clean up your mess first.'

'I do not remember asking for your help, Your Majesty,' said Wilkin.

'I do not remember giving you permission to go against whatever I decide to do, Duke,' she retorted. 'If you had controlled yourself a little longer, I would not have had to send someone to them myself. If you were going to get them, you should have been thorough instead of doing a sloppy job.'

'But you do realize if Ella finds out what you did to them, her emotions will only increase her magick, right?'

'I do not care, Wilkin. You are a full breed, while she is half-human. If you're worried about the girl's strength, does that mean that you are not confident in yourself?'

Wilkin just remained silent out of shock. He was not

going to win against her words. He had to get out right now.

'You are thinking of leaving immediately so that you can stop what I am about to do? Well, it is a little too late for that, because I have already sent him to my army. They do not stand a chance, especially against your pack.'

'I allowed my pack to join the army and serve you as a soldier, but you sent them as werewolves?'

'Then go. Try and stop them yourself. At least it will be good for you to show your authority once in a while.' The queen just smirked and turned around. 'Because it was partially due to my husband that you got yourself into this mess, I took it upon myself to help you out, nothing else.'

Wilkin bowed and left the room. He turned back to look at the queen, touching her pack of cards. He knew that she was not planning to kill them but to trap them. He felt that since she had no intention of harming them, it may not be worth the effort to try and stop it. In fact, he was eager to see how the next move would play out.

As he walked out of the castle, he saw Fred get off his horse.

'Look who's here? My old friend's faithful dog,' he teased. Fred just bowed and ran in. Wilkin scowled at the lack of respect towards him. He heard the laughter in the distance.

As he walked a bit further, he saw Leofrick sitting on a tree above him and watching him. Leofrick jumped down and as he touched the ground, he transformed into Loki, landing on his feet.

Loki was beyond angry. He held a terrified Wilkin by the collar and swirled out, leaving behind a blow of dust.

The two of them appeared in the Kroukhesta mansion. Loki flung the wolf across the room. As Wilkin tried to stand up by holding onto a nearby table, he noticed his right foot was injured.

As Wilkin tried to balance and take small, painful footsteps towards his god, Loki just pushed Wilkin's head back with such force that caused him to be pushed back. As his head slammed against the wall, he barely managed to open his eyes when he saw Loki come closer again. He felt his life at risk if he continued to get flung around like that, so he closed his eyes and mustered enough magick to block Loki's next attack.

'This is the level you have been reduced to, Bodolf, a mere wolf that needs to be triggered to fight seriously.'

Wilkin's eyes widened. He was surprised to see Loki's eyes turn back to that of a human. He took a deep breath and looked down.

Loki knelt and pulled Wilkin's head up by his hair, and said, 'Think about your past fights. You always had the upper hand in every battle but did not take your opponent seriously. You have always been too full of yourself.'

Wilkin thought back to his many battles before … against Vasilisa twenty years ago and against Edmund at the temple before he was banished. He also remembered the unexpected cloaked lady in the king's dream world, where his magick had been forced shut.

'Looks like you remember that lady. Do you want to

know who she is? You'd be quite surprised to know of her identity. As someone engaged to Elizabeth Desouza, it's normal for you to know the people around her.'

Wilkin's eyes narrowed. He remembered the anger he felt that time. 'The cloaked lady is someone Ella knows? Who the hell is she?' he bellowed.

Loki pushed Wilkin's face again, and he slammed against the wall again, this time creating a crack on the wall. Wilkin was surprised his head was still in one piece. 'Mind your words around me, Bodolf. I am not on your side, even if you are my shadow. In fact, I will not save you if you die at the hands of either Edmund or anyone else for that matter. I only came to tell you the information, as it is only fair that both sides of the battle know the same rules. I do not want my precious wolves to die at the hands of anyone else because of you.'

Loki then bellowed the name of Wilkin's advisor, Raoul, who ran in filled with fear as he shivered uncontrollably. 'Get to the river. Recreate the circle you drew for your master twenty years ago.'

Raoul, who was still shaking in fear and was sweating rather profusely down his temples, quickly bowed, transformed and ran out.

'What are you doing, my lord?' asked Wilkin.

'Hush now. I have another thing to warn you about. After this, the next time we meet will be back at my abode when you are a full wolf and no longer human.'

'I will never lose, my lord. Do not help me, but please do keep watching me. I will make sure to get my hands on the peridot and gain a new level of power, something that will combine the powers of us were-wolves and the elves. When I do that, I am sure that we will be able to get to greater heights.'

Loki just grinned. 'I'm sure we will be able to. In fact, I will very much keep an eye on you, but do not trust the queen too much.'

'That is not for you to decide.'

'No. I am not going to stop you, but I have to stop Queen Adela. She is not planning on helping you. Every time she imprisons someone with her cards, a mirror portal is blocked off in Thavma Gi, and that is causing too many ripples. The people living in the river are worried and uneasy about the sudden overwhelming pressure.' Loki continued when he noticed Wilkin was not resisting and just slouched against the wall. 'You may get the peridot, Bodolf, but she has the Queen of Elves, the most powerful of them all, Vasilisa herself.'

He then stood up and transformed back into Leofrick. 'That's all I can tell you. Whether you win or lose, I do not care anymore, but if I should ever meet you again, it will be when you lose. I'll show you the pain of a fallen shadow, a shadow no longer supported by his god.'

Leofrick then jumped out of the window. Wilkin shut his eyes tight, trying to absorb everything. *No*, he thought. *I do not care about Vasilisa. I only want that stone, and I will create a species far superior than any other. Just watch me, Loki.*

CHAPTER 26

At the door of the room Ella had been staying in at the temple was Marcie, who was in her wolf form. She had run all the way from the Desouza mansion. As she transformed back, she glanced behind her, hoping no one had seen her. She then entered the house and went straight to the bedroom on the second floor, hoping that Ella would be there. She was about to open the door when a hand on her shoulder stopped her in her tracks. She quickly turned in defence, ready to retaliate, but calmed down when she saw the priestess.

'Elizabeth is not in there. She is where she is supposed to be. Follow me, I will bring you to her.' She walked to the rose garden, with the nurse following closely behind. At the garden, the nurse saw Ella lifelessly laid on a bed of rose petals and a dreamcatcher hanging above her.

The nurse walked towards Ella slowly and took Ella's hands in hers. As she stroked her hair, she cast a glance at the priestess, who gave her a nod. They then walked out of the garden back to the house. 'Priestess, is that girl really all right?' asked Nurse Marcie worriedly.

'She will be fine. We have something else to do right now.' She then looked at the back gate. 'Looks like he is not here yet …'

'Priestess, Wilkin has made his move already. He even revealed himself to Sir Desouza and my lady.'

The priestess did not say anything. She just closed her eyes and muttered a few words under her breath, and Ella was no longer visible.

'You use magick?'

'Yes. Something I learnt on my own from books. This spell is quite handy, I would say. Just hides her from plain sight.' She then turned to Marcie and handed her a locket, very similar to Wilkin's locket chain, but much smaller. The priestess did not speak further, as she knew that Marcie recognized it, probably having a hundred questions running through her mind right now. 'Don't let her be seen unless there is an emergency.'

Marcie looked at her and realized that the priestess knew exactly who she was. She just agreed, poring at the small locket, and her hands were trembling. She never liked that thing.

The priestess cupped her hands over Marcie's and said, 'Let's calm ourselves down, Marcie.' They then heard horses coming closer.

'Looks like they have arrived,' said Marcie.

The Desouzas reached Ella's room. Sir Desouza knocked on the door first but did not wait for more than three seconds before opening the door himself. Lady Desouza ran in worriedly, and when she didn't see her daughter, she went straight to the rose garden, as she knew Ella liked to spend a lot of time among the roses. She could not find her there either. Dejected, she went upstairs, calling her daughter's name.

Sir Desouza could smell a faint scent of rosewood and lilac and decided to follow it. He also decided not to make a fuss if Ella was not found, as it would only make Lady Desouza more worried. Rosewood and lilac were the two scents used by Ella during her coming of age dance and her engagement.

He knew Ella was definitely in the house.

Lady Desouza ran down, completely engulfed in a state of panic. 'She's not in the house, Derrick. She might be in trouble. The wolf must have done something.'

'Angela, forget Ella for just one second and look around. On a normal day in bridal training, there should be people around, but there's no one. Not even a servant.' At that moment, he saw the nurse coming in from the rose garden. 'Did you find her?' he asked.

The nurse looked at Lady Desouza's eager face, but she knew she would have to disappoint her for now. 'My apologies, but I will not be able to tell you where she is. All I can tell you for now is that she is safe,' replied Marcie, without blinking.

Lady Desouza ran up to her and slapped her across the face. 'You are telling me that you know where she is, you know how she is, but you cannot tell me, her mother. Don't forget that you are just a nurse, Marcie. I decide what to tell you, not the other way around.'

'My apologies, but I will not be able to tell you where she is, but I can tell you that she is safe,' repeated the nurse.

Lady Desouza was furious. As she raised her hand again, she was stopped by the priestess.

'Really? Every time I see you, Angela, you just prove to me time and time again that you are so full of yourself with your self-centred heart,' mocked the priestess.

'Let go of me, Cafelle. I am not in the mood to listen to you talking. I am here to find my daughter and get her out of here. That's it.'

'And you think slapping people around is going to give you answers? Don't let your emotions cloud your judgment, Angela. And Marcie is telling the truth, your daughter is safe with me, for now at least.'

'What do you mean by for now? What's happening? It is about that wolf Wilkin, isn't it?'

'Oh? You finally know about that creature's identity. That is going to make things a lot easier.'

Sir Desouza studied the look on her face, unable to tell what she was thinking. He then said, 'Cafelle, pardon me for saying this, but I do not think you should be involved with problems involving my family.'

'No,' said Cafelle firmly. 'I am very much involved, long before you were. In fact ...' She then turned to Lady Desouza. 'It's about time we have the second part of our conversation from the engagement night, don't you think?'

They heard a voice at the door. 'Hold on! Let us be a

part of this discussion,' said a gruff voice.

'Gordon,' said Sir Desouza.

'I did not wish to get involved with you ever again. I tried to break the string of life between my son and your daughter, but it seems that it is not going to be easy,' said Sir Gilmore. He walked in with Lady Gilmore one step behind him.

'What has that got to do with our daughter, Gordon?' questioned Sir Desouza.

'Have you forgotten, Derrick? That night, we saw the final moments of two people by the riverbed. We promised to never get involved in another situation like that, but the moment we said that, both my wife and yours got pregnant at the same time.'

'So? That is probably just—'

'Coincidence?' finished Lady Gilmore. 'That may have been the case at any other time, don't you think, Angela?'

Lady Desouza looked away, crying. Deep down, she could always tell that Ella was more than just a daughter of her household, but she never wished to admit that fact.

The silence went on for a few moments. The priestess rolled her eyes at the tension in the living room and coughed, breaking the tense atmosphere. 'All right, let's stop the staring contest and get down to actual business.' She then turned to Marcie and requested her to prepare some tea and snacks. The nurse agreed and went to the kitchen.

As everyone entered the study, the priestess closed her eyes and took a deep breath. To find a method to save her god-daughter and her lover, she was finally going to hear about the story of that night twenty years ago.

Sir Desouza started talking about that night first. 'That day, we got a secret royal order in the middle of the night. We were asked to find the king's niece's missing daughter, who was having an affair with someone from the royal family. We never knew much about the affair, and we never questioned royal orders either. We just did what we were told. All we were told was that the girl had red hair and that the young lovers would often spend a lot of time hiding in the Broken Woods. I wondered why they needed us to find them, because they seemed to know a lot already.'

Lady Gilmore asked, 'So you do not know if it's the king or queen who gave you the letter?'

Sir Gilmore said, 'Yes. It bothered me a lot at first, because the order was too vague and sudden. We had no time to plan a strategy. We had to leave when the moon was still bright. We spent the whole night and the whole day between the woods and the outskirts.'

Sir Desouza added, 'But what changed our thoughts that night was after we saw what the lady in green did to them. What we saw was completely different from what we believed in.'

Sir Gilmore continued, 'We could not even go to help them, as we heard a woman scream in the distance. Soon after, the howling of wolves filled the forest. So we left after placing the card on the forehead of the woman in green. We had strict orders not to fight the wolves prowling the forbidden forest grounds.'

'Why did you leave without bringing the two of them back? Those two may or may not have been alive,' said Nurse Marcie.

The priestess shot a death glare at Marcie, who looked away quickly. Cafelle started, 'A woman chose to get rid of the bodies. Using a tracking spell or any other magick on the body would have affected the soul, which may have been still attached to them.'

The nurse was getting restless as she heard the story she was a part of, and not in a good way.

Cafelle continued, 'That was quick thinking on her part, no doubt. They were definitely not alive. I know because I saw their death happen and knew exactly what was going to happen. I tried to stop it, but I was no use.'

No one spoke for a moment.

'Is that why you were so interested in this story, Priestess?' asked Lady Desouza. 'You tried to get me to talk to you about it the other day, on my daughter's engagement.'

Priestess Cafelle did not say anything. She could not answer the question without knowing more first. Her mind was trying to scheme up a way to change the direction of the question. She was afraid they would ask her about her past.

'Priestess,' Lady Gilmore cried out in desperation, 'is there something you're worried or scared about right now?'

'Why would you think so?' asked the priestess as firmly as possible. She was fiddling with her hands but hiding them under the table.

Lady Desouza started, 'Because, after everything I just said, you …'

'… are not surprised at all,' continued Lady Gilmore. 'You look like you lost something precious to you, someone you loved maybe, on that very day.'

The priestess could not control her sudden rush of emotions any longer. Her feelings took over her self-control, and a tear streamed down her face. She knew that she had to reveal at least something for them to stop asking too much. She pulled down the hood of her cloak and removed the braids of her red locks. 'Yes I did,' she finally said as tears streamed down her face uncontrollably. 'I lost so much that day. I lost my name and my life.' She then looked up at them, holding up a lock of red hair in front of them. 'I lost my daughter that night. The girl you were told to find. I lost my daughter, Virgo.'

'Priestess! What are you …?'

'Who are you, Priestess?' questioned Sir Desouza, obviously shocked.

The priestess bluntly ignored him. She wanted answers, not to be questioned. 'I answered the question you asked. Now it's your turn. What else happened that night?' she snapped back, glaring right at him.

'I do remember something else. Along with the letter, I got charmed, a pendant of some sort,' remembered Sir Gilmore.

'A pendant …?' The priestess' mind was trying to fit the pieces of the story together. *Did it belong to Vaughan?* she thought.

'Yes,' replied Sir Gilmore. 'I was told to give it back to the boy the moment I saw him, but it was too late.'

'That pendant,' asked Cafelle. 'Do you have it?'

'No, I lost it that day. I dropped it somewhere in the woods,' said Sir Gilmore.

Sir Desouza then said, 'Thinking about it now, it did resemble the one Wilkin always carried around.'

The priestess realized then that the pendant, which had belonged to Vaughan, rightfully belonged to Edmund now. It was the item which controlled his shadow magick.

'Could I ask you something, Priestess?' Lady Gilmore enquired. 'You say that the red-haired girl was your daughter? How is that possible?'

Lady Desouza agreed. 'You are a priestess, aren't you? I thought priestesses are not allowed to be married, let alone have children.'

The priestess realized she had no choice but to tell a small part of her story at least, to make them talk more. She sighed. 'I am now, because I was killed once by my husband. I was also saved by Priest Linus, who helped me get a new identity as the Priestess Cafelle so that I would not be found by my husband.'

'Who is your husband, Cafelle?' asked Sir Desouza carefully.

'Not is, Derrick, but was. My husband is now your future son-in-law, Bodolf Wilkin. Virgo was our daughter, whom he killed. He killed her, he killed her love, and he killed me. He has now set his eyes on your children.'

The sun had started to set, and Edmund realized that he had to reach his destination soon else it would get too dark to find his way. The temple of Athena and the lodging beside it had always been hidden in a place rather hard to find. As he walked, he found a wild berry bush. Edmund was glad, because finding the wild berry bush meant that he was almost there, since the berries were grown by the temple as offerings.

It also meant that he had something to nibble on, as he was starting to feel tired.

The sweetness of the berries would help him move on a bit longer, enough for him to see Ella again. He only had one day with her before he made his way back to the castle. He started picking the berries, munching on one every time he picked three. At that time, he heard something, something unknown yet strangely familiar.

He could hear the breathing of a beast.

His mind was suddenly filled with images of the encounter Vaughan had with Sir Wilkin. With that in mind, he turned around slowly. His eyes grew as he quickly dropped his things and ran. He ran so hard, hoping he would be able to find someone like Vaughan had. He kept going and did not look back even once.

The Desouzas and the Gilmores were face to face with almost thirty royal guards. The four of them were surrounded. They were confused as to what was going on, especially Sir Gilmore and Sir Desouza, who recognized a lot of their soldiers from their own Eastern and Western Gate sectors. A guard stepped forward.

'What's going on?' asked Sir Desouza sternly.

'We need you to come to the castle immediately, my lord. Queen's orders,' said the guard as he bowed deeply.

'I'll have to turn down the order then, as I swore to never take a direct order from the queen again,' said Sir Desouza.

Sir Gilmore stepped up. 'He is right. If there is anything she has to say, she can say it directly to us during the military meetings. Now if you do not mind, please step aside.'

The guard looked up, his eyes changing to a deep, dark colour. 'In that case, you will need to fight us, as we were ordered to take you by force if you refused.' He and the other guards then drew their swords.

'You are making a mistake by trying to fight us,' said Sir Gilmore as he drew his sword as well. 'Come, Derrick,' he said. 'Looks like these guys need to learn who their betters are.'

The guards started attacking. Sir Desouza and Sir Gilmore stood in a position that would cover their wives. They then fought, easily defeating many of them continuously. Sir Desouza wondered why these soldiers were throwing themselves at them randomly. They should be aware that they were no match for them. He then realized that they were distracting them.

'Gordon! Stop!' yelled Sir Desouza.

Sir Gilmore went into defence. 'What in the name of the gods is your problem, Derrick?'

Sir Desouza looked around. He realized that their wives had been captured. 'Oh no, we didn't notice at all! When did they get past us?'

At that moment, they saw a man step out from among the shadowed trees. Sir Desouza recognized that face from this morning. He warned Sir Gilmore that he was a wolf, the one he had seen this morning, and that there may be more among those they were fighting.

Sir Gilmore was shocked to know that there were werewolves among the royal guards, and even more shocked that they were taking orders from Wilkin. 'You sure have a lovely son-in-law, Derrick.'

'Shut it, Gordon. You didn't know about Wilkin either.'

'I was never involved with him since that night all those years ago. It was you who got all excited over the fact that your daughter would become the Duchess of

Kroukhesta. I never understood why she was not around when I came to her coming of age ceremony. Now, I think I have a pretty good idea why.'

The messenger spoke. 'Yeah, from her point of view, it would be a troublesome alliance.'

'If that is true, then why do you take orders from the queen?'

'That's where you're wrong, my lord. I take orders only from Sir Wilkin, and he asked me and everyone around you right now to pledge your allegiance to the queen.' He then nodded at a guard beside him, who went into the woods and brought out a tied-up Edmund.

Cassandra paced around the room nervously. Just before Nurse Marcie, the Desouzas and the Gilmores came, she had a vision of the house being surrounded by Wilkin's hounds. She was worried that they were targeting the girl in her most vulnerable state, hence had decided to hide her from sight.

But something felt off about it.

In the vision, it was just before sunset. That meant they should have been there by now, but they were not. She wondered if there was an unknown variable which affected the order of events. Her visions were not something anyone could change so easily, especially humans or even elves like Vasilisa and wolves like Wilkin. Yet something had changed.

As she looked at the sun go down, she turned around

and saw the moon starting to peek through the horizon. She noticed a tinge of red around it. She ran out in shock and looked at the sky. There were still a few days left.

The moon should not be changing now. *It is too soon,* she thought. Time was suddenly moving faster than expected. She saw a glimpse of someone walking towards the house. As the silhouette looked similar to Edmund, she ran to unlock the door, only to see a faceless person floating in front of her.

She was utterly confused, as she did not understand how a silhouette that looked so much like Edmund stood before her with no face.

'You can see me?' the figure asked.

'Yes. Who are you?'

'I am the personification of the magick Edmund Gilmore wields, but I got separated from him a moment ago, and somehow, I felt that coming here was what I am supposed to do. Am I in the right place?'

'Which god's magick are you?'

'I can't remember. I can only remember my own magick. I am not capable of having memories of my master, or even the god I belong to.'

'So you do not know?'

'I am the magick of time.'

'You are Edmund's magick? That means Edmund uses the time magick then.'

'Yes, I am.'

It finally struck her that the one slowing down time all these days had been Edmund. Unknowingly, he had been using his shadow magick the whole time.

She then realized that if time was normal now, it meant that Edmund's magick was weak. No, she thought. Someone had physically separated Edmund from his magick, and he was in trouble. 'Do you know where he is now?'

'I can bring you to him.'

'Then lead the way and hurry. We do not have much time.'

Lady Gilmore held onto her son, trying to wake him up. She was thankful that Lady Desouza was beside her trying to ease her, considering the situation they were in right now. However, it was still not safe, as their husbands were still fighting. Not humans, but wolves.

Lady Desouza placed two fingers over Edmund's neck to check his heartbeat. She was glad she was able to detect a pulse. They had managed to poison Edmund; she knew that from the cloth over his face. Lady Gilmore ran over to her son and knew that he was still alive, although weak.

'Gordon! We need to hurry. His face has turned pale,' said Lady Gilmore, with her lips twitching. She was digging her nails into her palms.

Even Lady Desouza's face was growing haggard with worry. Still, she was able to hold Lady Gilmore's hands, preventing her from digging into her own skin.

The two men now started to fight more seriously, since it was for their lives and to save the life of Edmund, but no matter how much they fought, there were just too many of them. They were getting exhausted.

The messenger then said, 'You know something? I'll give you credit for being able to fight the pack for so long, unlike your families. They will not last another minute.'

The two of them quickly looked at their wives. They were unconscious, with Edmund being held by two of the guards, away from his mother. Two wolves stood over Ladies Desouza and Gilmore then transformed into their human forms. They took out a familiar card each, placing them on their chests and muttered some words under their breaths.

'No, stop!' yelled Sir Desouza.

The two of them tried to fight their way to them, but they could not do anything, and they saw their wives disappear right in front of their eyes.

'Why the long faces? You will see them soon enough.'

'What are you sa—'

By the time they could say anything, the two of them were cut right across their chests. As they fell, blood oozed out from their bodies. The messenger came towards them. 'You want to know what I said. I said that you will be able to see them soon. I always keep my word, so don't worry so much.'

The two wolf guards placed the cards on them as well. They were about to start muttering when the others were suddenly slashed by someone.

'Who's there?' asked the messenger. He and the guards turned to see Cassandra there, with her hood and mask, the same as in the king's dreams.

'Who are you, lady?'

'Sorry, I'm not here to talk to you,' she said bluntly.

The priestess took a quick scan around. She had realized the mothers were trapped the same way Vasilisa was, but she knew she was too late in saving the fathers at least. She sighed. She would have to do something about finding those cards later. For now, she had to find Edmund first.

'Hey, Faceless, where is he?'

Edmund's personified magick floated towards the gap between the trees and found Edmund lying against a tree. 'He is here, Priestess.'

'Are you not able to go in?'

'No. I am trying, but his body has a kind of poison which separates the magick from its wielder. The person who did this most likely is someone who is also a shadow.'

'Things are just not going to play out the way we want them to, are they?'

The messenger clapped, and a whole set of wolves surrounded Cassandra in an instant.

'Don't make me fight you. You will regret it,' swore Cassandra.

'You took the words right out of my mouth, lady,' said the messenger.

'Then don't say I didn't warn you,' she said as she flung a dagger at him at full speed.

But the dagger was stopped right in front of the messenger's face, with his face shaking with fear at the sudden attack.

And the one who stopped it was Raoul, Wilkin's advisor.

214

Boris glared at Raoul. Everything was silent for a while. 'What do you think you are doing, Raoul?'

Raoul pushed the dagger away, and Cassandra did not try to attack again, for now at least.

'Let me ask you again, Raoul. Who are you to stop this? Are you going against the queen's orders?'

'I am not under the queen like you, Boris,' said Raoul. 'I only follow the orders of my lord. You should know this very well.' He then turned to face Cassandra. 'I also recognize those eyes. There is no way I could forget the one who managed to hurt one of the strongest of our pack, Roukan.'

Cassandra tilted her head. 'I only managed to hurt him? I thought I managed to get his head off.'

'Funny. That is something the queen would say.'

'Raoul,' called the messenger. 'I can still fight her. You know that I am no match for that wolf who tends to throw a punch before processing his words.'

'Yes you are, but now is not the time. Rest assured

you can fight her to your heart's content later.' He then pulled out a small vial from his belt and turned towards Cassandra.

Cassandra stretched out her hand. 'Hand it over, wolf. I know your master enough to know that if he sent you, it means that he didn't want too much bloodshed. Putting reasons aside, it will work to our advantage if we both pull ourselves out of this.' She then looked at Edmund, with his personified magick peering at him from above. If Edmund ever opened his eyes, he would probably pass out again just by looking at the black, faceless smoke floating over his face. She had to get to him soon.

Raoul handed her the vial. 'My lord has plans. For that, the boy needs to live, for now at least. You probably already realize it as well. There are too many people injured as it is.'

He then added, 'If it were up to me, I would kill the boy the same way I killed our lord's first wife. She was such a pain, not understanding our lord's greater plans. When he ordered me to kill her, I could not be happier.'

Cassandra froze. 'May I ask, wolf, how you killed her?'

Raoul did not hesitate to say, 'That woman, I chased her down, up to the cliff by the end of the river. A little push was all she needed to fall straight down.'

Cassandra asked, 'You never thought that she might survive?'

'Our lord did look for a body, but it was never found. He did find her blood, which he used a Leus Mort spell on.'

Leus Mort Spell, Cassandra thought. *A spell to find out if the blood belonged to someone alive or dead. But they would not be able to tell whose blood it was without seeing the body.*

'Dead, good riddance.'

Cassandra was boiling inside. She could not believe that she had been murdered in such a horrible way. She was thankful for Priest Linus who saved her that night and used the blood of an animal instead. She controlled her anger and turned her attention towards Edmund.

'A priestess who remains silent even though she heard the confessions of a murderer,' laughed Raoul. 'If the temple finds out, she will be expelled.'

Cassandra snapped. 'I will find you, Raoul. Wherever you go, I'll chase you down like a rat out of his hole and kill you,' she said.

He ignored her and ordered the guards to leave, as their task was over. He specifically made sure to tell Boris to sheath his sword and remember to hand over the cards to the queen.

Cassandra wondered for a moment whether she should go after the cards, but she knew that the queen wouldn't be rash with them, considering the fact that Vasilisa had been alive for so long and was trapped the same way. So she turned her attention to Edmund.

She opened the vial and sniffed it, surprised to find it odourless, which was rare in antidotes, as they were mostly recognized through their unique smells. Wrinkling her nose, she could not help but ask, 'What in the world is this? This is something I have never come across. Are you trying to kill him?'

'If it were up to me, I would aim for that. Too bad I

could not play a part in his decision this time. For my lord to get his long-desired wish fulfilled, that boy cannot die yet.'

Cassandra knew she had no choice. She took the gamble and poured the substance in the vial down Edmund's throat. Although slow, Edmund's breathing was getting steadier, and the colour on his face was turning normal.

'I am going back now,' whispered the faceless magick as he drifted away and disappeared. Cassandra figured he had gone back to Edmund, because Edmund was now able to move his feet and fingers.

Edmund stirred and weakly asked what happened. He could only remember being chased by the wolves and suddenly losing consciousness. He gave himself a mental note to re-learn some fighting skills from his cousin, Neal, as he'd found himself too slow in fighting back.

'I know what you are thinking of, Edmund, but it is not your fault for being slow, all right?'

'But ...'

'Edmund, there are things which only you can do, even if it is not with a sword. Even right now, Ella needs your help. You need to be mentally stronger, you understand me? We do not have time anymore.'

'What are you saying? What happened to her?'

'Come. We need to move first. There is still too much wolf scent lingering around here.' The two of them reached the house near the temple.

The priestess opened the door and went in. Edmund hesitated to enter and asked, 'Am I allowed to enter …? I thought sneaking in was not allowed inside.'

'Strange coming from a person who climbed into the Temple of Athena itself,' she pointed out with a smirk.

'You knew?' he asked, shocked.

'I know a lot of things, Edmund. If I start talking about them, I could go for days on end. So just be quiet and get in. You have things to do.'

As the two of them walked to the rose garden, Edmund's senses perked up. 'She's here, isn't she?'

'How could you tell?'

'This place reminds me of that day, during the party. Only one part of the roses were blooming.' He then pointed to a rose wall and said, '… like that.' At that moment, the rose wall opened up and faded off. Nurse Marcie, who had stayed back to tend to Ella, was standing right in front of him.

'I asked you once, Edmund, but pardon me as I ask again. I will not ask about your love, for I do know of it well. Your heart' – she looked at Ella tenderly – 'and hers.'

'Yes, do ask me what you wish to know.'

'Will you be able to accept her even if she is not human? Even if she has the blood of another species, even if she is an elf, albeit half-human?'

'If that is what worries you, then I can ease your concerns. I have nothing to fear, and I know that even more now than the last time, because we experienced the same things. We met after an entire lifetime, and I have promised myself to make that the last time we would have a sad ending.'

Marcie smiled. She realized that the feelings the boy in front of her had for Ella were exactly the same as what Vaughan had for Virgo. She decided to let them find their own ending while she stood on the sidelines to help them along the way.

She then stepped aside, and Edmund finally got to see Ella. He walked up to her and reached out for her hands. As he cupped her hands in his, he looked at her face. She looked deathly pale and sullen. He placed his hand on her cheek, feeling a wave of cold sweep through his body. He missed her soft touch so much, and really wanted to tell her so many things as soon as possible.

As he looked up, he saw a circlet sitting on the side table. He recognized the design. It belonged to Vasilisa, the one who saved him in his past life. He then noticed something weird about it.

'The stone is missing from it, isn't it? A green gem.'

'Yes, peridot to be exact. The circlet is powerless without it.'

'Would this help?' asked Edmund as he pulled out the two gems from his pocket – one dark blue and one yellow.

'These! Where did you find them?'

'At Thavma Gi, in my god's mirror. At least the yellow gem was from there. The other one was given to me during my quest there.' He remembered Kain giving it to him just before he entered the cave.

'Why don't I keep them with me for now?' said the priestess. 'It is probably safer with me considering where you are going soon.'

'Where will I be going?' Edmund asked, confused.

'To bring her back … She has been asleep for long enough and now that time is moving faster, I will have to forcefully pull her back, and I'll need you to help. But first, I need to make the king sleep.'

'And I will give the signal for you to go in,' added Nurse Marcie, who had just come back with the dream-catcher Ella used. She hung it in front of a lighted candle.

'You cannot use elven magick, so I will have to push you in. But this time, I cannot do that, as I will have to meet the king. I need Marcie to do it.'

Marcie's eyes grew. 'Me? I'm no elf either. Wouldn't it be better if I meet the king instead? Putting him to sleep is far easier than dream catching.'

'No, I'll go. I have things to tell him personally as well, so I might as well be the one to do it.'

'Then what about the spell?'

'It won't be needed. You are going to push him in. Meaning that the amount of time he will have to come back with Elizabeth is two hours. I will let you know about the procedures.'

'Two hours! That's an awfully short time, Cafelle. I may not be well-versed in spells, as I cannot cast them anyway, but if there is one thing I know, it is that it is extremely easy to get lost in a dream world, especially if it is not your own.'

'I am well aware, Marcie, but we do not have a choice.'

'I'll do it,' said Edmund. 'I'll be fine. I have been through worse.' *Much, much worse,* he thought. Besides, he was willing to take the risk for Ella. He had been doing that from the start. 'So when will I get the signal?'

The priestess looked outside. 'See the moon? It is slowly coming up from its sleep. It should take a while for it to reach its peak.' She then walked back into the house and to the bedroom. In the middle of the room was a birdbath that opened up to the sky. 'When the shadow of the moonlight turns the water black, that is the moment you go in.'

Back in the dream world, Ella was now able to do so many things on her own with her magick. Vasilisa was surprised at the way she had so much grace in every movement she made. A pureblood elf was usually taught grace separately, as it taught them to have pride in their magick and race. But this girl, who was not of pure blood, was doing much better than she had expected.

As Ella continued to focus on her training, Vasilisa had other thoughts in her mind. She had and always had been looking for a way out of this beautiful prison, and was contemplating if she should teach Ella the one spell she had personally created. This would allow Ella to not only fight against Wilkin and his wolf pack but also give Vasilisa a chance to leave this place. She longed to go back to her people, who had probably been living without a ruler for about a decade.

It was very easy to teach her, but she needed to control the way she channelled her emotions. The problem with the spell was that if it ever went wrong, it would backfire on the user. She knew the only way to decide was to let Ella choose for herself if she was ready to take on the last step before the final battle. She decided to give her a test.

There was also a queer feeling she had that something she had lost ten years ago was actually close to her now. She knew it was a matter of time anyway.

'Ella, do you wish to learn something else for a change?'

Ella stopped her practice and put her hands down. Her eyes were tired, but she could not feel physical exhaustion, as she was not in her real body. She wanted to sleep, but if she did, she would wake up back in her real world.

'What kind of spell?' asked Ella.

'It is called the Darkest Rose. It is a spell which will involve poison, and it is something I personally developed. It is something which should be used in a fight alone.'

'If it will help me fight Wilkin, Vasilisa, if it helps me fight that wolf in sheep's clothing, I am more than willing to learn anything.'

Vasilisa could tell that every time she talked about Wilkin, she got emotional. No, not just emotional. She built up so much anger that she unknowingly released her magick. The same way she had spewed so many petals when she was falling into the Abyss back then.

'All right, then. You have the will, so it is only right that I pass on whatever I know and have to you. The Darkest Rose is a spell I personally created to fight many. The one thing I found out about this spell is that it contains a weakness, something which affects Wilkin.'

'If the spell has been used against him before, then he should not be alive at all. You said it is a spell which involves poison.'

'You need to remember something, Ella. Elves never go for the kill. An elf that has killed loses their magick. This is because our magick is something which helps nature grow, not die. You may be human, but you are also an elf. You are bound by the rules of both races.'

Ella's face sank. She did not want to kill but was hoping to learn something to protect herself and to protect Edmund. She did not want him to die again the way she saw the boy die while she was falling down the Abyss.

Besides, she promised Edmund she would be there at the Moonlight Festival, and she was dead set on keeping that promise. They hadn't seen each other for so long, and it was slowly killing her. 'All right,' she said with complete resolution. 'Let's do this. I need to go back to his side soon.'

The priestess, in her hood, had snuck her way into the palace. As she walked along the rooms and past the dining hall, she felt a surge of nostalgia rush into her body. She could see the image of a young girl, around the age of twenty-two, seated across the table with her parents, and the current king and queen of Yovaria. As she walked along the hallway, she saw the swan pavilion, with a pond once filled with those white beauties. It was now barren, as the queen had sold them to the neighbouring kingdom of Amrita within a year after Prince Kai's birth.

Just then, she noticed Prince Kai walk up to the swan pavilion, and Priest Linus walking just a few steps behind him. They exchanged a few words and were joined by Prince Kai's older brother and heir to the throne of Yovaria, Prince Lukan. Standing near the pillar of the pavilion was a beautiful girl she'd never seen before. In fact, she did not look like someone from Yovaria at all. But she did look like someone of a higher class, and considering Prince Lukan's recent travels with the priest, she must be his betrothed.

She then walked towards a bridge that connected the royal family's quarters with the rest of the castle. She could see the king's chambers quite easily if she bent low enough and looked at the room from a particular angle, something she'd found out as a child due to her short height back then. She knew that once the curtains closed, he would be alone in the room. She could see a silhouette of him walking around the room. The king had finally drawn his curtains.

Good, looks like I can finally start, she thought.

There was less than an hour left to sunset, and Edmund was still on standby. She walked across the bridge, disguising herself as someone who worked in the castle, and stood in front of the door. When she finally heard silence in the room and the last light was turned off, except a scented candle by the bedside, she entered the room.

Cassandra could see that he was not in a deep sleep at all. She expected this, since he had slept long enough and probably developed a fear towards his own dream world, but she had no choice.

She walked up to his bed, not making a single sound with her footsteps, and stood by the window, opening the curtains. The best way to make someone sleep was to use the moonlight itself. She did, however, limit the amount of light in the room, as too much could end up waking him. She could wait a bit longer, but if the queen returned before she could complete her task, it would be a failure. The moonlight was strong, as it was only a few days till the Moonlight Festival. The lunar eclipse was just around the corner, and Wilkin and his pack's strength would be at its fullest.

'You sure waited a long time for me to be alone. Who are you?'

Cassandra panicked. She pulled down the curtain by accident, and the whole room was filled with blue light. She did not want to face her uncle, especially right now. 'You do not need to know of me, Your Majesty. I am just a person who has to do something that may harm you, and it would have been better if you hadn't noticed me at all.'

The king slipped out the dagger from under his pillow and stood up. 'I may have been away for years, but I am not foolish. I remember you, as you are the one who woke me from my long slumber. A person would not harm someone else without reason. I can help you, but I will need to see your face.'

The king was walking up to her, but the priestess did not move. She was holding a needle coated with the sleeping potion, prepared to aim at the right moment. She knew that it was probably faster to just aim at him when he got close enough.

The king placed one hand on her cloak's hood and pulled it out and stabbed her left arm when the priestess spun around and poked the needle into his neck. With her hood down, the king could finally see her face. He was overwhelmed with shock.

'Cassandra ...'

'I'm sorry, Uncle, but you'll need to sleep for a while. This is the only way I can save Vasilisa and fulfil the oath I made to stop my husband from making more people suffer.'

'How are you even alive?'

'I did die. I threw away the name Cassandra when I died, but at that moment, I had something in me that had to be saved. Vasilisa knew that and saved it by putting a protection spell over it. Thanks to that, I am still able to see the daylight.'

'Cassandra, you should—'

'I am no longer Cassandra. I am Cafelle, a priestess for the goddess Athena.'

'Listen, the one you need to be careful of is not Sir Wilkin.' The king was getting drowsy.

The priestess perked up. 'What are you talking about?'

'My wife, she knows who started this …' He fell asleep, falling to the ground. At that moment, the blue moonlight darkened, as if swallowed by the dark night. The priestess felt her dress blowing in the sudden surge of wind through the window. She could feel the chill.

But that was not from the coldness of the night.

Standing at the door was Queen Adela, and her eyes stood out in the darkness. Cassandra looked into the queen's eyes. She could feel her mind going blank and her body no longer under her control.

She saw the future again.

Everything was scarlet red around her. She saw two windows. She sighed.

Each window showed the possibility of a future event. The priestess thought for a moment, and she could only choose one door. She then walked to the left window and opened it.

She knew what she had to do.

'Edmund, it's time!' exclaimed Nurse Marcie as she was keeping an eye on the moon's reflection on the water. Edmund took the cue and lit the candle behind the dreamcatcher, which the priestess had hung before she left.

Nurse Marcie took out a crumpled piece of paper. As she opened it, there was a small translucent shell with white smoke fuming in it. Edmund noticed how similar it was to his shadow code, the conch the gatekeeper had given him at the entrance of Thavma Gi. He kept a mental note to get it back from Leofrick later.

'What's that going to be used for?'

'It's a Vanikoro shell. It contains the dream-catching spell, which only elves can use. We only have one chance to stand in front. I will push you in. Find the door, get in and jump. That's all I can say.'

Edmund stood behind the dreamcatcher, facing Ella.

Just a little longer and I'll bring you back. I have so much to tell you.

He focused on the flame in front of her. Nurse Marcie then stood behind and blew the fumes. As the fumes in the Vanikoro shell engulfed Edmund, the flame on the candle got blown out and Edmund was sucked in. His body fell to the ground.

The fumes from the shell slowly dispersed. Nurse

Marcie noticed the roses around the bed, probably due to Ella's magick leaking all over the place. This was another sign that time was running out and Ella's consciousness was not in one place. She bent down and broke every thorn out of the stalks. She then partially transformed her arms to that of a wolf, carried Edmund and placed him beside Ella.

She then transformed fully and looked at the moon. Her heart felt heavy for leaving the two of them defenceless, but there were only a few days left. She realized that this was the right time to join the Fenrir pack again. She had to get some work done before her long-awaited reunion with Wilkin.

She never wanted to be a part of them, but right now, the only way to protect those two was to keep her enemies closer.

CHAPTER 30

Back in the king's chambers, the priestess stood face-to-face with Queen Adela. After the glimpse of the future, she had narrowed down to two options. She could either fight the queen now or fight someone else later. Fighting the queen would be overwhelming for her, since she had to fight a royal, which would get her into trouble, but fighting the other person would be too painful. It would not be easy to get over it. She slowly bent down and picked up the king's dagger, which was lying on the floor beside him.

'You do not have to pick that up. I have no intention of fighting in the middle of the night,' said the queen.

'What?'

The queen walked towards the 'lifeless' king, without glancing at Cassandra at all. 'I shall thank you instead. You have made it easier for me to find the ones you have made to trespass into my cards.'

'I do not understand, Your Highness. I never made

them trespass. They are not entering with their physical bodies at all. It is only through astral projection.'

'Did you ever wonder why that girl ended up in the king's dreams when you were aiming for the Queen of the Elves' dream world?'

Cassandra's mind was filled with thoughts of confusion, but a part of her was telling her to just stand her ground and follow her own judgment from the little glimpse into the future. 'I may be right or wrong, but I will definitely get out of here. I have done what needs to be done. Now, those stars need to do what they are destined to do.'

Queen Adela took out her stack of cards from the sleeve of her nightdress. She held them out, facing down, and let the deck of cards levitate. She then closed her eyes and touched the top card, revealing Vasilisa. Cassandra was not surprised. She knew very well her location.

The queen took that card and placed it at the bottom. She then flipped the next card, revealing something no one would have imagined.

On the card was King Alphonse. His dreams were no longer connected to the dreams of Vasilisa. Cassandra fell to the ground. *What have I done?* she thought.

She had made Edmund enter the king's dreams. Originally, if he had failed his quest of getting Ella out, he would be able to open the door on his own, even as someone who did not cast the dream-catching spell directly. But now, he could never leave on his own without someone opening the door from the other side.

If he failed, he would be stuck the same way the king had been asleep for nineteen years.

Edmund found himself inside the forest, which the priestess had told him was the king's dream world. He took out his pocket watch and took note of the time.

There were fifty-five minutes left.

He put the watch back in his pocket and started walking into the woods. He was told to find a large hole and jump, a rather vague description but enough to get a rough idea, but the only thing he had found in the last five minutes was footprints. They could be either Ella's or the king's.

He contemplated whether to follow the footprints or not, because if they belonged to the king, they might lead him to pretty much anywhere in the dream world. Edmund sighed. He decided to just follow the trail for now. It was better than nothing. Realizing it was going to be a long walk, he bent down to tighten his shoelaces, bracing himself for it.

Suddenly, he heard the sound of something being dropped. A half-chewed carrot rolled in front of him. He looked up to see a rabbit poke his head through the bushes. Edmund pulled his shoelace tight and picked up the carrot. As he stood up, the rabbit jumped out, looking at him with its large round eyes. Edmund assumed it wanted the carrot back and held it out to the rabbit, but it just turned around and hopped a few steps away.

It's probably scared of me, he thought as he moved a bit closer to it. The rabbit moved a couple more steps back again. Edmund realized it was making him follow it somewhere. He slowly put the carrot down. The rabbit then started going faster, and Edmund ran behind it. After a full three minutes, the rabbit suddenly stopped in its tracks. Edmund looked around him; in front of him was a dead wolf.

Was it a part of Wilkin's pack? he thought. He heard the sound of the vultures and realized that the wolf had been dead for a long time already. But this was not the end of his quest. In front of him was the Abyss. He knew he was one step closer to getting to where Ella was. He looked down. The vast depth made his stomach churn as the memories of him getting pulled into the water back at the river by the kappa came to mind. He took out his pocket watch again.

There were forty-five minutes left.

He jumped.

The walls of the Abyss grumbled. Ella and Vasilisa looked up.

'What's going on?' asked Ella.

'It looks like Cassandra has managed to bring Edmund in, but something is wrong. I am unable to see Edmund fall the same way I saw you.'

'What are you talking about? You said I would be able to see him soon, didn't you?'

'Wait, let me try to find him,' said Vasilisa. She

walked to the walls of the Abyss around them, and slowly touched it.

'The connection is broken …' she muttered under her breath.

'I beg your pardon?'

'Without the connection between the king and me, he will end up in the king's Abyss, not mine. It will take him five minutes to go down, and we need to do something fast, but I can't leave this place, because the queen has trapped my body—'

'I'll do it then. Leaving this place is possible for me, since mine is safe.' She looked at the purple walls flowing down, getting absorbed into the ground.

'But you are not of the same blood as him. Only someone of the same blood as him, a family member, can do that. Even though you are his wife, you have yet to take the Oath at the flame in your new household. It won't be enough!'

Ella plopped to the ground. She had no idea what to do. She stared into the walls blankly. After a few moments, she felt a presence beside her. She looked beside her and saw a red-haired girl looking at her. The girl slowly put her hand through the wall. Ella was surprised to see it slip right in.

What are you? she wondered in her head.

The girl looked at her and smiled. *I'm you*, she replied back. She then walked into the wall.

Ella quickly stood up.

'Goodness! Ella, what are you doing? I am already in so much thought as it is.'

'Let me do it.'

'We already spoke about it. There is no way you can do this. You haven't made the Oath yet.'

Ella looked at her hands. She slowly reached out to the gushing walls.

Vasilisa tried to persuade her. 'Ella, stop, you are going too far.' Ella's fingers were now touching the cold yet molten purple sludge. Ella's eyes grew in amazement. She knew she could do this.

But Vasilisa thought otherwise. 'This is not something you can …'

But she couldn't complete the sentence. Ella ran in, leaving behind nothing at all.

There were thirty minutes left.

Ella continued to run in the darkness. The only thing she could see was the red-haired girl running in front of her. She could feel slime all over her skin, yet she could breathe and see what was in front of her. It felt as if the walls were separating in front of her and coming back together behind her.

The place split in front of her, but she could not see it. Ella continued to follow the girl. For some reason, she knew that this girl was the girl she'd seen on the walls when she'd fallen into Thavma Gi. She clearly remembered her dying and her blood flowing into the river. She remembered seeing Wilkin there as well. She had so many questions going through her head, but getting to Edmund was her highest priority. And the red-haired girl was slowly fading from her sight. She held up her dress and ran faster. She had reached the other end, and she saw Edmund standing there, looking rather lost.

'Edmund!' she cried, running to him. Edmund turned around. He was elated to see her. Ella ran to him and threw her arms around him. He wrapped his arms around her.

'I've missed you so much,' Ella cried out, her eyes getting moist. She held onto his clothes, tight. She did not want to let go yet.

'I know … I know … I've missed you, too,' he said as he ran his fingers through her long tresses. Ella could feel the warmth through her body, something she had longed for for a long time. He could feel the scent of roses lingering around her, much stronger than before.

He knew her elven magick had gotten stronger.

Ella then said, 'I have so much to tell you, and so much to show you. And—'

'Shh … Let's take our time with that later. I am not going to go through this ordeal of being away from you for so long. It's so painful that the only thing that pushed me through every step of the last couple of days was you.'

'I'm sorry. I should have told you about my magick sooner. I'm sorry.'

'Don't be. You did not know yourself. It is not your fault. It is something the gods put in front of us as a test.'

'Then we must leave. Right now.'

Ella and Edmund turned around. They could see a boy, probably around their age, standing behind them, near the stream. The red-haired girl, who was a few steps behind Ella, was starting to well up. She let a tear drop.

Edmund was shocked. 'I recognize you. You are Vaughan Petyer, aren't you?'

'It's a pleasure to meet you. Not exactly. I am a part of you anyway.'

Edmund was puzzled. 'That can't be possible. I thought you were …'

'Dead?' asked the red-haired girl.

'Virgo,' gasped Ella. She finally recognized her.

Virgo simply smiled, looking at her with the eyes of a mother looking at her child grow before her. 'We have been with you the whole time,' she said calmly. 'I told you. You are me, and I am you, but right now, we need to go.'

'And how are we going to do that?'

Vaughan looked at Virgo and smiled. 'Leave that to us. We will help you. This is our fight as well.'

'Wait! That does not tell us what to do at all.'

Virgo came forward, looked at Ella and said, 'The person whom you met when you first came here. Do you remember him?'

Ella nodded.

'Find him. He will bring you to the door you came through.'

'The dream world is a funny place,' Virgo added. 'Fall into your own Abyss and you can never come out, but if it belongs to someone else, coming out is a piece of cake.'

The two of them vanished.

CHAPTER 31

Back at the king's chambers, the priestess and Queen Adela stood facing each other. The queen held onto her stack of cards, ever ready to use it.

She was surrounded by the guards. Cassandra felt the cold wind caress her cheeks, and she shivered. One wrong move and she would end up joining the queen's numerous prisoners in their eternal slumber. She pulled her clothes tighter around her and took a step back. Her dress got caught on a bowl of fruits, overturning it and creating a juicy mess on the floor. The silver bowl was barely balancing on the table.

'Don't move,' said one of the guards.

Cassandra peeked at the king out the corner of her eyes. He was still deep asleep. She sighed. She did not want to drag other people into her problems, but she had to get out. She had more important things to do than deal with the queen's tantrums. With no choice, she sheathed her dagger.

'Cassandra, stop moving towards the window. We

are not uncivilized enough to bring in others to our problems.'

But the priestess knew better. She ran to the window and pulled the curtains open. She picked up the bowl and used it to reflect the moonlight on the people at the pavilion. She knew that Priest Linus would notice.

She was right. The queen probably noticed, too. She tucked her cards away and scowled. 'We are far from over. I should have been finished with you twenty years ago.'

Cassandra looked out of the window and grinned. Priest Linus had noticed, but he was not the only one.

Following him were the two princes and the new princess.

Cassandra faced the queen and bowed. 'My apologies, Your Majesty. I may be uncivilized as you say, but I have unfinished business from those years ago as well.' She glared into her eyes and added, 'I have no intention of losing again.'

Cassandra could pick up the distinct sound of the princess' anklets. Within minutes, they barged into the room.

Prince Kai looked at his father lying on the floor, almost lifeless. His older brother, Prince Lukan, ran to him and held him over his shoulder.

'Well, don't just stand there! Get over here and help me!' said the prince. Prince Kai snapped out of his shock and helped him carry the king to his bed.

Prince Kai then turned to his mother. 'Have you

called the royal physician yet, or should I do it myself?' he questioned.

'Goodness, my son. That is no way to talk to your mother.'

'Just answer my question!'

The whole room went silent. The queen stood there, unfazed by her son's raised voice. She turned to Prince Lukan and said, 'Now that you're back, I expect you to focus on state affairs. Your father won't be able to hold it up by himself much longer, and now that you have found yourself a wife' – she looked at the Amrita princess standing a few feet behind him, and the princess bowed – 'you should start preparing for the wedding as well.'

She then turned to Prince Kai. 'One thing you should never do, Kai, is to reveal a weakness in the royal family to your people.'

Prince Kai was shocked. 'Are you telling me to ignore the fact that my father is almost lifeless right now?'

The princess stepped forward. 'Forgive me for saying this, as we have never formally met, but would you permit me to tend to him? Where I come from, healing is something I mastered. I may not be on par with the royal physician, but I will be able to help.'

'You stay away from family problems, Princess,' said the queen.

'No, you stay away from this, Mother. The minute she stepped foot into Yovaria with me, she became a part of my family. You asked me to handle state affairs, and I'm going to do just that.'

Prince Lukan then turned to his princess and gave her a permitting look. The princess bowed and walked to the king, placing her hands over him and muttering something under her breath. Cassandra was surprised to see the colour of the king's face getting better.

Guess this is a good thing to speed it up, Cassandra thought, but she still had to get out. She was still surrounded by the guards, and she could not put down the dagger she was holding.

Prince Kai noticed her condition. 'You may put down the dagger now, Priestess. You will have to face trial for what you did, but I will make sure no harm comes to you,' he said.

At that moment, the priest stepped into the room with something in his hands. The priestess looked at him, hoping to get an answer.

'I can drop it, right, I will be able to find my peace now?' she asked Prince Kai, indirectly directing the question to Linus. The prince agreed to help her get out of her predicament, as long as she did not do anything wrong.

The priest smiled and nodded. He then opened a piece of cloth in his hands, showing her a lock of red hair. A teardrop fell from her eyes, and she dropped the dagger. She held out her hands to the guards, and let herself be cuffed.

The guards walked up to her, but she suddenly asked for just a minute more. She turned to the queen and asked, 'Will you ever release the Queen of Elves, Your Highness?'

'If there should be a deal, I should get something in return, don't you think?'

'I'll do anything you say, even if I have to leave Yovaria for good.'

'Oh? That's a bold yet tempting suggestion. I will think it over and talk to you during the trial, but I doubt someone who stayed hidden for almost twenty years did all this to help an elf she barely knows. What is it that you want?'

Cassandra pondered for a moment, wondering if she should tell her after all, but right now, telling her about her defeat was like pouring a glass of poison right in front of her. Besides, the sun was going to rise soon, and she was worried about whether Edmund had managed to get Ella out.

She turned to the priest and asked, 'Did you … did you find it, Linus?'

The priest opened the palms of her cuffed hands and gave her the cloth with hair. 'You can see for yourself.'

The Queen, knowing that Cassandra was not going to open her mouth right now, ordered the guards to take her away to the palace prison for intruding in the royal residence, forcing the king to consume something against his will, and raising a sword towards a member of the royal family.

Cassandra walked out and spared one last look at the king. He was twitching. He was waking up, and she grinned. Edmund and Ella were going to be fine. Her job was done.

The queen noticed it as well. 'Get the Gilmore boy

here immediately!' she yelled at the guards. The guards quickly ran off.

'Be easy on him, Your Majesty.'

'I have no reason to show any concern for that boy.'

'Oh, you do, and you will.' She smirked as she allowed herself to be brought out.

While the chaos in the palace continued, the temple was not so quiet either. In the room where Elizabeth and Edmund lay, appeared the apparitions of their past lives.

Virgo and Vaughan were standing over Ella and Edmund's bodies. Vaughan could feel natural energy outside the room.

He walked out and saw the two gems in the bird-bath shining brightly against the moonlight. The water was vibrating, probably because of the attraction between them. He realized that they were able to materialize their past memories because of them. The gem he stored their memories in was slowly releasing them, allowing them to go back to where they belonged.

Virgo walked towards him. 'We have been lonely long enough, haven't we?' she said.

'Maybe, but we found each other again. Even if "we" don't exist, our memories will continue to live in them. Our love will be passed on to them through another story.'

'That's right. The only thing we cannot do is to leave

it to them to stop Wilkin from repeating the past. It is time for us to return.'

Vaughan looked at Virgo, held out his hand and said, 'It's time for the final showdown.'

Virgo smiled and took his hand. They walked to Ella and Edmund. They each touched the foreheads of the two lying down. Back in the birdbath, the two gems combined into the original peridot.

Edmund held her hand and pulled her forward, as he could remember the way out. Within moments, he felt the trees in front of him fade into the forest.

'What's going on? It is like this place is disappearing,' pondered Edmund, covering his face from the light.

'It is normal. This is His Majesty's dream world. If this place is disappearing, it means that he is waking up back in the real world,' said Ella.

Edmund stopped for a moment and looked around. Looking up was making his head woozy. He made a mental note not to look up for now and focused on the floor. Thankfully, he noticed his footprints on the mud and soil.

Edmund took Ella's hands again and quickly ran towards the door. Edmund held the large handle tight and was about to pull it open when the king walked towards them from the back. Ella felt her heart jump a little from the unexpected appearance. The two of them bowed.

'Use your initiative a little. What makes you think

you will be able to open my door without my permission?' he said as he opened the door for them.

Ella quickly thanked the king and stepped through the door. Edmund was about to follow suit before the king stopped him for a moment.

'Edmund, I may be selfish for saying this, but do forgive your mother,' said the king.

'My mother? What did she do?'

'You will find out soon enough, but I do ask this of you.'

'Edmund,' called Ella from beyond the doors. 'Hurry up.'

'I'll keep what you said in mind, Your Majesty.' He then bowed and ran through the doors, with the aged king looking at them go.

Well then, it is time for me to wake up as well, he thought.

Edmund and Ella ran for a while and found a light in front of them. As they went through the light, they found themselves awake and back in their own bodies.

CHAPTER 32

Leofrick paced around the room restlessly. He kept glancing at Edmund and Ella, who were still lying down. Out of frustration, he pulled a bunch of leaves and threw them at Edmund. 'Wake up, you flapdoodle. I can't keep waking you up every time.'

Ella was stirring. She slowly opened her eyes and noticed Leofrick standing in front of her bed. 'Who are …' she started.

'Leofrick, Edmund's friend and currently your only source of escape, so let's cut the introductions, as I am sure we will have the time for that later. Now, I'm going to be blunt. Why isn't this guy waking up?'

Ella looked at Edmund. He did not look like he was waking up anytime soon.

'That's odd. He was in front of me when we ran out of that door.'

Leofrick was clueless. 'So you're telling me that he should be awake before you?'

'Yes, that is how it should be.'

'Then I'll force him awake. I have done it before, so I should be able to do it again. Not surprised actually. With time magick like his, he might be slowing down his own time.' Leofrick took out a vial from his belt.

At that moment, Ella noticed Edmund's fingers moving. 'I do not think he will need your help. Look,' she said, placing her hands on Edmund's cheeks. Edmund's eyes opened, looking into Ella's eyes, with her face so close to his.

'Looks like I should make you dream walk more often,' said Edmund with a smirk.

'And why is that?' Ella whispered softly.

'I could see a blooming rose every time I woke up.'

'I am honoured that you want to see me every day, Edmund.' Ella smiled, pulling herself up to sit.

Edmund held her waist and pulled her down, kissing her. Although they were still mildly drowsy, Ella's heart beat fast, as just the gentle touch made her shiver from the feeling. It was the sound of Leofrick clearing his throat that made them realize they were looking at each other not as themselves, but as their past selves.

'Yeah, sorry to interrupt this passionate moment, but do you realize that you just got back the memories of your past lives? For example, Ella, look at your hair.'

The two of them sat down. Edmund pulled down a lock of Ella's hair, then he traced his fingers through it. Leofrick walked up to them.

'The tips of her hair are turning red,' said Edmund.

'Yes, Edmund, but that's not the point.'

Ella pondered. She could somehow feel a flood of images going through her head. They were so vivid, almost too real, and her head throbbed. Somehow, she felt like she was looking through the eyes of another, yet it felt like her own.

Edmund could feel it too. 'Then do you know what is going on?' asked Edmund.

Leofrick started, 'Of course I do. You are ...' Suddenly, they heard a howl in the distance. 'We need to get out. Now,' said Leofrick, with his voice low and stern and anxiety written all over his face.

Edmund, Ella and Leofrick ran out of the door into the living room. Ella ran up the stairs to grab the cape and the circlet from her bedroom. Edmund tried to look for the two gems in the birdbath, but he could only see a green peridot in front of him.

'It's back to normal,' said Leofrick. 'We need to put it back in the circlet, but there is no time for that. We need to flee immediately.'

Ella came down with her things. Edmund could now feel the gem vibrating like it was getting attracted to the circlet. Ella noticed the gem Edmund was holding.

'Oh, that belonged to Vasilisa!' she exclaimed.

They heard the howl again, and this time they realized it was much closer.

The three of them ran out. Leofrick told them to keep running, but he was not sure about where to go. He knew more than anyone that it was nearly impossible to run from wolves.

As they kept running on into the woods, Ella's legs were feeling numb on one side, probably because of the fact that her body had been asleep for so long. She was running not that long after waking up.

Luckily, they had run into Fred along the way. From the looks of it, it seemed he had been waiting for them for a long time already.

'This is not what you said, Leofrick,' said Fred.

'With all this running, I lost my mind along the way.'

'The sun is not up anymore. I am sure the royal family is aware of things now. They will not wait for things to happen on their own and with the sundown, you should know very well what comes out next.'

'The moon?' joked Leofrick.

They then heard howling in the distance. Leofrick could now feel a familiar scent getting closer.

'If we go together, we will not be able to make it in time,' said Fred.

'What do you suggest then? It is not like we will be fighting them,' asked Edmund.

Ella was reluctant. 'Fighting them does not change the fact that we will not be able to overpower them. It is just enough to get us some time.'

'Then that's exactly what we need to do,' said Fred. He then turned to Leofrick and added, 'Take them to the inn. I will not be able to fight them for long, but I will be able to hold them off. They need to stay in hiding for just one more night, as the following night is the lunar eclipse. Once the festival ends, they will no longer be in danger.'

Leofrick looked at Fred. He chuckled softly, genuinely surprised at how easy it was for him to believe all this, because he had not seen magick until that day at the inn. But looking at the way Fred watched Edmund, it was almost as if he was seeing someone close to him after a long time. There was an air of familiarity around them. He felt that there was a lot more between him and Vaughan that he didn't know.

Fred was not himself. He could see the boy in the painting standing in front of him, and it was just too surreal. For some reason, he felt like he knew him. In fact, he had not known himself, till a few days ago, while revealing that day to the prince.

'So, you plan on fighting the entire pack?' asked Leofrick.

'I don't think anyone else here has any other idea,' snapped Fred.

'Why are you even involved in this fight?' asked Edmund. 'Let's be honest, this is the first time I have even spoken to you.'

'I will do what I need to do to protect the royal family.'

'Neither Ella nor I am part of the royal family,' Edmund reminded him.

'Maybe not now, but you once were.'

With that, Fred entered into the deeper part of the woods. Edmund tried to stop him, but Leofrick asked Edmund to let him fight, as he had a higher chance than any of them there. Besides, if either Edmund or Ella got caught, there was no turning back a second time. He knew that Wilkin was not planning on missing his second chance in getting what he wanted.

It was now a full-on fight.

Edmund and Ella stood in front of the marketplace; festive preparations were in full force. They looked at the overwhelming crowd of people around them who were making their last-minute purchases for the festival, which would be starting when the sun went down.

People kept walking past them, holding meat, cheese and wine for their respective banquets in their own households. Some of them were placing candles by their windows, to light up the place when the brightest moon was up. They saw many wearing intricate and colourful masks, signifying their last day as a youth of Yovaria.

The two of them could not avoid the side glances of the people and their silent judgments on their appearance. They were not surprised to hear occasional whispers from onlookers.

Edmund had to think of a way to get in without drawing too much attention to themselves. Their clothes were clearly more worn down, especially Ella's – she had been asleep for way too long to care about her appearance.

Ella had noticed that, too. She looked at her dress, which was tattered in many ways. She was only glad that her mother was not there to see her like this, else she would have been reprimanded like there was no tomorrow. She quickly put on the red cape, with the hood down.

'Guess that covers my clothes,' said Ella.

'That's great, but what about the circlet? You may want to wear that, too.'

'But the priestess told me not to.'

'It's just temporary. Till we reach the inn. It is better to blend in than holding it all the way.'

Ella looked around again. Almost all girls her age were wearing flower crowns and circlets themselves to show that they were the youth of that season. She had completely forgotten about that.

Ella wore the circlet on her head. 'I look like any other girl right now, don't I?'

Edmund just looked at her for a moment and chuckled under his breath.

'Why? Do I look too weird?' asked Ella clearly puzzled.

'No. It's quite the opposite actually. You look lovely, almost like the first time we met.'

Ella took out her mask and put it over her face, and Edmund followed. He then held her hand, took a deep breath and walked into the crowd. They were blending right in with the crowd, but in their eyes, they were the only ones walking down the road.

They soon turned into the back alley. Contrasting to the rest of the marketplace, it was a very poorly lit area, filled with a strong smell of beer from all the taverns around them. Edmund could not help but wonder why Leofrick would always spend his time there. Thankfully, they could see the flickering light of the inn. Once they reached the place, Edmund knocked on the door.

'Edmund, I think we can just go in.'

'But there might be people inside.'

'No, there is no one inside. Listen,' she said, pressing her ear against the door. 'I can't hear even a dog bark in there. Forget about people talking.' She then opened the door to find the place completely empty.

Edmund could feel the vibrations of the peridot again. He was feeling uneasy about something, but he could not wrap his mind around what that could be.

'What is it?' asked Ella.

Edmund snapped out of his thoughts. 'What? No, nothing ...' he stammered.

Ella knew he was hiding something, as she could feel something ominous as well. When Sir Wilkin had given her this circlet that day, she had felt strong energy from it. Today, it was much stronger. It was almost as if it was completely embedded into her skull.

Though they could not wash away the uneasiness, they walked in.

CHAPTER 33

Knight Fred was ready. He could feel the wolves' eyes on him.

As one wolf pounced at him, he slashed it, and it flew to the ground, injured but not dead. As more wolves pounced on him, he continued to fight, but soon he started to get overwhelmed. His sword was covered in blood. He was cut in various places. He unbuckled his belt and wrapped it around his hand, giving him another weapon to use. He used the belt to catch his target and put his sword through a wolf. He flung the dead one aside, ready to get the next one.

'Okay, stop now!'

Leofrick was suddenly standing in front of him with his hands up.

'Sir, what are you doing here? What about Edmund and the girl?'

'As long as they do not run into Wilkin, they should be fine,' Leofrick said. 'Oh and wash your wound, Fred. You do not want to get that filled with dirt.'

Fred looked at his shoulder. He had not noticed it before, during the fight. He had a long, deep scratch, which was not filled with dirt. He took out the leather sack that held water and poured the remaining water on his shoulder, grimacing at the sharp pain as he tried his hardest not to shriek.

He then asked again, 'You left them behind? What if something happens to them?'

'I did not have a choice. It's about time I step into this battle.' Leofrick then stepped forward, placing one palm over the other, ready to release his magick.

Among the wolves, Raoul, Wilkin's advisor, changed back into his human form.

'If you wish to tell me something, tell me now. You will not get another chance,' said Leofrick.

'Think before you fight, my lord.' Raoul smirked. 'Because the one you should be wary of is not among us right now.'

'What are you talking about?'

'That aside, we know what your magick is. Do you think we wouldn't have come here prepared?'

'Oh, really? So you have something to stop me?'

'No way, you are far too strong to stop. That lad, on the other hand, is weak,' Raoul said, looking towards Fred. At that moment, Fred noticed a brown rope tied around his wrist. He then looked at the other wolves. They all had the same white rope around their necks.

'Leo, their necks …'

Leofrick saw them and grinned. 'My my, Bodolf has been spoiling you way too much, hasn't he?'

'Maybe, but if it helps him fulfil his desires, then we

will be more than willing to cater to his needs,' said Raoul. He then added, 'Lord Wilkin warned us about your strength. Therefore, he gave us this rope. With this, we will be able to see through any illusion.'

'He sure is lucky to have an entire pack behind him.' Leofrick then looked at Fred and said, 'Whatever you see from now on will be a secret between us. You do not tell the prince, and you most definitely will not tell Edmund.'

'What are you …?'

But Fred could never finish his sentence. Within moments, the trees around him were falling in all directions, and the rocks were rumpling on the floor as if it was an earthquake. The first thing Fred remembered was the pillar at the tavern. He now knew that what he saw that day was not exactly unreal.

'Leofrick, what are you? Stop doing this!' he shouted as he barely dodged a falling tree. He saw many wolves fallen under trees and rocks. 'You do realize that both you and I will end up getting hurt as well, right?'

'Just stand still, Fred.'

'Who are you?'

'Ha! You've been friends with him, and you do not even know him?' said Raoul, whose rope was no longer visible.

Leofrick was shocked. There should be no way these mere wolves would be able to break out of his illusion. He could feel his illusion breaking apart, bringing things back to normal.

'No way …'

'Looks like I just wrote a page in the history books. I managed to trick the god of trickery himself.'

'How is that possible? I thought I …'

'You set your illusion on us even before you faced us. So, I released my protection charm much earlier than you think.'

But Fred was more shocked. 'God of trickery …? What is he talking about, Leofrick, and how come your magick is the same as Sir Wilkin's?'

Leofrick remained silent. Raoul spoke up instead. 'That's because he's the one who gave our lord his magick. He is the god Loki, and our master is his shadow.'

Fred fell to his knees immediately, completely in shock. He wanted to bow in respect, but could not command his body enough to do so. Leofrick went up to him and placed his hands on his shoulders.

'Stand up, Fred. Now is not the time for this. You and this vile wolf in front of us may be seeing reality, but the rest are still under my illusion.'

'But—'

'This was the promise I needed you to keep. No one should know about me. Do you understand?'

'Yes, my lord.'

'Drop the formalities and call me the same way you did before. I am not the uptight kind like the others.' Leofrick then smirked. 'Now then, I guess I can go all out now. Since the secret is out of your mouth, I'll make sure you regret doing that.'

'I'm sure you will, but are you sure you want to? You

should have realized by now. I released my protection only after some time,' said Raoul.

Fred could somehow feel that Edmund was in danger. He looked around and then realized that things were wrong. 'Lord Wilkin is not here with us. That's why he gave you these to protect yourselves.'

'What are you saying?' asked Loki.

'You waited through the illusion to give enough time for your master to go after Edmund.'

Leofrick, or Loki, was still holding onto his illusion. The other wolves soon started to tire themselves out. He slowly dropped his hands to the ground. 'We need to go, right now,' said Loki.

'What about these people?'

'They are no different from dogs without even a shred of strength to wag their tails.'

'What?'

'The person he is after is not Edmund, nor is it Elizabeth. It is the gem in their possession. He knows that they have it, and now, he will no longer show any sort of leniency towards them, even if it costs them their lives.'

'So you're saying that he will actually kill his fiancé just to get a piece of stone?'

'No, he will kill them because those two will stop his plans. He knows that the two of them are the ones he killed in their past lives, and he plans on repeating that night again.'

'That's not possible. Those two should be safe with Nisi right about now,' said Fred.

Leofrick suddenly realized that something was seriously wrong. He could feel his magick tingling under his skin. As the moonlight shone on him, he looked at the ground around him. There was no trace of his shadow. He could not believe he'd never realized it.

Wilkin was using his illusion magic, and he had been for a few days already.

'Fred, from now on till I say otherwise, close your eyes,' said Leofrick, looking right at Raoul. 'Open them, and you will die,' he warned.

'What are—'

'Don't ask. We have no time. Those two are in danger, and Wilkin is there with them, but first …' said Leofrick as he snapped his fingers, emitting a bright light around him. Fred could not help but squint at the light, shutting his eyes in the process.

'I will need to get rid of these vagabonds,' said Loki.

Edmund looked around. 'We are supposed to meet a person called Nisi, right?' he asked.

'Yes, but it looks like she is not here yet,' said Ella. 'Or maybe we are at the wrong place …' she added. The place was dusty, and it looked like there hadn't been anyone in there for the past few days.

'No, you are not,' said a voice from the second storey. Edmund and Ella looked up to see a lady walking down the stairs seductively yet full of power. Her midnight-black hair fell beautifully around her shoulders, her deep blue eyes shone under the light in an entrancing manner. She stood tall in her white dress as she climbed down the stairs and walked towards them.

Nisi asked them to sit at a table near the tavern counter, offering them a chunk of cheese, meat and vegetables. Ella chomped down ravenously on some meat, swallowing her first meal since she'd fallen asleep. She had not been hungry as a spirit when training with Vasilisa, maybe just a little thirsty, but she realized that her body had been left empty with no food the whole time.

Edmund stayed quiet, letting her eat without worrying about their future. After a while, he asked Nisi what was to be done from now on. Edmund needed to face Sir Wilkin again, and ever since he'd come back from Thavma Gi, he had felt something different in his body, even though he had not gone through any sort of training like Ella.

Ella put her hands over his shoulders and leaned on him as if she was telling him she was going to be with him through the fight as well.

'This is just a thought,' started Nisi. 'But I may know of a way to keep the gem safe.'

Ella perked up. 'There is? Because keeping it broken was the only way Vasilisa could protect it while she was gone. Now that we've brought it back together, it is only a matter of time before Wilkin finds out.'

'You are wrong in one thing, Ella,' Nisi seemed to be almost whispering in a low voice. 'But us merely talking is going to bring us nowhere. For starters, maybe you can show me how the gem looks?'

Edmund did not want to take it out. He asked, 'What do you plan on doing with it?'

'I will hide it again. I have a few ideas in mind, but I will need to see it first.'

Edmund felt that she sounded desperate to see it, but agreed to trust her as she was someone Leofrick trusted. He took the gem out of his pocket.

'You too, Elizabeth, take off your circlet. I'll need it to put them back together.'

Ella nodded. She tried to take it off, but for some reason, she felt the circlet weigh down on her head more and more by the minute. As it got a bit too heavy, her head throbbed almost as if she had a massive headache.

'Ella, what's wrong? Why aren't you taking it off?' asked Edmund.

'I don't know ...' said a struggling Ella. 'It's not coming off. Gods, why is it so firm on my head? Feels like some roots have grown in. It feels awful.'

'Oh, I wouldn't worry too much about that. It's probably just reacting to your magick. I'll just attach the peridot directly to the circlet for now,' said Nisi as she touched the circlet.

Ella flinched at the touch, as she hadn't even replied to that, but she stayed still anyway.

Edmund, on the other hand, was feeling suspicious. 'Ella, are you sure about this?' he whispered.

'Of course! Your friend trusts her, you trust your friend.' She then put her hand on Edmund's and said, '... And I trust you.' She faced him and smiled.

Nisi looked hurt. 'Okay, talking about whether you

can trust me or not right in front of me just makes me feel bad,' she said.

Edmund couldn't shake the feeling of distrust. Suddenly, in his head, he heard Vaughan's voice.

Edmund, Run ...

'What?' said Edmund aloud; Ella and Nisi looked at him. 'Sorry ...' he muttered.

Edmund, Run ...

Vaughan? thought Edmund in complete surprise.

Her neck ... Fake ...

Speak louder. I can't hear you clearly, thought Edmund.

That locket is the last thing I saw before I died!

Edmund was shocked. He pushed Nisi away immediately. Nisi was puzzled by his actions.

Ella was surprised as well. She looked into Nisi's eyes, hoping to see if she was not who she said she was. She was hoping she was telling the truth, but she was not.

From within her, Virgo shouted, *Father!*

Ella realized she was wrong to trust Nisi.

Edmund felt himself lose control over his body. Vaughan took over, lunged towards Nisi's locket and shut it, causing their surroundings to change. Tables were broken, and there was beer all over the floor.

Standing in front of them was no longer a lady with midnight-black hair, but Wilkin.

'Where is Nisi?' Edmund asked.

Wilkin chuckled. 'How can you be worried about someone else when you already have enough on your plate?'

He lifted Ella's face. 'Stand up,' he ordered. Ella was

still scared. 'Come with me yourself, and I'll forget about your affair with him even though you had a fiancé,' he said.

Ella went ballistic. Edmund had no idea what to do or what not to do.

Edmund, let me blend in a bit more, said Vaughan.

No, not yet. We still have unfinished business, replied Edmund.

I can hear horses. This means that the royal guards are coming this way. We can finish what we need to do later. For now, let me blend in more. You will be able to stop time and get Lady Elizabeth out.

Edmund hesitated for a moment, and then looked at Ella. Her eyes were blue and green. He could see her hair fading from red to blonde and back to red, as if the girl inside her was emerging, while Wilkin fidgeted with his locket the whole time.

Wilkin noticed that Edmund was planning something. He chuckled. 'Whatever you're planning, do it now. I'll even let you hit me with everything you've got,' he sneered. He then looked outside. 'On the other hand, it looks like we do not have much time left.'

Edmund's now grey eyes looked right into Wilkin's. 'Oh no, this time I have all the time in the world,' he said as the sound of the horses abruptly stopped.

Wilkin looked outside and quickly noticed the sound of the horses stop. Ella, who was still holding his hand, noticed the change as well. She was not affected by the magick due to direct contact.

He looked at the grey eyes and said, 'You're my daughter's lover, aren't you?'

Vaughan, who was now in control of Edmund's body, chuckled. 'I'm glad you remember me, Sir Wilkin, for you have always been in my memory,' he said, the moment of watching him murder the maid and running away from him that night still etched in his memory.

'Let's cut this short. I knew it was you who saved the Edmund boy from my sword during our duel. Why would you save him when your target is me?'

'I am him, and he is me. My memories will be a part of his son.'

'So it's true that this boy and my fiancé are the reincarnations of you and my daughter.'

'I guess you could say that.'

'Her mother would have been happy to see her. Too bad I killed her immediately after I got rid of the two of you. I was hoping that she would keep her company in the afterlife.' He then opened his locket, changing the ground around them to rocks, but within seconds, the rocks faded.

'You've completely misunderstood the situation here, sir. You may have control over space and imagination, but I control time.' Vaughan then moved his right wrist as if he was turning an invisible doorknob. Time was slowly moving backwards.

Ella held onto Vaughan tightly. She could feel Virgo trying to come out too, but felt that her coming out could be disastrous at the moment. Without the gem, she had no control over her magic. Vaughan could feel it as well; he held onto her tightly.

At that moment, they heard a chirp. Vaughan was

surprised. Under his magick, there should be no sound, let alone movement. 'Ella, do you hear it too?'

'Hear what? I can't hear …' The sound of a bird chirped again. 'I hear it. That doesn't feel right …'

'Let go for a second,' said Vaughan as he let go of her hand. The moment he let go, Ella was frozen in time.

Vaughan ran to the window, looking for the source of the chirping. In the distance, he saw a bird circling above them. It suddenly swooped towards him and perched on a tree right in front of him.

'Who are you?' asked Vaughan.

The bird was then covered in light, and the one who stepped out was Loki.

'Who am I? I think you already know the answer to that.'

'You are Edmund's friend, someone who has been around him for as long as I remember.'

Loki tilted his head. 'You are not wrong. I am his friend.'

'But you don't look like you are here to help him.'

'My my, it seems that the former prince still has his well-known intuition.'

'So the god of trickery and illusions has come to save his shadow.'

'I am not saving him. I am going to bring him home and give him a piece of my mind. That's my role as his god, right?'

'Then are you planning to betray Ed—'

'Hush. Your time freeze is only temporary.' Loki then lunged forward, pushing Vaughan with so much force that things behind him were getting pushed down like a crumbling wall. He pushed Vaughan straight to Wilkin, who then started to move.

'What are you doing? Are you really planning to go against us?'

'If it helps the people closest to me, then yes, I will,' he said as he used his illusion to create an imaginary link between Vaughan and Wilkin.

With this, Wilkin was no longer under Vaughan's time magick. This also caused Vaughan's magick to dissipate at the sudden interference, causing him to fade back, which let Edmund gain control of his own body again.

However, the magick spurt took a toll on their body, causing him to get dizzy for a moment. He vaguely saw a figure of someone familiar in front of him. He rubbed his eyes, hoping to get a better look, but Loki was already gone. Edmund fell to the ground and saw Ella run towards him.

'I told you, didn't I? That no matter how strong you get, you won't be able to stop me,' said Wilkin.

Edmund, whose legs were still weak, trod towards Ella and hugged her tightly, reassuring her that every-thing was going to be fine. Ella pleaded with him to go away, as she did not want to hurt him. Edmund reminded her of his promise to her and held her tighter.

Wilkin laughed out loud. 'You two are absurdly fool-ish. I can't believe that you once were my daughter.'

The horses were close, just a few metres away. Wilkin grabbed Ella's arm and pulled her away from Edmund. 'I am the only one who understands that gem,

Ella. I will be the only one who can get rid of that shackle and ease you of your pain.'

'Don't you dare touch her!'

'Letting her feel the pain all the way will slowly remove the elf side of her, turning her into a full human.' Wilkin then lifted Ella's chin and looked at her fearful, tear-filled eyes. 'But on the downside, she will no longer have her elven magick.'

Edmund was baffled by Wilkin's calm and sinister thoughts on getting what he wanted without a thought for others. He wondered if that was how Vaughan felt that night. He decided that if Vaughan could stop time, he could too. He focused on his thoughts, taking slow steps towards Ella.

'No matter what happens, do not let go of what is yours, okay?'

Ella noticed the strain in his voice and his already weak body breaking down even more. 'Edmund, stop! You're hurting yourself. Just stop!'

'JUST LISTEN!' Ella's eyes widened with surprise at Edmund's raised voice. 'Just listen. I can't hold it for long.' He took Ella's hands into his, clasping them as if he was going to promise her.

Ella nodded furiously as a tear rolled down her eyes.

Edmund muttered under his breath, just enough for Ella to hear him, 'I'll find you. No matter what, I'll always find you.'

With that, Edmund let go and fell. Time started again.

Ella screamed at Wilkin to let her go, but Wilkin just

ignored her. Struggling again, Ella pushed his face away from her.

Wilkin applauded Edmund for stopping time for the first time, but he wouldn't be able to do it for long. The guards had entered the place, and they were taking Edmund away by force.

It was the queen's orders.

Wilkin smiled. He carried Ella and left the inn.

Edmund was also cuffed and taken away.

Sometime later, things got quiet, and Leofrick, who had re-transformed from Loki, waited at the door for someone. Soon, Fred ran towards the inn. He was in shambles, covered with blood and sand. There was a random twig in his already messy hair.

Leofrick laughed. 'What took you so long, Freddy?' he joked.

'I don't want to hear that from someone who can just change into a bird and fly off.'

'One of the perks of being me,' said Leofrick.

'It must be convenient. I had to take a shortcut through the woods instead of walking on the streets.'

Fred scanned the room, hoping to find Nisi, while Leofrick felt the air around the room. Wilkin's presence could still be felt. This meant that it had not been lifted since he left. He knew Wilkin had taken Ella with him. He did not know of a better way to put the gem back in the circlet than through his pack. Werewolves were extremely talented in woodwork and the making of weapons, and the Fenrir pack was exceptionally talented. Wilkin was no different.

It was still noon. This meant that for the next few hours, Edmund and Ella had to do whatever they could to stay alive. He thought for a while and then looked at Fred, who was now on the second floor, looking into every room.

'Fred, go back to the palace immediately,' said Leofrick.

Fred yelled back from the room, 'But I just got here!'

'You are not going back empty-handed.'

'What?'

'I kind of need you to introduce the prince to his older brother after a long time.'

'And how exactly are you planning to do that? With other relics from upstairs?'

'Those are much too important. I'm pretty sure Nisi put some crazy spell on it. No, I have already asked for a certain someone to wait for you at the east gate. He will be able to help you.'

'Who is it, another good friend of yours?'

'I have normal people around me, too, you know,' said Leofrick. 'Aren't you, a human, being much too casual with me?'

'You aren't the kind of person I expected a god to be. Broke all expectations—'

'You're one of the rare ones who have the honour of knowing a god in their lifetime.'

'And for that, I am eternally grateful. So, who is this other person I have to bring to the prince?'

'Someone you do not know, as he is not your kind.'

'What's his name?'

'Kain. Kain Glendower.'

Leofrick waited for a while to make sure that Fred was far from the inn. He had noticed a change in the air near the ale tubs. He knelt in front of the tub and put his hand into it, diffusing the air around the room. He could feel Nisi right in front of him.

He quickly clenched his fist, drawing the dark air into his palms. He could now see Nisi in front of him, unfazed by whatever was going on. Her hair was still the same messy side braid. Leofrick looked at her for a while, but she avoided looking at him.

'Why didn't you stop him?' asked Leofrick. 'Even though you are a goddess yourself.'

Nisi sighed. 'I tried to bring myself to do it, but I just could not.'

'Don't hold onto your past, Nisi. It will just hurt you. You should have stopped Bodolf earlier. I would not have had to take action otherwise.'

Nisi stood up, walked behind the counter and opened a small box hidden under a bunch of cups. She then took out a small silver ring, holding it in her palm.

'You are still holding onto that life, Nisi?' asked Leofrick.

Nisi looked at Leofrick and asked, 'Aren't you hoping to find that shred of hope in Bodolf too?'

'I have to. He is my shadow. You know that very well.'

'No god watches their shadow's every move, Loki. How long do you intend to hide it from him?'

'I told you to never bring that up again,' snapped Leofrick.

'He is our son, Loki,' cried Nisi. 'He is your son. Don't try to deny that when the very reason we are no longer allowed back to the heavens is due to the mistake of bringing that child to existence.'

'We are not allowed to speak of it, remember?'

'Yet you kept him close to you from the beginning. You let the Fenrir clan adopt him, to give him the family he would have never had.'

'Which is why I made him my shadow, and that is the one bond even the heavens cannot break.'

'What will happen if the heavens find out?' asked Nisi.

Leofrick paused for a moment and looked at Nisi. He then said, 'Let's just hope they never do. We are already banned from the heavens. We spent the last fifty years in hiding. There is nothing worse that could happen.' He then stormed towards the door.

'What do you expect me to do?' Leofrick was surprised to hear that. He stopped in his tracks. 'We may not be the same as before, but you are still a valuable part of my memory. I can't throw that away.'

'Then so be it,' said Leofrick. 'If you need time to get over it, then take all the time you need. I don't care either way.'

'If you're planning to go to the river, you're going to need help.' Leofrick saw Hermes swoop down. 'Here, take them. It's faster than your bird form.'

Leofrick took them immediately, but he couldn't help but question, 'What crazy thing do I have to do in return for this? If it is something outrageous, I'd rather fly myself there.'

'I'm just returning an old favour. I do not plan on forgetting the numerous times you stole them.'

Leofrick grinned in thanks and flew off. Hermes then turned towards Nisi and bowed.

Nisi returned the greeting. 'It must be hard coming to this land so often.'

'Yes, it's actually more interesting than up there.'

'I don't want to get you into trouble, you know.'

'It's fine. Like I said, I owe you a lot, you and Loki both.'

'And I am always grateful for that. You shouldn't have joked around with him just now.'

'I know. It's just that this version of Loki does not sit well with me. The original, joyful version is the true him.'

'The true him? I have not seen that side of him since the day we were banished.'

'Going that far back is too much. I meant the version of him after he moved on from that and was finding his goal in life again.' Hermes said what he knew. He felt that this version of Loki was not right, it would not help him get what he wanted. 'If he really wants to end this story, he has to get back his old joyful self.'

'He is not going to hurt his son, is he?'

'No. He is going to stop his shadow from committing a crime far worse than that.'

'It feels more like a game.'

'Oh, it is very much a game, Nisi. You and I both

know that Loki always looks at everyone around him as a pawn in his mind games.'

Nisi just remained silent.

Hermes noticed her uneasiness and reassured her by saying, 'But this time, it is different. The game already ended when the two reborn lovers woke up. Now, it is time for the final battle.'

Kain stood in front of the entrance of the waterfall in Thavma Gi. He put his hand through it and felt a wild shock of current. As he removed his hand, he felt the burn through his skin.

'Still plan on leaving?'

Kain turned around to see Evian standing there. 'This is my punishment for stopping the ripple that very day,' he said as he held a broken bracelet.

'You broke your seal by force. It means you are certain you will find the woman up there.'

'I have to, Evian,' said Kain. 'I have to warn her about what happened. The boy's final moments.' He put his hand out.

Evian sighed and placed a yellow piece of paper with red letters in it. 'These are only allowed by the gate-keepers of Thavma Gi. For the sake of the gods, bring it back in one piece. I do not want to be filing a report if that goes missing,' said Evian.

'What is this?' asked Kain as he put his hand through the waterfall, this time without any jolt of current.

'A talisman, used by the eastern gates of Thavma Gi

as an alternate to the shell code we use here,' said Evian. 'You have no idea the amount of trouble I had to go through to get my hands on this.'

Kain laughed. 'I'll return the favour when I get back.'

'Do me a favour now instead and don't get caught,' said Evian.

Kain nodded as he walked through the waterfall. Soon, he reached the surface. He looked around to find someone standing here, as if waiting for him. 'You are …?'

'Fred. Knight of Yovaria and the personal guard of Prince Kai. I have been asked to escort you to the palace, Kain Glendower.'

*

'Did you just say Kain … Glendower?' asked the prince.

'Yes, Your Highness,' said Knight Fred. 'He will be awaiting your presence at the swan pavilion. Right now, he has requested an audience with Her Majesty Queen Adela.'

'With mother, huh. So things always lead back to her,' said the prince. 'Where is she right now?'

*

'Your Majesty, a certain Kain would like to speak to you,' said a messenger.

'Kain? What's his full name?' asked the queen.

'He would prefer to not say, Your Majesty. He asked me to tell you that he is here with information.'

'Send him in.'

Kain emerged and bowed. 'It's a pleasure to finally

meet you again,' said Kain as he stood up. 'Your Majesty.'

'We have not met before, but it seems that I may be mistaken. Care to remind me of our previous encounter, young man?'

Kain answered, 'I have seen you many times, Your Majesty, but you have not seen me before.'

'Is that so?' said the queen. 'Well then, do state the reason for wanting to see me, Kain.'

'I have witnessed, by pure accident, the planning of a great conspiracy, Your Majesty. Something which would throw everything around you in utter chaos.'

The queen then asked, 'And what did you see and hear?'

'A woman dressed in blue and green, puts a crusted basket in front of a mirror …' started Kain slowly.

The queen froze. 'Who are you?'

Kain ignored her and continued. 'She looks behind her, gets fearful, then picks up the basket and starts to run.'

'I order you to tell me who you are!'

Kain continued to ignore her. 'She then reaches a waterfall, looks back one more time, before running right into it. Along the way, she drops a ring,' he said as he walked towards the queen and took her hand in his. 'A ruby ring, same as what I see around your finger,' he added as he held up her hand.

The queen was speechless. 'How in heaven's name do you know all this?'

'I even know what happened after that. Shall I say it, or will you say it with your own mouth?'

'Don't say it!' she pleaded with widened eyes.

'On the other side of the waterfall, you see a man waiting for you. Surrounded by wolves, he gives you a single offer … protection, if you do his bidding.'

'I said don't say it!' she screamed in anguish.

'But you ended up selling your son and the love of his life in exchange for your own protection. I'm guessing even covering up the very murder that killed them both.'

Queen Adela lost her posture and staggered.

'Let me tell you something, Your Majesty. You will be meeting the person you killed very soon, and I promise you, he will ask you to give your best excuse,' said Kain. 'I pray that when the time comes, you set things straight yourself, or I will personally take matters into my own hands.'

*

Marcie had reached the Kroukhesta Mansion. She could sense that it was mostly empty, just a few maids and servants wandering around. Even though they walked past her, they were not surprised by the intrusion.

I guess Wilkin must have placed them on a permanent illusion, she thought.

She opened the doors and took a step in. She realized that the floor was as cold as the day she'd left this place. As she walked in, the first thing she had to do was get to the basement, but before she could take another step, a maid walked towards her and bowed.

'Lady Marcie?' she asked.

Marcie scoffed. 'I am Marcie, but I am definitely not a *lady*,' she said. 'Where is everyone?'

'Sir Wilkin has been on a business journey for the past few days.'

'Has he? Well, it's been a while since I have been in this place, so mind if I look around.'

'No, you may not,' said the maid as she slowly transformed into a wolf. Other maids and servants started transforming as well.

Marcie quickly realized something was off. 'You! You were not a werewolf before, were you? You were human!'

The maid said, 'We were all once human. Thanks to our lord's graciousness, we are now able to protect the mansion for him. You, who no longer belong to the clan anymore, have no business here.'

That despicable wolf has completely lost it, she thought. She could not believe that she was once head over heels for him. It made her thank her lucky stars. 'I never would have thought a day would come where I would have to fight with a bunch of half breeds who have not even reached their maturity.'

'We live to protect our lord's clan.'

'So be it. I will personally break the illusion that a wolf has put on all of you,' said Marcie, as she transformed into a wolf.

Marcie swerved as two half breeds ran at her and almost immediately, she was able to subdue them. As if there was some sort of magnet attraction between her and them, more half breeds kept running at her, and she kept her pace. This went on for hours until finally, she was able to subdue them all just as memories from the past flowed through her mind.

In the past years, a long time ago, a young Wilkin entered the palace officially for the first time. He had come many times before as a child, but they were never this formal. Wilkin was here to fix an alliance with the king's niece, Cassandra.

He brought along two of the most trusted members of his pack, Marcie and Raoul. As Wilkin reached the gates, he ordered them to stay outside, as he had to go in alone. Marcie and Raoul obeyed while Wilkin walked in.

For the next few moments, the two of them stood against the castle walls awkwardly. Marcie sat on the ground with her head on her knees. She sighed deeply, indicating that she had a lot on her mind.

'Are you okay?' asked Raoul. 'If you are tired, you can try and sleep for a while. I can wake you up before our lord returns.'

Marcie just stayed and shook her head, denying the offer. 'I don't think that is what I need, Raoul.'

'I know what you need, Marcie but you know that is something we, as servants to the alpha, should never hope for.'

Marcie lifted her head. 'How long have you known?'

'Did you seriously think I wouldn't notice, after being around you for so long?'

'Who else knows?'

'That depends.'

'What do you mean?'

'I know that you have feelings for our master. I have known for a long time. You follow his every step, and you have never failed his orders. You are someone he trusts, one of

the best werewolves in our pack and an amazing assassin. The blood you have spilt over the years can never rival anyone else's, not even that of our master himself.'

Marcie looked at him and asked, 'If you knew so much, why didn't you take action against me? I broke the pack's law, didn't I?'

'I wanted to. As his advisor, it is my job to ensure that all rules are kept, regardless of who you are. Losing someone as gifted as you is, however, not worth it, not yet at least.'

Raoul then added, 'Besides, I don't think it is needed anymore. Once Lord Wilkin gets engaged, it is only a matter of time before the wedding takes place. You and I both know how important this marriage is for his goals. I am sure you realize that doing anything stupid will only anger him.'

'It is for that reason that I am remaining silent. I will stay that way until the end. I know I will never be able to give him my heart, because if I give it, it will come back to me broken.'

'I will trust you on this, Marcie. No matter what happens, we are bound by our pack laws to obey his every command. We should never forget that till our death. Else we will be banished from our pack, and that is the worst insult we can ever get.'

'I know, Raoul. You do not have to tell me twice. I do not want to ruin his chances of getting the elven peridot. I know just how important that is to him.'

Edmund reached the palace. He was taken to a room to clean himself up, as the queen had asked him for an audience.

Edmund was confused. *The queen? Why on earth would she want to meet me at this time?*

Edmund knew about Vaughan's past now, and the queen seeing him would only result in her asking a lot of questions. Edmund looked into a mirror to fix his clothes and neaten his hair. He could see Vaughan in front of him instead.

No, he thought. It was not Vaughan; some of his features were blending with his past. The main change was his eyes. This was similar to the change in the colour of Ella's hair.

Suddenly, the door opened. Edmund turned around to see the queen enter. He quickly went on his knees.

The queen asked if he was Edmund Gilmore, and he replied yes. The queen thought for a moment. She had to delay the time of him leaving as much as possible to give Wilkin enough time to get his hands on the gem.

The queen then said that she did not want him to go around the garden, and would like him to stay there for the night. Edmund declined politely, saying that he had to do something important.

As Edmund was still bowing, the queen asked him to rise. Edmund hesitated. He did not want her to see his face, but he had no choice. He heard Vaughan whisper in his mind, *Mother*. He stood up, with his head still down. He then slowly looked up, right at the queen.

The queen looked shocked. Her exchange with Cassandra earlier that day repeated itself in her head.

'I have no reason to show any concern for that boy.'

'Oh, you do. And you will.'

The queen's mind was now completely clear. 'You are not Edmund Gilmore. You are my son, aren't you?'

'No, Your Majesty. I was your son but not anymore. My name is Edmund Gilmore. I am the son of the Gilmore family.'

'No, no, you are my son. You are alive.'

'How can that be? There were rumours that the young prince was out in the dark forest and drowned near the river.'

'This can't be ...'

'But I am Vaughan Petyer. I am him, but I am no longer your son.'

The queen looked baffled. Edmund noticed her confused expression.

'If you want, I can let you talk to him,' said Edmund.

What are you doing? asked a surprised Vaughan.

Getting out of here. You should know what Wilkin is capable of. A royal order will speed things up, said Edmund.

Queen Adela walked up to Edmund slowly, saying, 'No, no wait …'

Edmund did not stop. He was giving Vaughan even more control. The air around him was getting cold, and soon, Edmund felt himself deep inside his soul. Vaughan was now in control of his body.

Vaughan, we are the same person anyway, but I can only give you thirty minutes. My time cannot hold for long, said Edmund.

'I understand, Edmund. I will finish this soon,' whispered Vaughan under his breath. He walked towards the queen with his deep grey eyes. 'It's been a long time, Mother.'

The queen fell on her knees. Tears welled up in her eyes, and her voice quivered as she called for her dead son, 'Vaughan …'

'You really were selfish, you know.'

'I didn't have a choice, Vaughan.'

'No, you did have a choice. You just chose to let go of me to keep your own secrets hidden.'

'I cannot change anything now. What's done is done.'

'Till the end, you are choosing to sacrifice others for your selfish goals. Well, I'm already dead, so I will let that go and ask something else. Why are you helping Wilkin?'

Queen Adela stayed silent.

'Okay, next question. Were you happy after what happened?'

'Of course not!' the queen cried. 'I did not realize

that the duke's daughter's lover was you. I would not
have harmed you otherwise.'

'So you're saying that if that boy was someone else
and not me, you would have killed them even now?'

'I …'

'Enough. I am done with your selfish reasons. This is
the end of the line for me. From now on, I am no longer
Vaughan Petyer, but Edmund Gilmore.'

'Vaughan, please. Even if I want to change things
now, I can't. You know the duke is much more powerful
than you think. Even more so, as the full moon is almost
on us.'

'Yes, I know. He will be the strongest tonight. Which
is why I am here to give you one last chance for
retribution. Can you promise me this?'

'Anything, Vaughan. That's the least I could do to
make up for this.'

Vaughan wondered if he should say it out loud.
There were things he couldn't let Edmund know yet. He
looked around, went to the study table, picked up a quill
and wrote it down. He then put the pen down, read it
and re-read it till he was satisfied. He then handed it to
his mother.

The queen scanned through it first to see his three
wishes and was surprised. 'Vaughan, you knew that I
was a—'

'Shh … People will hear,' he whispered. Deep inside,
he didn't want Edmund to know the queen's secret as
well. 'You promised. I will trust you one last time.'

'I will, my son.'

'Oh, and maybe, as a bonus, you could look after this

boy for me?' he said, pointing to himself. 'He and I will become one soon, and I do wish to see my father and my brothers again someday.'

'I will work something out to let him be in the castle.'

Vaughan smiled, and a tear rolled down his face. 'Guess it's time for me to leave now.'

'Vaughan, wait ...'

'Goodbye, Mother.'

Vaughan fell to the ground. Edmund felt himself back in his own body, but this time, he could no longer feel another presence in him. On the other hand, his mind was full of memories of his past. Edmund could see his past life through the eyes of Vaughan. He stood up and looked at the queen. He knew she was his own mother, but he also knew that she no longer was.

'Your Majesty,' he said, and bowed.

At that moment, the door opened and Prince Kai barged in. 'Why are you still here, Edmund?' asked the shocked prince. 'Don't you have somewhere to be right now?'

'Yes, I was about to ... but ...' stuttered Edmund, looking back and forth between the prince and the queen.

'Leave NOW!'

Edmund scurried out but paused for a second to glance back at the still shaken queen. However, he knew that was the least of his concerns right now. Queen Adela had the prince around, but Ella, she had no one. He was just glad that his past was slowly getting the closure it deserved.

With Edmund gone far enough from the room, the prince looked at the queen, who had slumped on the floor, weeping. 'This was not how I wanted for you to find out, although this was a much better way than I thought.'

'You knew? That your brother was the boy in the rumours back then?'

'Not at first. Definitely not back then. I only found out a few days ago when my knight brought back a painting.' He then asked Fred to bring it in.

Fred walked in, holding the huge painting which he had brought back then from the locked room in the inn on Loki's orders. He placed it in front of the queen, holding it straight.

The queen yanked on the veil and pulled it down. She grabbed onto the painting and sobbed even more.

The prince let her cry for a little longer. He then bent down and wiped her tears. 'Let's stop him, Mother,' said Prince Kai. 'I do not want to lose my brother again.'

The queen tried to regain her composure. She put the painting down, which Fred picked up. 'I have unfinished business to attend to first, Kaiden. Leave me alone for a while.'

Prince Kai just sighed. 'Yes, I shall do that. Like always, you need time to find a way to get out of it. Father is getting back his health, and it is only a matter of time before he takes over your temporary rule.'

'No, this time I am not running away. I need to fulfil a promise, which will help Edmund defeat Wilkin.'

Prince Kai's face lit up. 'So you will help me stop Wilkin's pack with your private army?'

'No, that I shall not do. In fact, the only thing I can do is this,' she said, looking at the paper Vaughan had given her. She then looked at Prince Kai and said, 'I am not capable of stopping Duke Wilkin. He is not for me to defeat.'

'What are you talking about? You have magick, too, don't you? Why can't you fight him?'

'Because he is not fully human, unlike me. Only a half-human will be able to be on par with his strength, and from what we've already realized, his pack will never go behind his back.'

'I wouldn't be so sure about that. We know that a member of the pack is one of Elizabeth's closest confidantes.'

'She is bound by a promise to Lady Cassandra. Don't forget that she was the trigger for their deaths in the first place. Without which, Wilkin would not have been able to find my son and that girl in the first place.'

'So you know absolutely no way of defeating him? What about those myths on killing werewolves with a silver stake?'

'Those are just rumours. Your father tried to do just that, but you saw what happened instead.' The queen looked away and added, 'Only the gods can stop him now.'

The prince turned back and walked towards the door, saying, 'Well, I am not going to give up now. There is still time left, I will go to the royal library to see what I can find.'

The queen stopped him and asked something that had been bothering her for quite some time. 'Kaiden, where did you get the painting from in the first place? If I remember correctly, this painting was destroyed a long time ago.'

'Who knows? Guess we can thank the gods for this one,' said the prince as he walked away.

CHAPTER 36

Ella stirred. Her eyes opened slowly, taking in her surroundings. She was seeing this for the first time, yet it felt so familiar. As she looked around, she saw a tree, a large oak tree.

Visions of Virgo's memories flashed by her, and she remembered that this was the place where she and Edmund had shared many memories in their past lives. She was able to hear the river in the distance as well. As she tried to stand up, she realized her legs were not able to move. It was as if she was paralyzed. She looked up to see Wilkin's pack standing around. There were so many unfamiliar faces in one of her most familiar places.

The huge drawings on the floor were intimidating. Just looking at them, she knew that those drawings were most likely drawn a fairly long time ago, but what bothered her was what the pack was doing. They were setting up the place to something like a spell circle.

She remembered what Vasilisa had said back in the dream world.

'A spell circle is usually used for either breaking or binding.'

'What kind of objects can we break and bind?' Ella asked.

Vasilisa brought Ella to a birdbath filled with water. 'Look closely, Ella. What do you see?'

'I see the sky sitting above the vast depth of the Abyss,' said Ella.

'Is it? What I see when I look in there is myself.'

'What do you mean, Vasilisa?'

'What I mean is that in a spell circle, you can bind and break anything as long as it is in contact with the water from the rivers of Thavma Gi.'

'What happens if you touch it?'

'If the stone happens to be with you at that time, it may either bind you to it or break you completely.'

'Where's Sir Wilkin?' she asked.

'He'll be here soon. Just sit and wait,' said a pack member.

'No need to wait, Ella,' said a voice. 'I am here.'

'Nurse!' exclaimed Ella, who looked up to see a familiar face. She reached out to her, unable to stand up.

Nurse Marcie ran to her side and put her arms around her. 'It's okay, Ella. I will do what I can to get you out of here. Everything will be over soon,' she said as she took out a vial of clear liquid.

'Nurse, what are you talking about?'

Marcie leaned forward. 'I always keep my promises,' she whispered as she stabbed the tip of the vial into Ella's thigh.

Ella screamed.

'Nurse, what have you done to me?' She was feeling

dizzy, as if her soul was slowly being pushed out of her body. She noticed the tips of her loose hair turning red.

Marcie looked at her. 'I have nothing against you, Ella. If anything, I have a whole lot of catching up to do with the one inside you. So I am just forcing her out.'

Ella knew she was getting sucked in, and Virgo was pushing her away. Her eyes were feeling disoriented, and she could feel the familiar tingle down her neck. Soon, she stopped moving.

'We meet again, Virgo,' said Marcie.

Virgo opened her eyes. Marcie noticed that the colour of her eyes was the same. The only difference was the hair.

'Yes, Marcie. It has been a while, hasn't it?' said Virgo.

'Now, now, that is no way to address someone who looked after you for so many years.'

'Ah,' exclaimed Virgo sarcastically. 'You did look after me in both my lifetimes, right? If I could stand, I'd give you my respects for that.'

'Even after you were reborn, you chose to walk the same path. I always doubted fate throughout my life, considering my own, but seeing you grow up now makes me doubt myself more.'

'Well good for you, because I had always believed in fate as much as I would believe in god himself, but that is not why you forced me out, is it?'

'You do sense that Vaughan's presence can no longer be felt, right?'

Virgo closed her eyes and took a deep breath. She then opened them again and said, 'No, I can still sense him, like Edmund.' She then turned her head in that direction and gave a little nod. 'He's on his way here.'

'Although you are no longer alive, you still have your enhanced senses.'

'It appears that once I cease to exist, my new self will no longer be the Daughter of a Fenrir but the Rose Elf.'

'Do you hate it?'

'Back then, I would have given anything to take away the werewolf blood in me. I was afraid to turn twenty-one, as that was when a young wolf got her first full transformation.'

'If you had it, it would have protected you. Why did you choose to run away before that?'

'I was always prepared to lead the pack one day. At least till my own father turned his sword against me.'

'You were too young to make that decision, Virgo. Your mother and I could have protected you.'

'You would have protected me, no doubt, but you would not have been able to protect him.'

'Don't you have the least bit of regret for leaving your mother behind?'

'Even after twenty years, I do not regret it one bit, especially for a woman who did not nurse me even once.'

Marcie sighed. She knew very well that Virgo was still as stubborn as she was back then. Even as Ella, she could always tell that it was a trait she kept the whole time. 'Don't make me regret this, Virgo', she said as she quietly took out a small piece of parchment. 'Touch it the moment you get the chance. Don't hold back,' whispered Marcie into Virgo's ears as she slipped the parchment into her hands tied behind her. 'That is the only thing I can do for you now.'

'What is it?'

'Something she asked me to give you a long time ago, but I failed to.'

'Thank you, Marcie.'

'Hush, your father is here,' whispered Marcie as she put her finger on her lips. They could hear the rustling of the trees, and the footsteps of a single man walking towards them.

'Welcome, my lord,' said Marcie as she bowed to Wilkin.

Wilkin walked past her without averting his eyes and headed straight for Virgo. 'You see your father after twenty years and not a single greeting from you?'

'I did not come back to see the face of a murderer.'

'Useless wench,' he said as pulled out the locket around his neck and opened it. The people around them slowly disappeared, including the alchemy circle on the floor. 'The full moon is only a matter of a few hours, Virgo. Go hide inside that body and bring Ella out. Only the one with elven blood can get this to work again.'

'We have the same body. No, that itself is wrong. There are no two people in the first place. What you do with her can be done with me, too.'

'No, you are getting it wrong,' said Wilkin. He then touched the locket again, showing an illusion of a person's form beside the river.

Virgo recognized that figure. It was Vasilisa, or what she'd looked like twenty years ago that night.

'So you remember her,' said Wilkin. 'Now you will see the reason why I need Ella and not you.'

With a wave of his hand, he created an illusion of the memory of what happened twenty years ago for Virgo to see.

CHAPTER 37

S he could feel the tendons in her legs tearing; gradually, she reduced her pace. They must have managed to catch up. She wasn't sure.

Bloodshot eyes, glares from hungry wolves, preying to pounce on her ... bright colours like mirrors of the moonlight with faces of murderers. For an instant, she yearned for help from humans. Her distinct camouflage betrayed her. They were going to wolf her down their throats.

The tree behind was the only alternative, but the branches pressed her downwards, bending and breaking from her weight. The rustle of the leaves as she fell to the ground drained all the energy she had left. Hiding was the only logical option, but those noisy leaves were giving it all away. Her thoughts of him overrode the idea of her freedom. Her death held no importance.

She had become prey for being different − those words reverberated through her. The only vivid image she could recall without any stress was when his voice echoed her name.

Not her name. It was the girl with the red hair or the cherry servant.

At least someone saw her as human.

As the voice grew closer, she realized that even though faith was adrift, she held on to hope. Although it was too late to live, she could always find comfort in him – her love. She let every part of him explore her dying mind.

When he wrapped his arms around her for the first time, their giant secret hideout tree, slowly she drifted into darkness. As her eyes were closing, she felt an open locket fall off her chest.

Someone picked it up and closed it.

Her knight in shining armour. He was human, and she knew that for sure. He watched her as the fangs of his hungry pack sank into her skin. This was it. She wasn't going to fight anymore. Just as she gave in to the last gasp of death, she heard her name ... not the girl with the red hair or cherry servant ...

'Virgo ...!!!'

Virgo continued to run, but the wolves were too fast.

Soon, she reached the riverbank, but there was nowhere to go. She looked around to see masked members of the pack surrounding her.

'Even though I have the blood of your leader, your eyes show hesitance to harm me. Yet you stand here, without moving an inch closer.'

A masked werewolf came forward. 'We were only given orders of containment. We are not to harm you in any way.'

'No, that is not the truth, is it? My father gave an order so weak ...? That is not like him. He killed a human servant every full moon to satisfy his hunger. He drank their blood,

completely forbidden and making him no different from the blood-sucking vampire.'

'You cannot compare Lord Wilkin to a lowly vampire,' said the werewolf.

'How are they any different? Every move he makes is for him to gain more power, as if what he has isn't enough already.'

'Lord Wilkin seeks power to protect our kind. We are hunters who gained a human form, not the same as the other humans you talk to.'

Virgo was infuriated. 'Neither can you use me to lure Vaughan here. He is not so foolish as to come running to this place, knowing that it is full of wolves. It's like walking into the enemy's dinner plate.'

Another wolf came forward. 'He will come here,' said a female voice.

'So you chose to betray your mother's trust. Isn't that right?' asked Virgo.

'There is no betrayal. You will not be harmed, and that boy will not let you get hurt.'

'What makes you so sure?'

The female werewolf pointed to the moon. As it came out from behind a cloud, Virgo noticed black smoke rising from the woods, making the moon look rather eerie. It didn't seem to be very far from here.

The werewolf pulled out a locket and opened it, using the moonlight to form a bright circle on the ground around Virgo. Virgo was taken aback.

It was Wilkin's magick locket.

'No, no, no!' gasped Virgo, unable to breathe.

The wolves stood around the circle. In unison, they slit

their palms and drew various symbols on the ground. Each symbol hardened on the ground and crawled their way into Virgo as numerous thin strings. Without the circle, someone might mistake them for roots or a tree.

Virgo tried to fight back. Each string, once it touched her skin, would penetrate into her body, causing unimaginable pain. As a werewolf herself, she tried to block out the strings from touching her feet, but there was a limit to how long she could stop it. It took a well-trained werewolf to be able to create such a barrier against every string. It was no easy feat.

And the number of strings she had to create a barrier against would be one thousand and one.

Wilkin suddenly appeared, asking all the other wolves to leave except Marcie and two others.

Vaughan, who had now arrived in the woods where his beloved was being held captive, ran towards Virgo and held onto her. Facing Wilkin, he asked why he was doing all this.

Wilkin replied by telling Vaughan that he didn't care if Virgo died, leading to the inexistence of a successor to lead the pack. He thanked Vaughan for stopping time inside the circle. Even though the magick was not affecting Virgo, it was stabilizing the stone, and allowing it to merge with the elements of a werewolf.

A barrier was formed, like Virgo, a werewolf, was affected by the stone of another species.

Marcie, seeing Virgo in danger, ran to the circle to protect her, but a barrier had already been formed.

Wilkin placed his hand on the barrier and muttered a spell, making it possible for him to enter the circle.

As the stone began to heat up, Vaughan was forced to drop

it, causing time in the stone to start to flow again, and Virgo felt the pain again.

Wilkin took out his sword, then single-handedly used magick to create lots of rose bushes, hurling them at them.

The two were cut by the thorns and writhed in pain. Vaughan ran to Virgo, with the gem in hand, slammed it on the circle, absorbing all the strings.

Virgo, too weak to do anything, held onto her lover tightly as they hugged each other.

Just when Vaughan tried to pick up the stone, he was stabbed by Wilkin, causing Vaughan to be wounded. Virgo cried out, desperately trying to move over to him but unable to move well, and so crawled towards him.

As he began to vomit blood, Vaughan tried to touch the stone again, but it was picked up by Wilkin, who walked out of the barrier. From the corner of his eye, Vaughan saw a single rose grow from the ground and turned around to see Vasilisa while Wilkin ordered Marcie to attack.

Marcie drew her sword and came closer to Vasilisa, who created a sword out of roses and waited for Marcie to come closer.

Marcie moved closer, seeing in Vasilisa's eyes a reflection of Wilkin. Pleading to Vasilisa to help Vaughan and Virgo live, she turned around and went straight to Wilkin, stabbing him in the process.

Vasilisa entered the circle and stabbed the stone, taking in all the pain of the circle.

Wilkin had used an illusion on himself, so he was not hurt at all, but on the other hand, Vasilisa was hurt more than before. Wilkin then cut Marcie, scratching out the clan mark on her body.

Wilkin looked at the unconscious Virgo and Vaughan and told Vasilisa that he'd won.

Vasilisa told him to think again, and Wilkin asked what she was talking about. Vasilisa asked Wilkin to look at the sword on the ground.

It was the rose sword, meaning that Vasilisa had poisoned it before Marcie took it. Wilkin would no longer be able to touch the gem and would be forced to transform into a werewolf.

She relayed that she was losing her magick and decided on one last spell. However, Wilkin attacked her but was stopped by Loki, who suddenly appeared out of nowhere.

He told Wilkin that he had lost, and as a punishment, he would never be able to touch the stone again.

Vasilisa removed all the bad memories of Virgo and Vaughan and transferred them into the stone with her last strength, using her elven powers, which made it possible for her to manipulate a person's emotions.

At that moment, Sir Desouza and Sir Gilmore came to the location on the queen's orders to capture Vasilisa, who instantly noticed them.

This would end their current lives but would save their souls. She let the female soul inherit her magick. She also prophesied that their current battle would be postponed till the day the two souls found their way back to each other, and they would stab the heart of the one who killed them.

Sir Desouza went up to her and placed a card on her forehead while Sir Gilmore watched.

Vasilisa told them that the two souls would be born that night under the blood moon, and that no matter what, they would never be able to stop their fate even if it cost them their lives.

Sir Gilmore stopped Sir Desouza for a moment and asked, 'What will trigger their revenge?'

'Memories,' said Vasilisa. 'Their love for each other will bring back their memories of today.'

'Who is the one they will get their revenge on?'

Vasilisa pointed to the wolf lying on the ground before being trapped in the card.

Back at Thavma Gi, a mirror showed a sleeping Vasilisa, surrounded by rose bushes, but with not a single flower blooming.

As every mirror has two sides, the other side of the mirror was in Queen Adela's private chambers, where she smirked cunningly at the mirror and ordered a maid to cover it.

CHAPTER 38

Queen Adela walked to the mirror and pulled down the cloth, watching Vasilisa pace around. 'It will be time for you to come out soon,' she said.

Back at the forest, Wilkin's illusion broke away, bringing Virgo back to the present.

Virgo said, 'Why did you just show me this?' She remembered the words said by Marcie. She quickly opened the paper in her hand and touched the powdery substances and tucked the paper in the sleeve of her dress.

Wilkin responded, 'They say that to get over a humiliating moment in life you go back to the same place. It all started to change that moment. Now then ...' he said as the pack moved forward in the same circle. One of them came towards her and cut the rope around her legs, forcing her to stand up. Her hands, though, were still tied up. 'My mistake then was placing you, a person who had the same blood as me, in the centre,' said Wilkin. 'The way to do this is with Ella, an elf, not as you.'

'No,' Virgo protested.

'Then I'll force you to come closer.' Wilkin came up to her, holding the peridot in his hands. He placed it in the centre of the circle. The pack around the circle repeated the same ritual they had back then.

Blood spilt onto the floor, and symbols hardened on the ground. The one-thousand-and-one-string shot straight at the peridot.

Ella's head hurt immeasurably. She felt herself take a step forward without wanting to. The circlet on her head was getting pulled towards the peridot. Each of the one thousand and one strings penetrated the stone, causing the same vibrations she felt when she had left the temple with Edmund.

Wilkin beamed. 'Ah, it is working! I made a few assumptions after my previous unfortunate defeat, and had enchanted the circlet to react to this circle.'

'You, you gave me the circlet, not because of the engagement but because you anticipated this far?'

'I must say that it was due to the promise to your parents to look after you, that I had planned to do it a bit more painlessly at the inn earlier today, but that boy managed to see through my plans.'

Virgo could not stop herself from moving. She also knew that by touching the barrier, it would break her body on the outside, forcing her to break the memories as well. She knew that, because the closer she moved towards the circle, the more she felt herself sleep.

As she touched the barrier, she felt a wave of current pass through her body, and her heartbeat was much faster than usual. She felt herself slowly fading away into Ella.

As she collapsed to the ground, she heard her name being called just as she had twenty years ago when she'd run from her father's wolves.

'Virgo …'

Wilkin and the pack turned to see Edmund walk in behind her.

'As predicted, you came again,' said Wilkin. 'Here to stop time again?'

Edmund ignored him and took slow steps towards the circle. 'Ella, look at me. I will help you.'

'Time inside the circle will not work anymore. You are a minute too late,' said Wilkin.

Ella heard his voice and turned towards him but could not see properly because of the pain in her head. She reached out to him instead. 'Edmund …'

'It's okay. I will stop it, I won't make the same mistake again. Keep looking at me.' Edmund reached out to her as well.

Ella looked at her husband, but just as she reached the barrier, Wilkin stood in between them, breaking the connection. He then cut him with a sword.

Ella screamed. As she felt herself break, walking into the circle, she saw Edmund's blood dripping on the ground.

Edmund's face fell. Ella kept calling for him.

Wilkin put his hand over Edmund's head. He tried to create an illusion in his mind. 'Stop getting in the way over and over, lad,' he said. 'Just look. You can see her body breaking away. The beauty of it is that all your painful memories are no longer here. You can live a new life, without a messed up girl.'

Edmund looked up, eyes a shade of grey, and smirked.

Ella's eyes grew as smoke formed in the circle within the barrier.

Edmund laughed.

Wilkin said, 'Having fun now, aren't we, boy?'

'Yes, this is going according to your plan, right?'

'Of course, and it is almost complete. The stone and circlet will finally fuse together again. Finally, I will be able to take control of the elves.'

Edmund laughed some more. 'Then I really did make it in time,' he said as the smoke started to clear.

Wilkin was shocked at what he was seeing. He grabbed Edmund by the collar. 'What have you done, boy?'

'Messed up, girl?' asked Edmund. 'After what you said about my wife, did you think I was just going to sit back and watch her suffer?' Edmund's body was clean, with not a single scratch on him.

'This can't be. I definitely cut you,' said Wilkin.

'Oh, yes. You did. I just brought my body to a state in the future, although I had to estimate whether I would live or die.'

'If I had cut you a little deeper?' asked Wilkin.

'I would have died on the spot. It is a good thing I took the gamble, though.'

'You are not worthy alive, shadow. Virgo is dead, and Ella is legally engaged to me.'

'I told you, Wilkin,' said Edmund. 'Ella is my wife. She is not your betrothed to be spoken as such.'

Wilkin raised his hand to order. The moon was right above them, red as blood, and the pack started turning into werewolves.

'Speak all you want, Edmund,' said Wilkin. 'This time, you do not have Vasilisa to protect you.' The werewolves ran towards him.

At that moment, rose creepers shot out from the smoke, piercing many of the werewolves nearest to Edmund. Wilkin was shocked. This was the same magick as Vasilisa's, and he knew that she was not around.

'Did you think I stopped time in the circle, Wilkin?' said Edmund.

Now, the smoke had cleared completely. All the werewolves stayed back, as they could feel something different.

The barrier fell, and in the middle of the circle stood Ella, eyes as green as Vasilisa's and hair the shade between blonde and red. On her head sat the circlet. The peridot was fully attached to it, and it gave off the green glow it used to have.

With roses continuously blooming around her, Ella was now completely merged with Virgo.

～

In Thavma Gi, a mirror started to crack. The cracking stopped as a woman's hand slid across the rim of the mirror. She then muttered a spell under her breath and brought her hand closer to the mirror, causing the surface to ripple. She slowly put her hand in the mirror, as if she was reaching out to someone. As she pulled it back out, she was holding someone's hand.

Within moments, Vasilisa stepped out. 'Thank you, Cafelle,' said Vasilisa.

Cassandra said, 'I'm done playing the role of Cafelle. I am going to go back to Cassandra now.'

'You knew it was going to happen to him. That day, the first time you came to me crying.'

'Even if I hadn't come to you, it would have happened. Being a sibyl is nothing but a curse to me.'

Vasilisa put her hand on Cassandra's shoulder. 'There is no such thing as a gift or a curse. They are just powers given by someone greater than us to use.'

Cassandra said, 'Let's go, Vasilisa.'

'To help finish this fight once and for all, are we not?' asked Vasilisa.

'You can go ahead and join the fight. For me, I am just cleaning up my former husband's mess,' replied Cassandra.

They then walked out of Thavma Gi, the mirror glowing around the edges as if the door to enter it was still open.

~

'No, no … How did this happen?' a shocked Wilkin muttered. The rest of the wolves quickly took a defensive stance in case they needed to save their master.

Wilkin, Marcie and the other wolves looked at Ella. Wilkin, especially, could not figure out what was going on. He knew one thing, and it was that his daughter, Virgo, was gone for good. The one standing in front of him was an elf alone, but something felt wrong.

The girl in front of him did not feel like Ella at all. It was almost as if she was not the half-human she originally was, and she was standing still, too still that if someone walked past her right now for the first time they would think of her as a statue. Her body was still not fully recovered.

What made it worse was that Edmund was standing just outside the circle. Wilkin knew he had to stop Edmund from using his magick first so that he would have a chance against Ella's full elf powers. He raised his hand, signalling his werewolves to kill.

The wolves stepped forward, some holding swords, while some showcasing their long, sharp claws.

Edmund took a step back, placing his foot on the circle. He then drew his sword and closed his eyes. He opened them again, seeing everyone moving slowly. He waited for them to come closer before he stabbed the one closest to him. He proceeded to take down a few more, when he felt Wilkin run towards him between the other wolves, sword smashing down the same way they fought at the temple. Edmund felt himself being pushed down. The brute force of a werewolf was overwhelming. Wilkin opened his locket, changing the location to the same place they fought at the back at the temple after he had secretly married Ella.

Wilkin, who had been standing calmly, finally spoke up.

'Your Highness, I have a bride waiting inside the temple.'

In an instant, he pulled out his sword and drifted towards Edmund.

'So, it will be best if we finish things right here and now,' he screamed.

Edmund, aware of the impending danger, took a few steps back. Dodged the attack lunged towards him. He grabbed his father's sword and took a stance.

'I doubt you'll be alive to make her your bride,' he said, his voice dripping in danger.

Edmund kept an eye on Wilkin and his surroundings, hoping to find a way to break out of the illusion. He then remembered; Wilkin had always opened and closed the locket to control his illusions.

For some reason, he could remember Leofrick saying something in the past. Every time Edmund climbed trees to sneak in and out of places, Leofrick would always say, *'I'd better start cutting all the trees around you for you to stop snooping around!'*

As he dodged another swing of Wilkin's sword from above, it finally came to him that simply closing the locket would not help, as he would just open it again. He had to break it completely, but getting close enough to Wilkin to reach for the locket was impossible. It was not going to be easy as a human going against the strength of a werewolf.

There was only one way.

If you can't go to him, let him come to you, he thought.

He exchanged a few more blows and then loosened the grip of his sword. As Wilkin's sword reached close enough, he quickly stopped time, just long enough to snatch the locket out of his neck. He quickly restarted time, letting himself get stabbed in the stomach.

'I've got you for good this time, brat.' He pushed the sword into Edmund's stomach, and Edmund felt a blinding pain spread through his stomach as he groaned.

'No,' said Edmund. 'I have won.' He lifted up the pendant.

Before Wilkin could react, a rose creeper shot right through it.

CHAPTER 39

Wilkin turned around to see Ella completely recovered from the circle's magick. It had happened much faster than he expected. Ella took a step forward.

'Ella,' said Wilkin.

'Didn't you notice yet? I am no longer affected by your illusion, Wilkin,' said Ella. She looked at the moon, still bathed in red.

Good, there are at least thirty minutes left, she thought. She had to finish the fight by then.

'No, that can't be,' said Wilkin. 'Not unless you used the …'

'This?' said Marcie as she stepped out from the woods. She held a bottle of white powder with a semi transformed werewolf arm and then crushed the bottle. The powder spilt on the ground. 'I got a little hint from someone who told me about how you developed this to prevent people from being hypnotized. In other words, your illusions won't work on them.'

Wilkin saw her. He then started to laugh. 'Now I understand how you broke the illusion. You snuck back into the manor and fought with my half breeds, and you let Ella touch it before I came here.'

Marcie ignored Wilkin and walked towards Edmund. He was hurt badly, and she only had enough knowledge in healing to stop the bleeding for a while. She would not be able to carry him out with Wilkin watching.

'They say in the east that a wife must make sure her husband is not burdened. Yet I made him fight alone,' said Ella, who looked at Edmund lying on the ground, feeling helpless as she stayed trapped within the circle.

'Elizabeth Desouza,' said Wilkin.

'Desouza …? You really are foolish, Wilkin. How long did you think it would take for me to realize that you were not who you said you were? I smelt the evil in you from the very beginning. Did you think I would not take the necessary precautions?'

Marcie turned back to Wilkin and said, 'You, a were-wolf, used a spell you developed to combine the stone back to the circlet, but you didn't notice that even the two separate memories of Virgo and Ella would get combined as well.'

Wilkin said, 'The barrier would get rid of the outer one the minute she steps out of the circle. Even if you protected her body from breaking, you could not remove her from the circle without removing the barrier.'

'But what if I sped up time inside her?' Edmund said between heavy breaths. Marcie had stopped the blood from spilling further for now. Still, he had lost too much already, making it difficult to stand. Forget about being able to use his magick.

Wilkin said, 'There is no way you entered the barrier without me noticing. You are only capable of stopping a person's time on direct contact. I proved that theory in the inn earlier.'

'Who said I had to have direct contact?' said Edmund as he pushed aside his vest to reveal his pendant hanging on his belt.

That cannot be the original one, thought Wilkin. *It was lost that night twenty years ago, as that is what Loki told me.*

It then struck him. 'Loki!' he yelled, realizing that he had been tricked and the one he had was not the original at all.

Edmund added, 'I sped up the process long before I entered the stage, Wilkin. Remember? At the inn, when the past versions of us recognized you, I quickly sped up the time required to combine the two when I held her hand.'

Wilkin could not believe his ears. He felt angry for being tricked, his eyes blazed with rage. 'You, back then and now, you never changed one bit,' he said. 'Underestimating your scheming prowess was something I miscalculated, no doubt.'

'That is why I could let her go with you, because what I did was just adding the catalyst. You had to start the process,' said Edmund.

'It is over now, Wilkin,' said Ella as she took a step forward. She slammed her hands to the ground, and the ground beneath cracked in a line towards Wilkin. It then shot right at Wilkin as he used his sword to cut down the creepers.

Wilkin could feel something weird happening in his body. He felt a sharp pain in his foot. As he looked down, he saw that he had stepped on a rose thorn. He knew that Ella's thorns would be poisoned, just as Vasilisa's thorns were. He pulled out the thorn and threw it aside. A single thorn would not do much harm, although he could feel a little numbness in his legs as his feet tingled in slight pain. He knew that now that his locket was broken, only direct connection magick would work. Using his shadow magick was not possible at this point.

'A couple more thorns and I'll be able to paralyze you.' Ella pointed at him, ready for her next attack.

Wilkin laughed. 'That's fine. What you did makes no difference to me. What matters is that I get my hands on that stone.' He pointed to the moon. 'I will make sure I get my hands on the stone on your head before the eclipse ends.'

He transformed into a werewolf. Marcie noticed his eyes. He was not going to fight back at Ella. He was looking at Edmund, who was barely able to stand.

There were fifteen minutes left for the barrier to fall. It was making it hard for her to get closer, but she had to fight. Ella could not let Edmund fight anymore; he was already too hurt, because he'd had to give her an opening to break the locket earlier. The minute she saw Wilkin run towards him, she shot a rose creeper straight at him.

Marcie yelled, 'Ella, stop!'

But it was too late – the creeper shot through Edmund.

Ella screamed. Her eyes rounded in shock as she watched Edmund fall to the ground in anguish.

History was repeating itself.

Blood flowed on the ground and into the river, with Marcie running towards the person lying on the ground and desperately trying to wake him. Edmund could barely keep his eyes open. The last thing he saw was a bloodied pendant in his hand.

'What … have you … done … to us …?' whispered Ella.

'A wolf's speed with a shadow's illusions was all I needed to make you think that you were aiming at me,' sneered Wilkin.

Marcie said, 'You had to touch him directly to make the illusion work.'

'Your analytical skills are just as good as before,' said Wilkin.

Marcie noticed the change in energy from Ella. 'Ella, don't do it!' yelled Marcie.

'What exactly do you want from us, you vile, treacherous man?' she yelled as she ran towards the barrier. She felt the barrier tearing her skin, but she kept going. She felt the weird crack of lightning engulf her entire body.

'Ella, stop being foolish! If you hurt yourself, I won't be able to save both of you,' said Marcie.

'If you do it, Ella, you will end up destroying your past memories,' said Wilkin. 'And you will break the peridot completely this time, causing you to lose your elven magick.'

Ella ignored them both and pushed forward. She felt her past memories fading away. As she saw Edmund struggling to breathe, her anger grew.

She tried to keep breaking through and heard Edmund call her name softly. The memory of them dancing and the memory of them waking up together after dream-walking made her cry as she remembered the moment.

Even if I lose all my old ones, I can just keep making new ones, she thought. She managed to break through, with the peridot still in one piece.

She barely ran to Edmund and fell to his side, telling him that she loved him as she kissed him and absorbed the pain and poison in his body. The roses growing around her began to grow darker.

Marcie tried to stop her but noticed that Edmund's injuries were fading away and getting healed. On the other hand, Ella was getting worse.

Ella took one last look at him as he slowly opened his eyes, and she fell heavily on him.

Wilkin walked towards the circlet and picked it up. 'See? I told you it would be impossible for you. It would have worked if you had listened to me and handed over the circlet on your own,' said Wilkin as he walked towards them.

Marcie quickly stood between the two of them and Wilkin. 'Enough, Wilkin. If you want to win so much then take just the circlet and go. Don't kill them a second time,' cried Marcie.

'You are weak, Marcie,' said Wilkin. 'You used to follow me around so much. You trusted my words more than anyone. Yet you stand before me and block my way.'

'You were our alpha. I swore, just like every other member, to follow your words and do as you bid.'

'Do you know what happens if someone from a pack is expelled?' he said as he grabbed Marcie by the neck.

'We lose our Venedros. We will no longer be able to transform into a full wolf,' said Marcie, coughing uncontrollably as it became more difficult for her to breathe.

Wilkin placed his claws pointed on her forehead. He then turned her around and forced her against a tree. 'I never formally expelled you, Marcie. Even now, I am giving you one last chance to choose.' He then whispered in her ears, 'Save them or keep your Venedros?'

Marcie was in a bind. If she lost her Venedros now, she would not have any of her werewolf strength left. Without it, she wouldn't be able to protect Ella, but giving it up might save their lives if he was telling the truth.

She then remembered. Wilkin never told the truth.

She looked at the eclipse. And realized it was ending in a matter of minutes. She transformed her arms and scratched Wilkin, making him let go. 'You ask me to choose? No, I will not answer you. Do you know why? Because you are no longer the alpha to the clan,' she said as she did a full transformation and pushed Wilkin.

'You can say that again, Marcie,' said a female voice from afar.

'You managed to come, my lady,' said Marcie, holding her injured neck.

'Right on time as well,' said another voice.

The eclipse was over as the moon slowly changed into a bright white colour.

Wilkin turned around and saw Vasilisa standing behind him. Before he could say anything, Vasilisa raised her hand and hurled rose creepers to him, slamming him against the tree.

'Gotten weak, have you, Wilkin?' said Vasilisa. As Wilkin tried to stand up, Vasilisa waved her hand, causing the creepers to turn direction and tie him to the tree, worsening Wilkin's leg as he struggled, still unable to move properly due to Ella's earlier attack.

'How did you get out?' asked Wilkin. 'The key was with the queen.'

'Oh, she let her out,' said Prince Kai, who had just arrived on a horse with Knight Fred riding close behind.

'Your Highness,' said Wilkin.

'We meet again, Wilkin,' said the prince.

'Marcie,' called Vasilisa, who saw Marcie trying to wash away the dirt on Ella's wounds. 'Take those two to the lady.' Marcie scrambled up and carried them out, trying to limit her skin contact by holding just their clothes.

'Now we deal with you,' said the prince as he went towards Wilkin.

'Did you think I spent the last twenty years idle?' said Wilkin as he broke away from the vines, crushing a rose under his feet. 'After my crushing defeat the last time, I made sure to make the pack stronger. Every one of them can push themselves out of their physical limits.'

Vasilisa and the prince quickly took a step back. They knew something was coming.

There was no way Wilkin would go down so easily.

CHAPTER 40

Marcie put the two of them down. She saw the priestess standing there looking at the cliff in front of her.

'It was here,' said the priestess, '... where I died ...'

Marcie asked, 'Are you here as Cassandra or Cafelle?'

'A mother,' said the priestess. 'I am here as a mother.' She then placed her hand over Ella's forehead. 'Her magick energy is too weak. I can restore that with crystals,' she said, before doing the same for Edmund. 'He, on the other hand, is bleeding. His wounds are beyond my abilities.'

Marcie asked, 'Will he be all right?'

The priestess looked up. 'He will be fine, for now at least,' she said as she saw a familiar black figure standing over him. 'He still has his shadow magick looking after him.' But she did find the shadow a little erratic. Like it was trying to say or do something.

'Then it is best if I bring him to the royal infirmary

then,' said Marcie.

'No, they cannot be moved. You may need to bring the doctor here. Maybe try looking for the Princess of Amrita, who is to be wed to the prince heir,' said the priestess, remembering the girl who was able to heal the king before. 'She will be able to heal them both.'

Marcie changed into a wolf and was prepared to run when she was attacked by another wolf. Marcie fell back, on complete guard against the other wolf. When the wolf pounced again, Cassandra stepped in with her sheathed dagger.

'Go, Marcie. I'll handle him.'

Marcie looked at Cassandra's eyes. She could see great hatred for the other wolf in front of her in them. She decided to leave this to Cassandra and go to the palace.

Cassandra pulled out the dagger. Once Marcie was far enough, the wolf transformed into Raoul.

'So you were alive, Cassandra,' he said.

· 'I waited so long, Raoul,' said Cassandra. 'Hiding in the temple for so long sometimes made me forget my rage.'

'You plan on avenging your daughter's death by killing him. You know I can't let you do that, Cassandra,' said Raoul.

'I am a sibyl. Cursed, yes, but you are forgetting something, aren't you?' said Cassandra. 'Others may not believe me, but I always knew the truth.'

'So you knew,' said Raoul.

'I knew. I was well aware that the real beast hiding behind my husband and pulling strings had been you the whole time,' she confirmed as a particular memory filled her mind.

Cassandra, who was lying on the bed, asked the midwife, 'Is it true? Am I really …?'

'Yes, you very much are. Congratulations, Duchess Wilkin,' said the midwife.

Marcie, who was standing beside her, asked, 'Is there anything our lady needs to be aware of?'

'Nothing special,' said the midwife. She then turned to Cassandra and added, 'You know the basics, Cassandra. You have been through this once. It is still too early to say anything.'

'Thank you for your help. Let's pray to Athena that we see each other again in due time,' said Cassandra. The midwife left soon after.

'This is great, isn't it? Virgo will be thrilled to have a little brother or sister,' said Marcie.

Cassandra smiled. 'I've been ignoring her for too long, Marcie. I have barely been a part of her life.'

'You have your reasons,' said Marcie. 'When she gets older, she will understand.'

Cassandra stood up and looked out of the window. She could see Virgo playing in the backyard, alone. She then made up her mind. She smiled, putting a hand on her stomach. Suddenly, she felt dizzy, and her eyes were forced closed.

She realized it was another vision.

As she opened her eyes, she found herself standing in the backyard, seeing Wilkin killing a maid. No, not killing; he was turning a human into a werewolf, a taboo in the pack. He turned to ask his advisor, Raoul, if this would truly prevent the pack from losing their Venedros.

Raoul moved closer to Wilkin and told him that the only way to stop the malediction would be by getting the elven stone before Virgo turned twenty-one.

'What would be the option should she turn twenty-one before we achieve our goal, Raoul?' asked Wilkin.

Raoul said, 'We are werewolves, master, and you are our alpha. To protect the pack, sacrifice is always needed.'

Cassandra ran towards Raoul in anger but suddenly found herself back in her room. Marcie seated her on the bed and asked, 'Are you feeling unwell, mistress?'

Cassandra placed her hands on her stomach, saying, 'This child, my husband should not know about it.'

Marcie asked, 'What are you talking about, my lady?' She then added, 'This is not a small matter to hide from Lord Wilkin.'

'He is going to kill her ... He is going to kill her ...'

'Who is it? Who is going to harm Virgo?' asked Marcie.

'Ra ...' she started, but she sensed that Raoul would have placed many of the half-werewolves as maids around the house to keep an eye on her. That was probably the reason why he made her husband turn normal humans into beasts to start with – to create his own army within the pack.

'My husband,' she said. 'He is going to kill her.'

'The Fenrir clan had always been about illusions and manipulations,' said Cassandra. She had her dagger in front of her as the memory vanished. 'But even my husband could not see that the weakest wolf would be the biggest manipulator of them all.' She shook her head. 'In the end, he created an illusion of himself that he was the most powerful in the clan,' she added.

'It had always bothered me, you know,' said Raoul.

'Why was I the only one who could not develop my Venedros physically?'

'You never had a werewolf form,' said Cassandra. 'It was that way from the beginning.'

'The elven stone would be able to help me complete my transformation,' said Raoul. 'But things changed when Wilkin was seen by Prince Vaughan on that day.'

'That day was when you had intended to confront Vasilisa directly,' said Cassandra.

'It failed,' said Raoul angrily. 'Time was running out, and Wilkin was not able to win against Vasilisa even though I fed him so much power.'

'Which is why you killed my daughter and that boy, isn't it? You needed more time and Wilkin was going to lose his Venedros soon.'

'It worked,' said Raoul. 'I prolonged his powers for another twenty years.'

'No,' said Cassandra. 'You have failed, Raoul. I am sure of it now.' Cassandra leapt forward in an attempt to strike him with her dagger, but he quickly dodged out of the way.

'I do not manipulate, my lady,' he said mockingly. 'He asked me to find a way to remove the malediction on the Fenrir bloodline. I only gave him what he asked.'

'Enough. From the beginning, you were always quiet, hiding behind him and slowly stabbing his back so that the pain would take a long time to feel. You made me lose my children, Raoul. That's all the reason I need,' said Cassandra.

CHAPTER 41

'What are you saying?' asked Raoul.

'Virgo ... she wasn't the only one,' said Cassandra.

'Are you saying the other still lives?' questioned Raoul.

'I will not say, but let me tell you this. If Bodolf tries to turn into a werewolf now, after the fight he just went through, especially when poisoned, he will definitely lose his Venedros,' said Cassandra. She had cornered him at the same cliff he had pushed her off.

'It's not possible. You can't survive after you fell over a cliff like that. The fact that you survived is miraculous enough,' said Raoul, clearly unaware.

'You still don't get it? Who do you think saved me that day?'

Raoul thought hard. *After she survived, she had been hiding in the temple the whole time. So the one who saved her was most likely ...*

'It was the priest of the temple?'

'That man is not who everyone thinks he is.' She knocked his sword out his hand and it fell off the cliff.

'That man, who is he?' asked Raoul.

'You will never know,' said Cassandra as she pushed him off the cliff. She watched him fall the same way he watched her twenty years ago.

Wilkin transformed into a werewolf and tried to break out of Vasilisa's binding of him against the tree. It took almost his full strength.

'Those two fought well. From the beginning, they were only meant to defeat you, not kill you,' said Vasilisa as she stared at a weak Wilkin in front of her.

Wilkin said, 'It is still possible, breaking our curse of losing our Venedros just because of a child. Losing what we built up over many years just to give it to someone else.'

'It is how things are meant to be,' said the prince. 'Even a throne is to be given to the heir when the time is right.'

'But I have no heir. I killed her, the only heir I had.'

'Don't you feel it, Wilkin?' said Vasilisa. 'Your Venedros has been fading away since the moment the eclipse ended.'

'He feels it. He is just in denial,' said Cassandra as she stepped in front of him.

'You are ...' started Wilkin.

'It feels like I am saying this on repeat now,' said Cassandra.

Vasilisa smiled. 'You've been hiding for too long, Cafelle. People won't be able to recognize you.'

'I will no longer be called Cafelle, Vasilisa.' She walked towards Wilkin and lifted his head up. 'I will be referred to as Cassandra now. That's my name,' she said as she pulled down her hood. 'Isn't that right, dear husband?'

Wilkin fell back in shock. 'You … you are alive!'

'Did you think I would die without dragging you down with me? I made sure that even if I died, you would still lose.'

'You really are foolish,' said Prince Kai. 'Lying there like a broken puppet, after being played around with by your own pack members.'

Then, they heard horses coming from a distance.

'The royal doctors must have arrived,' said Cassandra.

The prince had sent Knight Fred to help them find Edmund and Ella. 'We need to wrap up things here and head back to the palace,' said the prince. 'I suggest you two come along as well,' he said to Cassandra and Vasilisa.

Vasilisa agreed. 'I have unfinished business with Elizabeth as well.'

But Cassandra refused. 'I finished what I needed to do in Yovaria, Prince Kai,' she said. Marcie walked in at that moment. 'Now it is time for me to go to a place to find the other. I will return to the temple for now.' Marcie nodded, in agreement that she would join Cassandra on the journey.

'You knew that I would lose my Venedros today. But

how …' Then Wilkin realized. 'You hid the other, didn't you? You never wanted to see me for this very reason.'

'She is alive. Our second daughter,' Cassandra said as Vasilisa came up to him and put a card on his forehead, trapping him within it.

CHAPTER 42

Edmund and Ella lay next to each other in the palace infirmary as the prince watched over them. The Princess of Amrita had treated them, and he was waiting for them to regain their consciousness. At the same time, Vasilisa discussed something with the princess in the corner.

At that moment, Sir and Lady Desouza burst through the doors.

'Our daughter, where is she?' asked Lady Desouza.

Vasilisa stepped up. 'Wilkin is weakened, Edmund almost died, and Elizabeth is gravely injured.'

Sir Desouza said, 'She looks so lifeless, Angela. Look at her, the blood on her dress and the cuts on her body.'

'How did she end up this way?' exclaimed Lady Desouza, reaching out to Ella.

'Don't touch them,' said Vasilisa. 'Elizabeth used the Darkest Rose spell, but it was incomplete. I told her to never use it in a battle, as absorbing injuries is like poisoning herself. Touching her will poison all of you as well.'

'Then how did Marcie carry them here in the first place?' wondered Lord Desouza.

'Your daughter, for a brief moment, turned into who she once was but never got the chance to become. That gave Marcie enough time to cover her up, preventing direct contact,' explained Vasilisa.

Sir and Lady Gilmore entered the infirmary as well.

'Looks like everyone is finally here,' said the prince.

'I have not seen him since you had banished him. His mother has been heartbroken the whole time, wondering if he was all right. Instead of coming home to his family, he lies here with a Desouza,' said Sir Gilmore.

Sir Desouza fought back. 'It is he who is to be blamed for my daughter's injuries. She tried to save his life, a foolish decision.'

'Be silent, both of you,' said the prince sternly. 'The lives of your children are very close to the scissors of Aisa, and yet you stand here arguing on who is right.'

'Make no mistake ...' said Queen Adela as she walked regally into the room. Everyone in the room bowed. '... His Majesty has given me full authority to punish the ones who need to be punished. If I find a reason valid enough, I will not hesitate to put either of you on the blade of Aisa's scissors myself,' she said, looking at both Sir Desouza and Sir Gilmore.

'As such is the matter, we shall discuss to our heart's content who is at fault in a moment,' said the prince.

'We shall let the princess continue their healing from here.' The princess bowed in acknowledgement.

'Will they be all right?' asked Lady Gilmore.

The princess replied, 'They have escaped death, but it is up to their will to wake up.' She saw the mothers' worried expressions and added, 'Do be at ease, as I will keep an eye on them at all times.'

'And so she says. Let's leave it in her capable hands then,' said the queen.

'Well then,' started the prince. 'Let the others come in.'

Priest Linus entered the room. 'You have called for me, Your Highness?'

'I am presuming you have something to say?' asked the prince.

'I will be straightforward, as there is nothing to hide. Edmund, lying there, is Elizabeth's husband, and Elizabeth is Edmund's wife,' said the priest.

Sir Desouza was enraged. 'That is not possible! She was engaged to another, yet she went behind our backs to marry a Gilmore. Despicable!'

'Edmund and Ella were destined to marry from the day they were born. You should know very well by now the kind of fate they had. I did my duty as a priest and had Priestess Cafelle marry them, which also happened to be the same day Edmund was banished.'

'So while she was going through with her bridal training, she was already a married woman,' said Lady Gilmore.

The priest continued, 'While the priestess looked after Ella's bridal training, she secretly started training her in controlling her magick. This was essential, as seen in their battle last night. Edmund, on the other hand, had to find the gem belonging to Vasilisa. That had the memories of their past lives.'

Sir Desouza fell back. 'The battle was inevitable,' he said.

'It seems as though the gods have decided on bringing the Gilmores and Desouzas together,' Sir Gilmore said.

'Indeed. We should put everything behind us now and embrace each other, just as the gods have ordained,' said Desouza as they shook hands, signifying the end to their family feud.

Prince Kai said, 'You tried to stop a prophecy that was impossible from the start. Had you let things go naturally, these two would not be lying here like this right now.'

'Then we need to get her to speak next,' hissed Sir Desouza as he looked at Vasilisa.

'I will, but first go see your children,' said Vasilisa. 'They have awakened.'

Six months later, Edmund entered the throne room and bowed to the king and queen. Standing at the side were the two princes, Prince Kai and Prince Lukan.

'Rise, Edmund, and accept your title,' said King Alphonse. Edmund stood up. 'Edmund Gilmore, son of the Guard of the Western Gates, Sir Gordon Gilmore, is thereby proclaimed the Duke of Kroukhesta.'

Edmund bowed again and said, 'If I may ask, Your Majesty, why did you choose to give me the title?'

'Many wolves died that night,' said the king. 'The few survivors are now nowhere to be found. Hiding further into the Broken Woods, I presume. Someone needs to guard the town. You can move into the Kroukhesta mansion immediately.'

'But why me, Your Majesty?' asked Edmund. 'I am neither educated in those matters, nor am I strong enough to fight.'

'You're still young, Edmund. You have time to learn. Prince Kai has agreed to help you along the way, so you do not need to worry about that.'

'That is the official reason, but we do have an unofficial one as well,' said the queen. 'I would like to make you my Keeper of the Knaves, Edmund.'

Edmund was puzzled. 'What is a Keeper, Your Majesty?'

'Keepers are not known to the public; hence it is of no surprise that you wouldn't know. A Keeper is a private magick army who deals with non-human problems in Yovaria. Although Wilkin was caught and the circlet was returned to Vasilisa, there will still be people vying for it,' said the queen.

'Thank you, Your Majesty. I accept the titles that have been offered,' said Edmund. He bowed and walked out the throne room.

Prince Kai followed. 'That's a good decision,' said Prince Kai. 'It will be a good way to protect Elizabeth as well, since she has been proclaimed heir to the elven throne by Vasilisa.'

'I am not sure if I am ready, though,' said Edmund.

The prince then asked carefully, 'How are things at home now?'

Edmund said, 'More or less all right. Taking in the fact that the two of us, who were meant to be normal humans, have magick is something we will have to get used to, especially more in the future.'

'You know I'm talking about something else, right?' said the prince with a grin.

Edmund smiled. 'They accepted the wedding, Your Highness. They offered a sacrifice to the temple of Athena as well,' he said, still finding it hard to believe it was all over now.

Prince Lukan came out and congratulated him, and Edmund returned the greeting by congratulating him for his upcoming wedding with the Princess of Amrita. They looked to see Ella and the princess smiling and chatting while Ella bloomed a rose in her hands and put it in the princess' hair as she giggled.

'It still feels new, right?' asked Prince Lukan.

Edmund agreed. 'Nothing has changed, yet it feels like something new every day,' he said as Ella turned to look at him.

The prince walked away, and the princess noticed it and followed him.

Edmund went to the garden. 'I just realized that no matter how all this turned out, you would have been the Duchess of Kroukhesta anyway,' he joked.

Ella hit him playfully, 'Is that something you'd say to your wife?'

They laughed, and Edmund asked, 'I know Marcie

and Cassandra left without saying goodbye. Are you okay with that?'

Ella said, 'I can't say I am fully okay with it, but they have gone to find Virgo's sister, who, in a way, is my sister as well. I can only pray that they will be safe wherever they are. Besides,' she added. 'it looks like we will be pretty busy ourselves. I will miss those adventures we had before,' she said with a wink.

Edmund took her hand. 'It's fine,' he said. 'We have all the time in the world now.' Edmund pulled her into his arms, one hand around her waist and the other in her hair as he placed a deep kiss on her lips while she responded eagerly.

'What happened to Wilkin, Adela?' asked the king as they stood in the throne room.

The queen stayed quiet for a moment before saying, 'The card I put him in was stolen the very next day.'

'You do know that if he escapes, the royal family will be held responsible for letting out prisoners,' said the king.

'He cannot escape. As long as my mirror doesn't break, he will be trapped in there for an eternity.'

'His transformation?' asked the king.

'Gone,' said the queen. 'He is no different than what he despised becoming – a dog.'

'We should call for the Keepers to find the card. Better to be safe than sorry.'

'Oh, I know who stole it already,' said the queen. 'But I don't plan on catching the thief.'

Right then, she saw a vermillion flycatcher sitting on the windowsill, listening to their conversation.

The bird then flew away to the Broken Woods as a hand picked up the red cloak that had been lying on the ground ever since the fight happened.

338

ABOUT THE AUTHOR

Vera Morgana is the author behind Darkest Rose, which is the first book of the Inevitable War Series. She is also an avid wedding and portrait photographer, as well as an enthusiast of fairy tales, myths and legends.

Vera was known in school as a daydreamer who spend her breaks at the school library. She began writing in 2013, when she wrote a short story about a girl's journey across a desert to find her love gone to war.

On a day she is not working, she can be found in her own little world. Overtime, the world in her head manifested itself into what you read today.

Find her at www.veramorgana.com

Contact her at vera_morgana@hotmail.com